FORBEARANCE

by
Deborah Menard

PublishAmerica
Baltimore

First printing

This is a work of fiction. Names, characters, places, and incidents either are the product of the author's imagination or are used fictitiously. Any resemblance to actual persons, living or dead, events, or locales is entirely coincidental.

PublishAmerica has allowed this work to remain exactly as the author intended, verbatim, without editorial input.

Hardcover 978-1-4560-5260-7
Softcover 978-1-4560-5259-1
PUBLISHED BY PUBLISHAMERICA, LLLP
www.publishamerica.com
Baltimore

Printed in the United States of America

To my husband and soul-mate
William

And in memory of
Game Warden James Patch, the best friend wildlife ever had.

ACKNOWLEDGMENTS

To God, who guides me

~

To my husband, Bill for his love and support

~

To my daughter, Amanda, who waded through the first seven
hundred page draft, offering her critique with a wonderful sense of
humor

~

To my son James who caught the spirit of the book in the cover

~

A very special thank you to Author Melissa Mather, for her
honest criticism and experienced editing

~

Penny, who encouraged me to pursue the story

~

CHAPTER 1

Emily Harrigan shut the locker door quietly and watched him. Except for a strip of dyed red hair, his head was shaved. Shiny rings pierced his ears and lower lip. A lot of kids dressed in the "Goth" manner. This early September afternoon was too warm for a long black coat, but with teenagers, it was how you look, not how you feel.

His shoe squeaked on the polished linoleum. She edged between two sections of lockers not sure why she felt the need to conceal herself. He was probably just late for class.

The boy hesitated, his eyes on the door of a classroom across the hall from Emily. Behind that door, she could hear a teacher say something light-hearted and the children laugh in response. He glanced backwards and his hand went under his coat.

As he passed by, she could see his cheeks, molded with baby fat and flushed, probably from overheating in his coat. The enraged eyes didn't fit the rest of his young face. As he reached the door, she saw the pistol.

Emily lifted her own gun free of the holster. "Don't touch that doorknob."

The boy flinched at the sound of her voice and then his young body heaved with a shrug of capitulation.

"Just put the gun on the floor. Turn around and we can talk about this."

The boy began to turn, raising his arms slowly in a pose of surrender.

"Put the gun down!" she commanded.

He faced her and the anger in his beautiful blue eyes was gone. His expression was like that of a young child, sad and wanting to be consoled. He kept raising his hands, the gun still in his right palm, his finger still on the trigger.

Emily's heart stopped mid-beat. Holstering her own firearm, she lunged for the boy. Before she could grab the gun, he turned his wrist and fired. She had been one step too far away.

She caught him as he fell to the floor. Desperately she called on her radio for an ambulance while trying to stop the bleeding in the side of his head.

The classroom doors locked in simultaneous precaution and the children behind each began to cry out with fear. Emily cried too, looking down at the dead child in her arms. Once more she had been too late.

~~~~~

"What was she doing here? She is a detective, Joe!" Henry Harrigan demanded.

"She's still a rookie cop. It was a routine locker inspection." Captain Joseph Horan looked towards his old friend. "You remember the drill. Geezum Henry, she re-holstered her gun—what if that kid had fired on her instead?"

"You've always said Emmy's instincts were solid."

"Henry, you taught her—put her on the fast track to detective. But you couldn't teacher her how to stay above this shit. She's had too much of it lately—first that little girl, then the nurse—now this—enough to jolt anyone."

"What happened?"

"The kid shot himself, died in her arms. The mother was yelling in her face that she forced her son to commit suicide, gave him no way out. She needs to get off the street for awhile. I've been trying to convince Seth to take her on a vacation."

"You know she's not going to go on a vacation, Joe."

The police captain stared angrily at the report from the teacher closest to the scene of the suicide. "Why'd you pushed her into this job? You of all people!"

"You know damn well I didn't push her. She wanted it from the time…"

"Well, that puts the finishing touches on my day—the two men I respect arguing my fate." Emily Harrigan's voice was humorless as she took the report from Joe Horan. The captain walked away, muttering to himself.

"Bad day," Henry stated instead of asking.

Emily squinted up at her father. "Not one of my best. How's yours going?"

"There is no comparison. Your mother has me moving furniture."

For awhile they stood in silence, idly staring at the chaos around them. Then Henry spoke, "You've had quite a string of bad days lately."

Emily couldn't meet his eyes, afraid of betraying her overwhelming sadness.

"Think you need to see someone?"

"Go to a shrink? What, and risk losing the greatest job in the world?" She raised her brows sarcastically.

"That's your mother talking." Henry wanted to take her hand but refrained. "No matter what mom says, seeing the police psychiatrist is a good idea. It's worse out here now."

"Don't give me that, Dad. You saw plenty."

"It was different, Emmy. There was still some sense of decency. Even so, when the work started to get to me, I talked it over with the doctor."

"And because of talking it over with a doctor, as mom puts it, 'you were let out to pasture'."

Emily and her father had always been honest with each other. For as long as she could remember, Emily had been treated as the third member of an adult trilogy, rather than the late-born and only child. Often caught up in her parents' volatile relationship, she sometimes felt like the only adult.

"I was ready to let go. Dr. Brandon didn't have anything to do with my decision."

"I hear you, Dad, but I don't want to take a chance of losing my job." She exaggerated her voice as if sharing a well kept secret. "I'm likely to get a sympathetic boot behind a desk, knowing the captain."

Henry didn't say anything. She was right. As a lifelong friend of the family and as a possible future father-in-law, Captain Horan was over-protective of her.

"And if Cathleen Droger decides to press charges, I'd better not be clinging to the leg of a therapist."

"Who?"

"That's the dead boy's mother." The words "dead boy" swirled behind her tired eyes, making her feel dizzy. "She wants to believe I drove her son to shoot himself."

Henry shook his head sadly. "Everyone else is to blame."

"Don't be so glum," Emily said, tilting her head so that if briefly touched her father's arm. "I know I need a break from this. Captain thinks I should take a vacation with Seth but Seth can't go away right before the real estate markets drop off for the winter."

"Saints be praised for such bad timing." Henry lifted his eyes to heaven.

She laughed at her father's expression of relief. "Seth isn't so bad."

In spite of her father's joking, she felt sick inside. "What about that job your friend, Bill Hines, asked you about?"

"What job? Henry watched a student run sobbing to her mother and took a deep, uncomfortable breath. "Oh. The temp-deputy job because his son wants to go on a cruise with his wife. I've got to call him about that. Thanks for reminding me."

"He was wondering if you'd stand in as constable for his son, Pete, in that—what's that little town up there, Kassy, Kisscassy…?" Emily prompted him, "the one near Errol?"

"Your Mother made up my mind not to go. She doesn't want to give up the last bit of warm weather. I think Bill just wants an excuse to go fishing with me, anyway. This time of the year, his son could leave and nobody would notice the constable was gone. Nothing ever happens up there."

"Tell him I'll come up and do it. Pete can go on his cruise."

"Emmy, it would be a whole month in a town where, maybe once a year, some hunter shoots his big toe off. That's it!" Then Henry scratched the side of his cheek thoughtfully. "It would be restful. Old

Ely Pike, the game warden, takes care of what's happening in the woods and there is nothing but woods up there. It's only bear hunting season, so there isn't much going on, even for him." He cocked his head and continued, "Emmy, it's really remote. Your mother will have a fit."

"We will *allude* that it's a ski town with rich ski bums milling around."

Henry chuckled. He had green eyes like hers. At sixty his hair still had some blond in it. Much to her mother's chagrin, Emily had been determined from a very young age to follow in his footsteps.

"I just need to get away for a little while. That's all! And I haven't taken any sick or personal time in two years."

"Emmy, Captain Horan means well, but you can't run away from your problems. I know all this is keeping you from sleeping."

"And how do you know I'm not sleeping, Detective Dad?"

"Because, Detective Daughter, it was me that you got your intuition from." He sighed heavily. "And your mother told me. All right, I'll call Bill and Pete tonight. Maybe this is a good idea. Wish I was going with you. It'll be boring for you, but it'd be great fishing in that swamp up there."

Henry spotted a well-groomed man in a blue blazer coming this way and lowered his head with an inaudible oath.

"Emily, my dad just told me about the shooting!" shouted Seth Horan, the police chief's son. He had hurried from his real estate office, a block away. "It was great you got that kid before he shot up the whole school."

"I didn't get him, Seth." Emily turned her head slightly so that Seth's kiss brushed her cheek instead of her lips. "He committed suicide."

"Well, if you hadn't been there he wouldn't have killed himself."

"Thank you, Seth," Emily said, sighing.

"I meant—"

"I know what you meant." She smiled and leaned into him, wishing he would take her in his arms and melt away this torture in her mind.

He pulled away beaming and took out two tickets from his pocket. "Hey, guess what I have."

"What do you have?" Her smile was bright but her voice weary.

"Remember that Broadway show that you've always wanted to see?"

"*The Lion King*?"

Instead of answering her, he said, "God, you look terrible, Em. What are those things under your eyes? They look like slugs."

"I haven't been sleeping well lately." Emily glanced at her father as if to admit his instincts were right.

"Sweetheart, try to look like my pretty red-head next Saturday. We're going to Boston, and we're going in style. I'm not telling you what we'll see, but be ready. I've got to go. I'm about to unload that old mill building for a very nice price."

"The old New Hampshire Wool Exchange?" Henry asked. "The one that's about to be condemned?"

"Buyer, beware. He knows it's in bad shape—wants to make it into a mall. That's what he is going to call it, 'The Mall on the River'. The guy is loaded. He could probably rebuild it from scratch." Seth hurried off smiling and waving.

"That boy is nothing like his father. Let's go home. Mom has dinner on." Henry put his hand on her back to guide her.

As gently as she could, Emily pulled free. "I'm not coming over tonight, Dad. I'm really tired."

He looked confused. "You have to eat!"

"Believe it or not, I do have some food at my apartment." She tried to say it kindly, but she could tell by her father's expression that he was disappointed. "Okay, but I'm going to leave right after dinner, as soon as you make those calls to Bill and Pete Hines."

Henry grinned. Meals with just him and Maureen eventually evolved into a disagreement.

"I'll be along soon." With a beleaguered expression, Emily watched her father walk away. Twenty-four years old and she was still having dinner with her parents. She did it to keep peace in the family.

CHAPTER 2

The drive north was beautiful. Being early September, the leaf color was still far from "peaking". Still, the White Mountains, with their dark ravines and breathtaking heights, made her smile in awe of the wild splendor.

After that pleasant interlude, she found her passage to the little town of Kaskitesiw, confounded by the very tool designed to provide accurate directions. Her GPS was useless. First it directed her down a desolate logging road and then a gravel dead end. Shutting it off, she searched through the map of New Hampshire. Kaskitesiw wasn't on it. However, Errol, the nearest, large town, was just where Pete Hines had described it. From there, she found directions to her destination.

Her father had spoken the truth. Kaskitesiw looked more like an abandoned bus-stop than a town. At least it had a gas station and Emily pulled in, deciding that she had better gas up when the opportunity presented itself.

There was a car parked by the single pump. Emily waited and glanced at her watch. She had ten minutes to get to the police station, and she thought she could see the building, which Pete had described, from here.

She got out of the Mustang and looked at the pump. It was cash only, no place to slide a credit card and only one nozzle.

A woman came from the shack-like building and glanced around quickly. She saw Emily and smiled, impulsively touching her cut lip. Her face looked bruised. "You have to pay inside first," she offered, meekly.

"Thanks." Emily smiled back and went into the dilapidated structure which smelled of oil and old newspapers.

The young attendant didn't look up, oblivious to her presence. His fingers clicked away at a computer game.

"I'd like to buy some gas," she said, putting a twenty dollar bill on the desk where his feet were propped.

The game still held his full attention.

She lifted one earphone. "I'd like twenty dollars worth, please."

The boy looked up, startled. Scowling, he popped his gum in her face and scooped the money into a drawer.

As he re-adjusted the earphones on his head, Emily went to the door and looked through the greasy window. The woman had finished pumping the gas.

Emily turned the sticky door knob and started out just as another vehicle came into the station. Before the black SUV slowed to a complete stop, a man jumped out and headed towards the woman. With terror in her eyes, she tried to climb into her car but the man grabbed her arm and pulled her back out.

"Bailey told me you was leaving town. This is the thanks I get for buyin' you a car?" the man shouted, unaware of Emily standing in the half-open doorway. "You been getting ideas from that game warden, haven't you? You been talkin' ta him 'bout me."

"Richard, no!" The woman tried to pull free. "You might need me to pick you up in Berlin. I'd need more gas."

A car horn sounded.

The man she called Richard yelled towards the driver of the SUV, "Hold on! Can't you see I'm busy?" He turned back to the woman, his lips blackened with chewing tobacco, his hair dark and greasy. "I'm gettin' a bear. Claret ain't stoppin' me. Got it? I swear I'll kill you if you don't get back to the trailer right now and quit talkin' ta that Indian."

"Excuse me, Richard is it?" Emily's voice was controlled, almost pleasant. "Take your hand off the woman."

Richard looked both angry and surprised to see another person standing near his wife's car. "This ain't yer business."

14

"I'm leaving!" The SUV driver yelled and started to back out. Apparently, he didn't like the altercation at the pump. "You'd better remember what I'm here for!"

Emily looked at the man in the SUV. He was plump, pale and perspiring in a red plaid hunting outfit.

"Now, Mr. Patterson, don't you go running off!" Richard yelled, momentarily distracted, and then turned his vicious eyes back to Emily.

"Let go of her." Emily lifted the police badge from her sweater pocket. "Manchester police."

Richard cursed his luck, and seeing he was about to lose his ride, he let the woman go and started running for the SUV.

"Get into the car, ma'am," Emily said, and held the door open for her. "Do you want to press charges?"

The woman shook her head, panicked.

"May I have your name?"

The woman jumped into the car and took off, heedless of her speed in front of a police officer.

Emily looked back to the SUV and saw Richard pounding on the passenger window of the slow moving vehicle until it stopped. The door opened and he got in. The black SUV swung wide and, thankfully, went in the opposite direction.

Emily wrote down the license plates, pulled the Mustang forward and began filling the tank as the boy attendant, minus his earphones, came out pointing to her car.

"Is that yours?"

Emily nodded and asked, "What's your name?"

"Tommy. It's a sixty nine Mustang, isn't it?"

"It is. Why aren't you in school?"

"It's after school!"

Emily looked at her watch. "You're right! Tommy, do you know that lady who came in before me?"

"That's Teresa Faidlee." He took the nozzle from her. "Here, I'll do that for you. Man, she's a beauty." He peered in the windows of the car.

"Did you happen to see the man with her?"

"What man?"

"Better slow down. I only gave you a twenty." Emily was watching the gallons roll by. "His first name was Richard."

"Musta' been her husband. V8 engine?"

"Yes. Can you tell me where the police station is?"

"Are you going to tell Pete that I was playing games? I'm sorry about being—" he searched for the word, sincere now that punishment might be a possibility, "rude."

"Not this time. I have an appointment there. Is that the building?" She pointed.

"Ayuh." The boy pulled out the nozzle and hung it up. "She could take thirty."

Emily got into the car with a smile. "She could take forty."

~~~~~

"You need a haircut." Pete swatted the back of the game warden's head with a baseball cap embossed with the word, "CONSTABLE". He put a paper bag on his desk and noticed Daniel's glance at his watch.

Pete looked at his. It was three o'clock. He was almost late for the new arrival and began his list of excuses, "Alley Rondo had a dog complaint and Ralph Whitmore is fighting over that east survey stake again. That woman from the conservation committee got in on it. I had to call the forester out. It's just getting too damn crowded up here."

The man in the green uniform, the seal of New Hampshire on the sleeve, kept on writing.

"I'm serious. You're giving Kaskittyway's finest a bad name," Pete said.

"Kas-ke-tay-a-say-uw," Daniel pronounced the name with uncharacteristic frustration. "I haven't had time. I'll ask Anna to cut it tonight."

"Geezum, Daniel, lighten up. Kaskittyway, kaskittywah, kaskittywumpum! I don't care! Can you believe it? Susanne and I are on vacation in two, count 'em, two days. In the meantime, I'm 'batching' it tonight with a grinder, beer and the first game of the season." He

16

leaned on Daniel's desk. "Then I'm going to watch boxing until my eyeballs fall out."

"Did Susanne go to her Mom's?" Daniel asked quietly, making an effort to converse though he was involved in the work before him.

"Yep, she took the kids to Littleton. Then it's on to the Bahamas, baby! Three weeks, just her and me!" All smiles, Pete tossed his cap onto the coat rack. "Oh, which reminds me, did you say you were going to see Anna tonight?"

Daniel nodded, studying the computer screen. "I'm going to split some wood for her."

"Susanne wanted me to drop this by her place, but if you're going?" Pete set the bag on Daniel's desk with a heavy clunk.

The warden lifted out one of the two half-gallon jars of homemade sauce and frowned. Unless supplies were needed, Pete knew he always walked much of the way to Anna's, instead of using the All Terrain Vehicle.

"At least it's downhill," Pete said, looking over Daniel's shoulder at the report he had been writing. "You're not going to catch Faidlee, and he's going to wind up suing you for harassment."

Daniel said, "If I can just get his wife to talk, we can bust him on domestic abuse and solve the poaching problem at the same time."

"Fat chance! She can't testify against him." Pete went over to the coffee maker. "Teresa's scared of her husband. She's not going to press charges."

"She's been telling me some interesting things about Faidlee's activities." Daniel picked up a pencil, not willing to commit all the information to the official log yet. "I think she's just about had it with him. He roughed her up again last night."

"So that's why you're ticked off. Daniel, you went to school with her. She's not going to talk and you can't prove he's the one putting that bait around."

"That is not true. Faidlee is getting sloppy. He got his legal bear the first day of the season and let everyone know about it. Now he's bringing in what he calls 'clients. He doesn't have a license to be a guide." Daniel thumbed through his notes. "I know he's selling the gall bladders though Canada to China."

"Can you prove it?"

Daniel looked uncertain. "I was sure he was going to shoot a bear over that bait pile on South Worth Road. A round ear tag was left on the sheep carcass. I traced it to the farmer. Felton is the only one who uses those tags. He says they don't get ripped out of his animal's ears as easy as the others. And he told me the slaughter house he used," Daniel said, looking up at the constable. "Mike White said Faidlee picked up a barrel of renderings for, as he put it, 'getting rid of a coyote problem around his house.'"

"What does that prove? Murky White sells more guts than meat. It's a wonder the health inspectors haven't shut him down. And besides, a lot of people bait coyotes if they're hanging around too close."

"The bait wasn't anywhere near Faidlee's house. I staked out the pile for two days." The warden looked down at his work, irritation showing in his face once more.

"Let me guess, no sign of Faidlee."

"I will get him, and I would give you the collar if it would stop him beating up on his wife," Daniel said, determined. "Too bad you won't be here and I'll have to do it alone."

"Unfair! Susanne and I haven't had a vacation in years!"

Daniel was back at his writing, ignoring the constable's outburst.

"Besides, you won't be alone."

He had Daniel's attention now and decided to taunt him. "Hey, Joe had a good joke today, one you'd appreciate. You know how geese fly in a V-formation?" he asked, sitting on the edge of Daniel's desk and taking a swallow of coffee.

Daniel nodded but looked back down at his work, knowing Pete would take his time about sharing any information which Daniel might be interested in.

"Well, here's a question for you, since you know all about that stuff," Pete said with the sarcasm. "Why is one line always longer? Huh?"

"There are more birds in it."

"You are the worst person to tell a joke to! You're supposed to say, 'No, Pete. Why?'"

"No, Pete. Why?"

"You're hopeless." The constable stood, shaking his head.

"It's an old joke!" Daniel stuffed the page into a folder.

"Geeze, you're on edge today!" Pete remarked.

Daniel took a deep breath. He didn't want to ruin Pete's vacation mood but he was upset by seeing Teresa Faidlee earlier today. Her husband had used his fists on the woman's face again; but there was nothing he could do unless she pressed charges. "Okay, so why am I not going to be alone while you're gone?" He interlaced his dark fingers, face impassive, waiting patiently,

"Manchester is sending up an officer for the month, to cover my vacation."

"Anybody we know?"

"My dad and her father are old friends." Pete enjoyed Daniel's slight scowl. "She's a detective down in Manchester, good one too. She wants a change of scenery, so you'll have a partner to ride around with."

Hunting season was a busy time, and Daniel didn't look forward to being a tour guide, but he said nothing, turning back to the computer screen.

"Now, now, I heard that panic in your voice," Pete joked.

"You're hearing things again."

Pete rummaged around his desk. A moment later, he dropped a folded newspaper in front of the warden.

Daniel picked it up. It was out of date by a week. On the front, a young woman was pictured being hounded by reporters. He knew of the high school freshman who had carried a loaded pistol into school. The boy had resorted to suicide when confronted by Detective Emily Harrigan. The boy's family was accusing the detective of threatening the child to excess, so that the boy took his own life. The story was all over the media.

The office door opened and the woman in the picture, minus the sunglasses and agonized expression, stepped inside. She gave them a pleasant smile as she tried to smooth a strand of hair into her bun.

Daniel set the paper down on the desk and stood up.

"Emily Harrigan!" Pete exclaimed, coming forward to shake her hand. "How's your Dad?"

"He's fine, said to tell your father that it's time to go fishing, unless he wants to cut a hole in the ice," the woman teased with friendly familiarity.

"I'll pass the word along. You and Henry finish fixing up that old Mustang?"

"State of the art and cop smart—parked right outside!" Emily smiled, noticing the other man in the room.

"Man, that car was a piece of junk. I can't believe what you guys did with it." Pete was looking out the door at the car. "You've even got a Blue Bar in the back window? You can hardly tell with the tinted glass. Bet that jolts tail-gaiters." Pete shut the door and followed the direction of her eyes. "Oh, this is Daniel Claret, our district game warden." He gave Daniel's last name a sharp 'et' sound.

She extended her hand with a bright smile. "Warden Claret? I thought Ely Pike was the warden."

Daniel leaned over the desk to shake her hand and wished he had stopped for that haircut earlier. In spite of her attractive appearance, dark shadows beneath her eyes told the story of sleepless nights. "Warden Pike retired. How do you do?"

"Fine, thanks!" Emily turned away from his dark eyes quickly, inexplicably, and felt in her sweater pocket. "I've got something for you, Constable."

"Call me Pete. And call him Daniel."

Daniel didn't know whether to sit back down or come around the desk. He could tell out of the corner of his eye that Pete was enjoying his awkwardness.

She handed the constable the license numbers she had written down.

Pete looked at her puzzled, hoping she wasn't giving him more work before he left.

"That first one belongs to a black SUV driven by a man named Patterson with one passenger named Richard. Richard was being rough on a woman, Teresa Faidlee, at the gas station and wouldn't let her leave. However, I mentioned I was a police officer, and he let her go," Emily said. "The attendant, Tommy, told me her name. He also thought that the man, Richard, might be her husband but he didn't see the altercation. Teresa took off going west in an old blue Malibu with this license." Emily pointed to the other number. "Richard and Patterson went the other way in the SUV."

Daniel stared at her in disbelief. "Teresa got away?"

"She was driving like her life depended on it," Emily said.

"Thank you." Smiling, Daniel took the paper from Pete. "She did it! She got away." He looked back at Emily and asked to make sure, "They didn't follow her?"

Emily gave the warden her full attention. "No. Richard said something about hunting bear, no, getting a bear, and Claret wasn't going to stop him. I assume he was talking about you, since I also heard him warn the woman to stop talking to the game warden."

Daniel looked thoughtful. "They didn't happen to say where they were 'getting bear', did they?"

"Sorry, the only other thing he said was—" Emily hesitated, studying the warden's dark features and black hair hanging over his forehead and ears in shiny clumps. She decided to leave out the part about the 'Indian'. "He said that he had bought her the car she was driving."

"Richard Faidlee totaled his truck and lost his license for DUI. That's why he bought her a car." Looking up from the paper, Daniel said again with a smile, "Thank you."

The constable was staring at the two of them. He honestly couldn't remember the last time he had seen Daniel Claret smile. "Guess I've got to eat my words." Pete patted Daniel on the shoulder and then changed the subject. "How was the trip?" he asked Emily.

Daniel sat back down pretending to shuffle papers and organize them.

"Long," Emily declared. "This is a long state going north. I almost gave up at Gorham."

"A lot of people give up at Gorham," Pete said, chuckling.

"And forget GPS," she went on, light heartedly, "It may work great in the city, but it wanted me to turn down every logging road that must have been on a map at one time or another."

"I'm surprised you made it at all. There are lots of those roads," Pete said.

She laid her sweater on the desk opposite Daniel. As her eyes rested on the old newspaper her expression grew somber.

Daniel quickly laid his folder on top of it. When he looked up, their eyes met and found it hard to breathe for a second.

Pete was talking to Emily but looking hard at Daniel. "How is your mom? Susanne wanted me to ask. They had a good time together at the Wives of Law Enforcement Officers Dinner."

"Fine! She's staying busy with that group." Emily turned her attention back to the constable.

"Susanne says she has a great sense of humor," Pete added.

"She sure can keep a party going," Emily agreed and then she changed the subject. "Pete, the name of this town—is it Native American like so many New Hampshire towns are? How do you pronounce it and what does it mean?"

"Daniel's the best one to answer that. He's Cree Indian."

Daniel shifted his eyes to his computer, his notes, to the desk, and then looked up. He had never seen anyone so pretty. "I was only raised Cree, and I am only part Abenaki." He got up, as if called on to give a speech in class, wiping his palms against his pants. "The town was originally called Kaskitesiw Nipiy, meaning black water." Daniel pronounced the name Kas-key-tay-a-say-uw Knee-pee. "The Algonquin, who first lived here, named the swamp nearby. Each tribe says it a little differently. The Abenaki call it Mkazawi Nebi but it means the same."

Daniel looked at her hesitantly, but she had a studious look on her face. Was she mocking him? He went on. "The name has been shortened and Americanized over the years, to Kaskitesiw, and it is often pronounced 'Kas-kitty-way' or 'Kas-ki-tay-wah'. Kas-ki-tay-wah is actually the inanimate word for black, but the swamp is considered animate, a living thing, with three faces. It was named for its dark face."

His voice trailed off as he realized that he was rambling. Walking over to a large wall map, he pointed to the vast body of water east of town.

"Nobody's going to know what town she's talking about if she says it like that. Call it Kaskittyway, just like everybody else does," Pete suggested to Emily.

"So the town is named for that swamp?" Emily ignored Pete, and stood next to Daniel, studying the map.

"Yes," he replied, looking down at her, trying to remember what he was going to say next.

"Kas-key-tay-a-say-uw Knee-Pee!" Emily repeated the lesson and smiled up at him.

Self-consciously, Daniel muttered, "Ah, if I'm going to get to Anna's before dark, I'd better get going. Thank you for the information, Detective Harrigan."

"Hope it helps."

"I will see you, tomorrow then, I guess," Daniel said, reaching for his jacket.

"Warden Claret," Emily said quickly, "before you go, if I may, I'd like to see your files on any cases you or Constable Hines are working on."

Pete snatched the folder off Daniel's desk and offered it to her. "Here you go."

He rocked back on his heels, proud that they had at least one active case to show her, but when he caught Daniel's exasperated look, he shrugged an apology.

"This is it?" Emily was accustomed to at least ten updates passing over her desk each day.

"Well, it's a slow time, calm before the storm. Just wait until rifle season starts. You didn't need that tonight, did you, Daniel?"

"I don't need it tonight."

"Don't forget the chili sauce." Pete shoved the bag towards him. "Tell Anna 'good-bye' for us."

"Good afternoon, Detective Harrigan." Daniel nodded politely to Emily. He picked up the bag and went out.

CHAPTER 3

"When did Warden Pike retire?" Emily looked up from the file.

"None too soon," Pete said with relief.

"Why do you say that?"

"Ely was about as useful as teats on a bull," the constable quipped. "Sorry, I mean, he was the kind to look the other way if there was poaching going on. People, around here, got used to that. He retired about a year ago."

"I take it this warden doesn't look the other way?"

"Daniel? Geezum, no, he's like a badger," Pete said. "So what do you want to see first?"

"I'd like to see the town, look at more maps, a topographical one too."

"Tell you what," Pete said, handing Emily her sweater, "let's walk around town and I'll introduce you to some people you should know."

"Walk around the whole town?"

"If we drove through it, you wouldn't have time to see anything," Pete said.

"I'll leave the sweater here. It's a beautiful afternoon."

"Supposed to get cold tonight though—maybe the first frost." He held the door open for her.

"A frost?" Emily exclaimed with disbelief. "There are still flowers blooming in Manchester."

Locking the door behind him, he told her, "I found a place for you to stay. It's in Mica, about 20 minutes from here. Nice family, the

Wrights. They have an apartment above their garage. It's small but it has a bath and little kitchen area."

"Sound's great! How much for the month?"

"Three hundred okay?"

"Absolutely!"

As they walked on, Emily studied the dirt roads which radiated from a central paved street. "It must be hard getting around here in winter."

"Would be in that Mustang of yours," he said, looking back at her car, "but that's one real pretty horse."

"Make it two hundred and twenty five horses," she said, glancing at the car with pride. Fixing up the Mustang had allowed her time to be with her father, now that he no longer worked with her at the police department.

They went to the center of the paved area, into what would be called a 'cul-de-sac' in suburbia. A half-a-dozen clapboard buildings stood around it, most with peeling paint. Little dusty roads led away from the pavement into the forested hills.

"I hope you don't take this the wrong way, but why does anyone live up here?" Emily asked. "It's so desolate."

"Some folks like the wilderness. Some, like me and Daniel, have lived here all our lives. A lot of people work at the paper mills, west of here. Some just want to get away from it all, like you."

Emily smiled, but said ruefully, "I assume my father has filled you in?"

"I know that Detective Harrigan thinks highly of his daughter and loves her very much," Pete said, turning to her, "and is worried about her. He says she doesn't talk or laugh like she used to, and has trouble sleeping."

Emily said nothing.

"You won't have any problems here," Pete said encouragingly. "I run a peaceful town. When the deer rifle season starts, we might get a problem or two, but I'll be back long before then."

"Sounds like just what I'm looking for."

"Here's somebody," Pete remarked, as if he had just encountered another human being on a deserted island. "Joe!"

"Hey, what's up, Pete?" The man was locking up the barred door of his shop, 'Joe's Guns & Ammo'. A pretty, black Newfoundland dog circled his legs expectantly.

"This is Detective Emily Harrigan. She is going to be standing in for me while I'm on vacation."

"Hey, nice to meet you, Detective," the man said politely. He turned back to Pete. "Are you and Susanne still going to the Bahamas?"

"Oh, yeah, three whole weeks of cruisin' and snoozin'."

"Cut it out, Gwen," Joe scolded the dog, who was licking Emily's extended hand.

"You're a pretty girl," Emily said, stooping to pet the big dog.

"Hey, Detective, you want a puppy? She is going to have puppies," Joe asked hopefully.

"I'd love one but my apartment in the city won't allow it." Emily rubbed the dog beneath her chin. "Otherwise, I would love to have one of your puppies. Yes, I would."

"Hey, while I've got you," Joe refocused on the constable. "Tell Daniel that Faidlee was in here with this other guy buying some heavy duty 'munitions. Name was, oh, what was it?" He scratched the goatee on his thin face. "Patterson, Eric Patterson—looked like a real flatlander."

"Yeah, I heard something to that affect. I'll let him know, Joe. Thanks for the tip." Pete walked on as Emily said good-bye to both Joe and the dog.

"Don't you think that's something the warden should know, now?" Emily caught up with him.

"Daniel will have that figured out. You gave him the license to the SUV. I'm sure he is searching for the car as we speak."

"But he said he was going to Anna's."

"He'll search first. He's got a pretty good idea where to look. Bringing a client into the picture gives Daniel the timing he needed."

"There were two of them. Won't the warden need back-up?" Emily asked, concerned.

"Game wardens usually don't use back-up when it comes to poaching. It's too hit—or-miss. Fish and game department can't afford it. They're stretched thin with just search and rescues. Daniel's area is the whole county, about eighteen hundred square miles."

"That's a lot of territory to cover," Emily said, thinking of the amount of law enforcement officers it took just to cover Manchester. She had worked with game wardens before, on recoveries, but never realized how solitary and lonely the job must be.

Next, Emily met the town's postmistress, Ila Brown. The grim-faced woman leveled her eyes at Emily like she was just one more person who would come and go. She couldn't even be bothered with taking the time to learn her name.

"Is Officer Claret around?" she addressed Pete pointedly, ignoring Emily's introduction.

"He's off duty." Pete shoved his hands in his pockets. "You need something, Ila?"

"I need to talk to him." The postmistress didn't seem to trust Pete completely.

"Can I help?" Pete offered.

"You? No!"

"Well, you're not going to be able to reach him. He'll be in tomorrow," Pete was all too happy about his coming trip to harbor an insult. "See you, Ila."

As she followed Pete out, Emily studied Ila's sullen eyes and decided that the woman must be worried about something. The phone rang just as they were going out the door and Ila turned away, hunching over it. Her hand was shaking as she picked up the receiver. One word drifted to Emily's ears, "*Safe.*"

Once outside, they approached the house of Dr. Pomfret. The sign beside the door said Health and Dental Clinic, but he was the only one listed. The door was open and they found him cleaning dirt out of a cut on a man's hand.

"What the hell did you do to yourself, Frenchie?" Pete asked.

"You know those two hounders, Bailey and Josh. They were whooping it up last night and broke a bottle." The man winced as the doctor took out a suture needle. "Just cut my hand cleaning up after. I thought it would close by itself."

27

"Why didn't you call me?"

"Wasn't a fight or anything; nothing I couldn't handle. You know those two, not a lick of sense between 'em."

"Detective Harrigan, this is Al French, owns the watering hole in town."

Emily shook his left hand saying, "It's nice to meet you."

"The Detective is going to be taking my place while I'm on vacation, so keep that bar of yours respectable."

"Yes, sir," Frenchie said obligingly, but Emily saw him roll his eyes in the doctor's direction.

"And this is Doc Pomfret. I don't know what we'd do without him," Pete said.

The gray-haired, bespectacled man with a kind face, looked up and said, "It is nice to meet you, Detective. Sorry I can't shake your hand."

"Doc was a dentist in Errol, but he left us for a few years after his wife died. She had a heart attack. He went to Canada and came back as a doctor too. He can handle just about anything in this town from birthin' babies to…"

"Thank you, Peter," the doctor interrupted, as if the constable had relayed a little too much information. "Put the closed sign on the door on your way out, please."

The old Doctor winked at Emily as if sharing a joke.

As they stood outside the clinic, Pete swept the area with his eyes. "That's enough for one day. Over there is Kevin's 'Kountry' Store. He sells pretty good meats and his vegetables are about as fresh as they come up here. His wife runs the Bear Bones Diner. We'll check out the other places tomorrow."

Emily wondered what other places? There wasn't much here as far as she could see. It was so different from Manchester. She followed him as he strode determinedly back to the office.

"I'm going to give you a map to the Wrights and call it a day." Pete was obviously anxious to get to his 'one night' bachelor pad. "Let's get inside. State Bird is coming out."

"What?" Emily asked, smiling.

28

Pete had to admit she was a pretty; no wonder Daniel was so smitten. It was apparent that she was a good detective, but he wondered if this slender woman could command authority in a town where authority was too often disregarded. Daniel would help her. He'd bet on that.

Pete slapped a mosquito and showed it to her saying, "New Hampshire State Bird. Tonight's freeze should put the skids on 'em."

Pete led her back into the office, tapping his pen impatiently as she e-mailed her parents with the apartment's phone number. He drew a map to the Wrights' house, gave her his phone number in case she had trouble finding it, and stuck it all into Daniel's folder. They left the office and with a wave he was gone in his cruiser.

Emily looked around before getting into her Mustang. A leaf fell on her car roof, and she actually heard it. Taking a deep breath of the clean, colder air, she got into the car and headed for the even smaller village of Mica.

CHAPTER 4

Daniel stopped at Anna and Russell's old house with its stone chimney and arched doorway. It stood solitary against a waning blue sky. The last owners hadn't been up here since spring; they were elderly and finding it harder to drive up from New York.

A quarter of a century had passed since Russell Miner built his wife a home atop Birch Hill, and it still looked good in spite of the overgrown grass. One window shutter hung askew, the victim of a summer storm.

Daniel had a vague memory of Anna standing in the doorway with a young, dark-haired woman who was crying. At once the memory vanished like the milkweed seeds blowing across the yard.

He went a half mile further and looked down the trail which led to the camp at the base of Birch Hill. Daniel had built the hunting camp with, Rusty, Anna's son. Now, after Rusty's death, it was Anna's retreat from the world. Every time Daniel came near it, the memory of his 'brother' stabbed his heart.

Daniel drove past the trail and ten miles further, looking for the black SUV which Detective Harrigan had mentioned. There had been no recent sign of the car or activity near the bait pile which he had staked out earlier on South Worth Road. Faidlee could be anywhere. It would take all night to search every one of the grass covered trails around the swamp and there was no certainty Faidlee was even poaching near the swamp area.

Pete was right; Emily Harrigan was a good detective. In a chance meeting, she had managed to find out 'who', 'what' and 'when', but it would have been nice to know 'where'. Perhaps Faidlee, realizing the detective heard him, called off his hunt or moved to another location. It was five o'clock and the shorter days assured an earlier darkness.

Daniel turned the jeep around. After dinner and splitting a week's wood for Anna, he would go back out. If the sound of gun fire didn't direct him, he would comb the area looking for jack lights illuminating a kill. For now, Anna was expecting him.

He turned down the steep logging path full of jutting stone and rain-carved gullies. As the jeep bounced and lurched, he had to hold the jars of sauce against the passenger seat to keep them from breaking. Daniel came to a stop at Kaskitesiw Nipiy.

A blue heron walked stiffly around the eastern bank of the swamp, searching for tardy hibernators. About twenty Canadian geese floated a third of the way out, soon to launch into their migration southward, for this evening would bring frost. In the chill of the late afternoon, the warmer swamp exuded mist which undulated over the surface, like water spirits inhabiting the air once more. Anna had given this wooded area of the vast swamp the nickname, nipiy nipahayawin, *water without life*, because of its shadowy trees and black peat bottom.

Daniel parked his Jeep next to the ATV which he sometimes used to bring supplies to Anna. The tamaracks were beginning to yellow on the far side of the swamp. Soon they would turn a golden red. Before they shed their needles, they would be the color of the summer deer, the color of Emily Harrigan's hair.

Daniel got out of the Jeep. It was bad to be thinking this way. What would someone like her want with someone like him? She would grow tired of this isolation, as his mother had. No one he ever cared for stayed. Even Anna had retreated from him, in spirit.

He concentrated on the clean, cold smell of the front coming in. The wind was getting stronger by the minute. No longer in uniform, he carried a spark plug in his flannel shirt pocket. It was to replace the useless one in the old ATV. This was his means of starting the old machine and protecting it from thieves since it had no key. The spark plug would stay in his pocket. He was glad Anna did not need gasoline for her generator, or propane for her lights and refrigeration. This afternoon he would walk to the camp, in spite of the heavy jars of sauce.

Daniel rolled up his sleeves, adjusted his knapsack, and set off down the path, which was no more than a game track now. His tall, lean frame moved easily over the loose gravel and stubbly vegetation. Scampering down the steepest sections of the trail, Daniel's feet moved respectfully over the earth. He avoided plants which he knew were uncommon, medicinal, or useful in halting erosion.

The forest floor smelled of rich humus. In spite of the dry summer, in the hollow of these hills, the mosses were vibrant green. Shiny-leafed bear berries carpeted the poorer soil along the path. Raspberries hung ripe within their thorny bramble. About half way down the hill, he stopped. Slowly, he turned to the side. A crack of a limb had echoed off near-by Grave Hill, loud enough to be either a man or a large animal.

Daniel smelled him before he saw him. A big black bear was coming towards the trail sniffing the air, wet nose glistening in the leaf filtered sun. A drool of saliva clung to the edge of its mouth.

The bear was on the trail of food but strangely ignoring the brush of berries near it. Something more tantalizing had caught its attention and its nose twitched, searching for the source. Its head was flat, its nose wide and its teeth yellow with age.

"What are you looking for, Grandfather?" Daniel spoke quietly to the bear rather than surprise him.

The massive animal planted its feet and swung its huge head in Daniel's direction, looking at him with small eyes.

"What is it you smell that is better than these ripe berries?"

The animal made a low rumble in its chest. It stepped to one side then swayed back to stare at Daniel again, sniffing loudly.

"Go back to your berries, Grandfather." Daniel's voice was firm and calm as he slid the backpack off his arms. "Whatever else cannot be as good for you. It might even be bait."

The bear opened its mouth with a deep resonating warning, and then swayed back and forth. With a snort, it rose on its back legs, nose high in the air.

Daniel knew this gesture was not a threat. The bear was just trying to get a better whiff of where his meal was, for bears are hampered by poor eyesight and their noses are the best sensors they have. To leave newly ripened raspberries behind, Daniel assumed what was on the bear's mind was a meal of carrion, a dead deer or moose. The black bear scavenged, therefore playing dead wasn't an option to escape the razor-sharp claws.

Dropping back down on all fours, the bear sniffed the ground noisily and looked at Daniel again. It popped its jaw irritably. This man was in its way.

Daniel knew the best deterrent to an attack was scaring the bear; especially since he was between the animal, and what it wanted. He slowly unbuckled the strap to his back pack and reached inside, always watching the bear, but not looking directly into its eyes. He had a revolver inside the pack but chose an air horn instead.

Daniel spoke again, calling the bear by its Cree name. "You might even be going to a trap, maskwa. You don't know. The raspberry fruit is good for you. What you desire may not be. Is it down the path we are both on?" He knew the bear was going to consider this conversation closed very soon now.

The huge creature moved onto the trail. It began pushing at the ground with his front feet.

Daniel turned with him, his sneakers making no sound. His eyes were wary, but amused. "Are you telling me to get moving? I apologize to you, Grandfather, but I was going this way first. You must go another time," he stated simply.

Head low, the bear stared at Daniel. He did not move and no longer made noises of warning. His ears were back.

Daniel watched him, knowing the bear was close to posing a threat. In a deep voice he commanded, "Namoya maskwa! Awas! *No bear! Go!*"

The bear sniffed the air once more and decided not to comply with the game warden's wishes. Half-way across the path, the bear turned and made an intimidating charge towards Daniel. Daniel lifted the can of compressed air and pressed the button.

The first blast of the air horn made the animal jump, all four feet splaying apart. The second blast sent him running back up the trail, black coat rippling in the late afternoon sun. Daniel admired the

big animal as it heaved itself into a powerful gallop. The bear could overtake a person, and would do so, if someone triggered a predator-prey response by trying to run away.

Daniel shoved the horn into the knapsack and swung it onto his back. Anna probably heard the sound and would be putting dinner on. He was hungry; there had been no time to eat this day.

Three quarters of the way down the hill, Daniel found a heap of ripe animal remains. It's what the bear had been looking for. Daniel stooped over it, hoping to find out who was baiting bear illegally. There was no identification sign. With a stick, he probed the gruesome heap searching for any clue he could use as evidence. The flies, sluggish from the growing cold, rose, and then alighted back on the meat.

This time the poacher had been more careful. There was no ear tag and no way to identify the remains. It was entrails, hide and head of a single cow, a home butchering, not done in a slaughter house. Anyone in the area could have done it. It would be much more difficult to trace the perpetrator.

Daniel looked around him, staring hard up the slope. He probed the brush and forest with his eyes. More than that, he listened. At one point, he thought he heard voices, but the wind direction made it hard to tell.

The bear he encountered would stay close to these remains, consuming them at leisure. The cow's skull would afford it hours of play, much like humans play with a ball. However, within a short time, the bear would be shot by a long distance, high powered rifle. Mother bears and growing cubs were especially vulnerable this way.

Sliding the pack off, he took oleoresin capsicum, pepper spray foam, and sprayed the contents of the can over the remains. The caustic foam would stay on the meat, making it inedible, and irritating to the eyes and nose of the bear. Daniel dropped the empty container into a side pocket of his pack and rubbed his hands on the earth.

He would be at Anna's in a few moments and could hear a rifle shot from there. If they shot the bear at this bait pile, the poachers would get more than they bargained for. He would run back up the trail and be here to meet them as they lugged their kill uphill.

Daniel, wanting the crime to stand up for a conviction in court, was forced into waiting until the poachers brought down the bear. Daniel hoped this bear would avoid the bait pile. If the poachers were watching, he hoped they were discouraged by his tainting the remains and would leave to kill another day.

CHAPTER 5

"Hi Mom!" Emily lounged back on the comforter and evaluated the mattress quality. She had walked in with her suitcase only moments before the phone rang next to the bed.

"How do I do what? I knew you'd call after I e-mailed the number. I've got to charge up my cell phone...Pete? He's nice...No I haven't met Susanne yet...met the doctor, postmistress, gun shop owner, game warden and oh, the owner of the bar...the doctor is very old, Mom... sorry to burst your bubble."

She stretched content with the firmness of the bed. "He will get over it...Seth is in love with Seth. Oh, tell Dad that Ely Pike has retired. There is a new warden...No, he's certainly not retirement age...Daniel Claret. He's American Indian...Whoa! Where is this coming from? No, I just thought it appropriate since those people are into nature..."

Emily sat up. "Mother what an awful thing to say about someone you don't even know...You don't hear anything in my voice...I'm only here a month. Besides he has a wife or girlfriend named Anna."

Emily listened dutifully as her mother switched the subject to Aunt Marge's condition. "Mom, I love you, but I'm tired. I'll call tomorrow... Yes, I promise. Love you. Tell Dad I love him—Bye."

Emily put her hands to her forehead and blinked hard a couple of times. She wondered how old she had to be before her parents stopped wanting to know her every move or, in her mother's case, trying to manipulate it.

With a heavy sigh, she looked around. The room was clean and smelled of lemon furniture polish. She made her way over squeaking floorboards to the curtain and pushed it back. Tilting her head, Emily smiled curiously, for the window was put in sideways to accommodate the roof line. Amazingly, it opened.

She took a deep breath. It was a clear evening, the wind crisp with the promise of autumn. In the driveway, two little girls about five years old were arguing. She leaned out and called down, "What's the matter?"

The little blond girl whined, "She says I can't take the scooter home."

"She had it last night!" The other little girl in overalls and brown pig-tails put her hand on her hip.

Emily couldn't help but smile at the child's grown-up posturing. "What's your name?"

"Tracy Wright, and my Mommy and Daddy own this place. All of it! Even up where you are!" She pointed to Emily as if to put her in her place.

"Where do you live?" Emily addressed the little blond girl.

"Right over there." She pointed.

"Well, Tracy, I have an idea. Do you want to hear my idea?"

Tracy didn't look so sure.

"How about if you let your friend ride the scooter home—now, wait a minute," she said laughing, "and you walk with her—making sure she gets home okay. Then you can ride the scooter back to your house again."

A bit of a hold out, Tracy screwed up her mouth but then shouted, "Yeah! Let's go! I'll beat you running."

Almost out of earshot she heard Tracy's demand, "But tomorrow I keep it at my house."

Emily laughed and started to close the window.

"Thank you!"

She leaned back out and saw a robust woman in a flannel shirt and jeans. It was Lisa, who had rented her this attic apartment.

"I don't think anything is solved, just postponed," Emily admitted.

"A temporary peace is all I ask for." Lisa put a folded towel into a basket.

Emily asked, "Could you tell me where the grocery store is in town?"

"There isn't any. You've got to go back to Kaskittyway."

Emily wasn't anxious to get back in her car and drive the approximate hour into town and back. She tried to weigh which felt worse, tiredness or hunger. "What about that place, just as you turn onto this street?"

"Wally's?"

"I guess."

"They pretty much sell soda, beer and night crawlers," Lisa said.

"I'll pass on that."

"Why don't you come and join us for supper tonight?"

"Oh, that's not necessary. I don't want to impose." Emily sensed the woman now felt obliged.

"Come down. It's no trouble," Lisa insisted.

"Thanks!"

Tracy met her at the door.

"Back already?" Emily asked.

Surprisingly, Tracy held up her arms to be picked up. Emily lifted the child and closed her eyes, relishing the tiny arms around her neck. "Oh, you smell so good, like baby lotion."

"Is everything okay upstairs?" Lisa Wright wiped her hands and beckoned her into the kitchen.

"Perfect!"

The heavy, dark haired woman was pretty when she smiled. "You make the salad?"

"Happy to!" Emily put the child on the stool next to where the vegetables were laid out.

"George will be home soon. Then we'll eat." Lisa stirred the venison stew.

"Where does your husband work?"

"Paper mill in Berlin—ways to drive, but steady work."

"How long does it take him to get there?" Emily asked, picking up some of the draining lettuce.

"'Bout a half hour—depending on the weather."

"It must be a half an hour to anywhere up here," Emily said, amused. "The constable said it was only twenty minutes from Kaskitesiw to Mica but it's more like a half an hour. I'm only five minutes away from most places in Manchester."

Lisa looked over at Emily, frowning. "You met the new warden."

"Warden Claret? Yes—how did you know?

"Way you pronounced the name of the town," Lisa said abruptly then added, "Tracy, go wash your hands. Stew's done."

The little girl dusted the last of the lettuce pieces off her hands and skipped into the other room.

"The last warden was liked by a lot of folks up here." Lisa said in a lower voice. "He made it easier for us to put food on the table, if you know what I mean." Lisa winced and then said uneasily, "I can't believe I'm telling this to a cop. You don't seem like a cop. Anyway, Ely Pike didn't just retire on his own. Claret had something to do with it. Just stay away from him and you'll be okay."

Emily studied Lisa's face gravely, hoping she would continue.

"It's different up here." Lisa shrugged. "People use hunting season to get rid of things they don't like; a neighbor's barking dog; another guy moving in on a man's wife—and they don't like the new warden telling them what they can and can't do. You be careful."

"What people are we talking about?" Emily asked, as if it didn't matter. She made a show of tossing the lettuce hoping to relax Lisa into a further discussion.

Hearing the screen door slam, Lisa whispered, "I can't get George in trouble at work. It's probably just mill talk."

A man walked in, curly brown hair plaited down his back and sporting a shaggy mustache. Tracy was latched onto his neck like a tick. "Who's this, our new boarder?"

"I'm Emily Harrigan. You must be George."

"Nice to meet yuh," he said, gently extracting his daughter from her strangulation hold and putting her hands under the kitchen faucet. "So, how is Pete Hines these days?" George asked over his shoulder.

"I've only just met him, but he seems nice," Emily said. "His dad is a friend of my father's."

"We're cousins." George wiped Tracy's hands and then his own.

"That explains why I was lucky enough to get this apartment."

Throughout dinner, Tracy chattered about everything from school, playmates, to her new baby sister who was coming in February. She was positive that the baby would be a girl because boys were yucky.

Emily listened, Lisa's warning still troubling her. Threats to fellow law enforcement officers were a priority on her list, along with threats to children, and her mind drifted back to that little hand she had found protruding from the leaves in Bow Park. She wondered how many times her name had been called before she came back to the present. "I'm sorry?"

"You seemed so far away," Lisa said, concerned. "You okay?"

"I'm fine. What were you saying?"

"I was wondering if on your day off, you might want to drive down to Littleton with me—outlet there has baby clothes."

"Oh, yes, I would love to go with you. It would be fun picking out things for a baby."

Emily helped Lisa clear the table and wash the dishes. All the while, Lisa, who seemed to want another woman's company, chatted about the new things that were on the market for children and the few things she could afford.

"I didn't think I'd like deer meat but the stew was wonderful. If you don't mind me excusing myself…" Emily said, drying the last dish.

"It's only a bit before six. We ate early. You're welcome to stay down."

"That's sweet and I'll take you up on the offer soon, but right now I'm tired and looking forward to that nice bath tub upstairs. Thank you again."

Lisa walked her to the door and said in a low voice, "You're not upset 'cause of what I told you? There are some real hard ass guys at the mill, but it might be just water cooler talk. George isn't one of them, okay?"

Emily nodded, understanding more now about the people she was going to swear to protect tomorrow. Lisa and her husband didn't have much, but they had shared their food with her. They were survivors, hard working in a hard land, and not opposed to taking advantage of an opportunity to add to their winter food stores, be it legal or not. The

40

less law enforcement they had interfering in their lives, the better. They didn't think long-term enough to realize that if there were no game wardens, eventually there would be no game.

"Tell me more when you can," Emily whispered back, and then changing her tone, "Night, George! Night, Tracy!"

CHAPTER 6

At the sound of the air horn blasts, Faidlee brought his head up from his rifle sight. He had been watching the pile of entrails, waiting.

"What was that?" Mr. Patterson started to rise off his knees.

Faidlee hauled him back behind the rock. "What the hell do you think you're doin'?"

"What was that?" The man repeated, pushing back his glasses.

Faidlee let go of the man's hunting jacket and then slapped at the sleeve, as if straightening out wrinkles he may have put in the wool. He grinned sarcastically at his client. "I said you was gunna' get a bear and you're gunna' get a bear. You don't want to scare him now, do you?"

Every pore in Faidlee's body exuded the stench of alcohol and cigarettes. His greasy hair was pulled back in a pony tail which stuck out from under his "I DON'T ARGUE WITH MY WIFE, I DICKER" baseball cap.

"Relax. That was just somebody that doesn't have the sense enough to keep his damn nose out of other people's business."

"Who is it?"

"You ask an awful lot of questions for someone who hires a guy from a newspaper ad to get him a bear." Faidlee looked back down the sight of his rifle at the pile of entrails.

"Look. I don't like what's going on here. Something is just not right. Who was that woman back there—at the gas station?" Patterson peeked over the rock.

"That woman was my wife, and if I don't catch up with her, because you tried to run off, that bear's is not going to be the only hide that's hanging." Faidlee spat out tobacco and pushed his cap visor off his forehead. His brow was oily with blemishes.

"Are you threatening' me?" The man adjusted his glasses and reached inside his coat.

Faidlee swung the gun towards him, eyes dangerous.

"Look, you can have the money. You kept your part of the bargain." Patterson handed him a wad of twenty dollar bills.

"Don't you want your bear, Mr. Patterson?" Faidlee spoke with feigned contrition, his eyes moving to the path. "Don't you want a picture of that big bear with that pretty get-up you're wearing? Show all the women in your office?"

"I'm beginning to think we're doing something illegal."

Faidlee snickered. "Now, just when did you figure that out? When you didn't have to buy a hunting license?"

"I thought it was all taken care of."

"You thought it was all taken care of," Faidlee mimicked. "Well it is!" He nodded and patted him on the back. "Now, just calm down. That old bear ain't gunna' to be scared off by that horn for long. They're territorial. He smells the meat and he'll keep coming back."

"Look, as I said, you can keep the money. It's all here. I'd like to go back now."

"Shit," Faidlee said softly.

Patterson squinted in the direction Faidlee was looking. "Who is that?"

"Officer Daniel Claret." Faidlee rolled the name out of his mouth as if trying to get rid of a bad taste.

"That's a police officer?" Patterson stuttered.

"Game warden—must be going down to the camp. Keep your mouth shut. He'll probably go right on by."

Both men knelt behind the rock silently. Faidlee could feel Patterson shaking, and felt empowered by it.

However, Daniel didn't go by. The smell of decay had drawn him to the entrails.

"Well, you ain't gunna' do it, are you?" Faidlee aimed the rifle at Daniel again. "You ain't gunna' keep your nose out of my business.

Questionin' a man's wife about him; causin' her to leave her husband."
He adjusted the site to his eye, speaking low and venomously, "I have
been huntin' these hills longer than you've been livin'. Just who the
hell do you think you are?"

"I'm, I'm just going to meet you at the car." Patterson started to
crawl away.

"Stickin' your—get back over here!" Faidlee physically pushed the
man down. He got a frightened nod from Patterson, and then turned
his attention to Daniel again.

"Shit, he spooked the pile! Ain't no bear comin' to it now. Last
one you'll ever spook though. I said sit still!" He gave Patterson his
attention once more and then turning back, squeezed the trigger slowly.
The rifle fired, its sound reverberating on the steep walls of Birch and
Grave hills repeatedly.

"Oh—oh—I can't believe…" Patterson began scooting away from
Faidlee on his plaid bottom. "You killed a game warden!"

"Think so?" Faidlee looked back down his site. "Hey, you're right!
Richard Faidlee hasn't lost his touch. Blood everywhere, musta' hit
the heart." Patterson turned onto his knees and was crawling uphill.

Faidlee asked, "Where do you think you're goin'?"

Patterson had made it to his feet and was stumbling back to the car
hidden on one of the grass-covered swamp roads.

Faidlee grinned. "Hey come back here, you little twit. You can't
outrun me. I'll even give you a head start." Faidlee stopped and sucked
on a decayed tooth, satisfied. Then he shouted down to the camp.
"That's both your boys, you uppity squaw."

~~~~~

Anna stopped washing the pot and listened as the gunshot echoed
off the surrounding hillsides. Taaniyal was due. He came twice a week,
refusing to let her submit to this reclusive life she'd chosen. He came
with food, knowing she would not let it go to waste. He came with the
supplies which she needed to live, though she had come here wanting to

die. She would argue with him about bringing such things and he would banter back about not wanting an old woman's death on his hands.

Anna opened the door and squinted up the winding path. The shot had been close. Granted, people were out sighting their guns for the coming season, but few ventured this deep into the woods to practice their aim.

"Taaniyal, what are you doing to an old woman?" She limped back to the sink. "Ah, Tahkayaaw. Namawiya Kinatoonaatin*! It is cold. I am not going to go look for you!"*

Anna went back to scour the pot and shifted the crock of soup onto a cooler area of the wood stove top. "Taaniyal, where are you?" She repeated, putting her hands on her wide hips.

It was a single shot—another sign of a serious kill rather than the sighting of a gun. She had heard the air horn. Taaniyal must have been chasing off a bear with it. Maybe the bear hadn't left. It may have attacked. Perhaps Taaniyal had been forced to shoot it.

Anna shook her head and walked back to the door. She stared up the incline through glass lenses so thick they distorted the size of her eyes. The sound had been from a powerful rifle. Taaniyal would be off duty and would not have a rifle with him, only the revolver she knew he kept hidden in his pack. He did not want to remind her that Rusty was killed by a terrorist's gun. "He should be here by now!"

Snatching a shawl and her walking stick from where it leaned against the wall, she started up the hill. The arthritis in her knees hurt with each step.

Soon she abandoned the angry stride caused by the thought that Taaniyal was somehow teasing her. Rusty would do that kind of thing but Taaniyal would not. He always came when he said he would, always did what he said he would.

Grabbing at bushes and small tree limbs with her free hand, she climbed pausing at times to listen for the sound of Taaniyal's descending foot falls on the stony trail. She stopped once more to catch her breath and then shouted, "Taaniyal, if you think it is funny to worry an old woman, you will get the end of my broom."

There was no answer.

A humming sound caused her to look back at the camp. She had forgotten to turn off the generator. She had needed it to pump tepid water out of the old water heater for scrubbing the pot. It was a waste of gasoline, but she did not turn back.

Once more, she climbed the rigorous slope. There was no sound but the wind and the distant hum of the generator. Not a bird chirped, not a chipmunk fussed, not even a leaf rustled. There was, however, a smell, a decaying stench, which caused Anna to screw up her nose. Pushing back a hemlock branch, she heard the hum of flies and saw the pile of animal remains.

She spat distastefully. "Lazy, no good poachers."

Then she saw his body covered in blood.

"Taaniyal! Kisemanito kisewaatisi*! Daniel! Oh, God be merciful!*" Painfully she knelt on the ground.

His eyes were closed. There was blood on his forehead, but the rest of it was something else.

Anna's fingers dug through the red ooze to his neck then touched her fingers to her tongue, murmuring, "brown sugar, vinegar—tomatoes?"

There was a sound of broken glass as she pulled the back pack from his shoulder and unlatched the buckle.

A torn label clung damply to a shard of a canning jar.

"A gift for Anna from Susanne's Kitc…"
"Chili Sau…"

"Chili Sauce!" she cried. "This is chili sauce, Taaniyal. Wake up! It is not blood. Taaniyal, wake up! What has happened to you? You must wake up!" She shook him.

Daniel stirred and tried to push himself up. His right arm buckled and he rolled to his side. The vinegar burned his eyes.

Anna roughly wiped his face with her shawl pushing the sticky hair off his forehead. She studied the gash frowning and snapped, "What have you done to yourself, Taaniyal?"

He tasted the sauce and blood dripping into his mouth. "The chili sauce must have exploded," he muttered.

"Nonsense, Susanne is a good cook. How did you get the cut on your head?" She scolded as if demanding to know he got mud on his shoes. "You fell on this rock? Did you fall?" Roughly she wiped his forehead again.

"Ow, I don't know. I guess," he said and tried to reach his right hand to his head but a stab of pain beneath his arm stopped him. "I think I have a piece of glass stuck under my arm."

"Here, let me have a look. You and Rusty! Always getting into trouble!" Anna clucked her tongue and adjusting her thick glasses, "Why I am gray! Why I am crippled!"

The back of his shirt was soaked. There was a tear in the flannel beneath his arm. Its edges were hard and singed. She peered within the cloth. Then Anna drew back quickly.

A grouse flew out of a stand of low shrubs and startled her. She glanced around nervously then back to Daniel, patting him on the arm as if doing it would help her think. "Can you stand? You must stand, Taaniyal!"

Daniel did not answer; he was already on his knees trying to shake the dizziness from his head.

"Taaniyal," she firmly demanded, "Maci Waniskaa! *Get up!*"

Daniel was used to that tone of voice. He'd heard it for the last twenty five years. As he staggered to his feet, Anna dragged him forward by his left hand.

"Is it Maskwa?" he asked, blinking the burning sauce from his eyes. He tried to make sense of the writhing snakelike path, tried to keep his feet on it. "Anna, is it the bear?"

"We need to get to the camp, and I cannot carry you," she snapped.

There was urgency in her demeanor, which, in spite of the way the woods pitched and whirled in his vision, triggered the need to see her safe also.

"Anna, is it the bear? We need to stop running," he urged her again, stumbling on a root.

Anna grabbed his arm, roughly keeping his tangled feet beneath him. She continued to push him down the steep hill. "It is not Maskwa. Keep going."

He fell and the pain in his side and head tempted him to stay where he was.

"Taaniyal, Pasi'ko semaak! *Daniel, Stand up right now!*" Anna shouted in his face. "It is not the damn bear! You must get up!"

Her short, stocky arms, with surprising strength, pulled at him until he got to his feet. Then she pushed him down the hill once more. A few more yards and they were at the camp door.

She shoved him inside and locked the door behind them. The racket of the generator vibrated the walls, but she didn't flip the inside switch to shut it off.

"Get into the shower," she shouted above the sound of the generator. "I cannot begin to see what's wrong with you until you get some of that sauce off."

Supporting himself on the bed frame and rocking chair, he did as he was told. Anna could pull that piece of glass out of his side, but she had to be able to see it. His hair hung thick with the sauce, making his eyes feel like they were on fire.

The water came on and he was surprised to find Anna in there with him unbuttoning his shirt.

"What are you doing?" Blinking hard, he stepped back.

"What do you want—to fall in the shower? Good luck me getting you out of there," she growled.

"Anna, I'm okay. Ow, Anna!" he protested as the flannel rubbed against his injured side.

"Then you do it! I will steady you, but hurry up. You will not be able to stand here long at the rate you are going," she shouted.

"Anna, I can do this by myself. I am no longer a child," he protested.

"Then do not act like a child. I am an old woman. You think you have something that will surprise me?"

He turned away and unzipped his jeans.

"I wiped your bottom from the time you were born. Your useless mother had no idea what to do with you." Her eyes squinted at the wound trying to see the extent of it, but it still was camouflaged by the sauce. She said, like a drill sergeant, "Underwear too. Either you do it now, or I do it later."

"Just a minute, I'm going to take my socks off!" he snapped at her, and reached down for them but lost his balance as a wave of nausea overtook him.

He couldn't argue anymore; he was just too tired and sore. She pulled off his socks then started for his underwear.

"I'll do it!" He turned away, feeling sick and humiliated. He got his underwear off, staggered against the shower wall and dropped to his knees.

Anna roughly shampooed his hair, "It is the concussion making you sick. You do not fall asleep in here. Do you hear me—you and Rusty always banging your heads, falling out of trees! Rusty hits you with a rock, 'Oh, Mama, I did not think I could throw so far.'" She scrubbed the sauce from his arms and shoulders. "Oh, Anna, I did not mean to push Rusty off the roof!'" She mimicked their childlike voices. "I would have to take you both to the doctor. I have no medicine for your heads. I think they are empty. Doctor tells me you have concussions," she said with irritation and then winced from what she saw. Gently, she wiped at his side and back with the soapy rag, rambling softly. "So I take my boys home and pray their heads fill with sense—but look at you." She grumbled louder when he seemed to be losing consciousness. "Grown into a man, but still no sense! Stand up, now! Stand under the water while I get this sauce off the rest of you. I may not have planted the seed, but I have grown you out. There is nothing wrong with my seeing what I have grown."

"Anna, I can do it!" he protested and reached up with his left hand, trying to get a purchase on the slippery wall.

"Alright, then rinse and do the rest while I find something for you to wear," she said with a stern look to determine he was still cognitive. "Do not fall down. I am too old to lift you up."

He leaned against the wall and let the water continue to rinse him. Then he turned off the water and tried to see what the problem was. Sharp pain stopped him when he tried to raise his arm. Red continued to drip down the drain. He rinsed his mouth with a swig of Anna's clove water to keep the taste of the sauce from making him sick and murmured, "If I never eat chili sauce again, it will be too soon."

The rattle of the generator sputtered, and then stopped.

"Here!" Anna came through the door clutching a pair of sweat pants. He looked at them, frowning. "Rusty's?"

"Yours! You always are leaving your things here for me to wash. I gave away Rusty's clothes, as is tradition," she said sharply and helped him pull the pants over his wet feet.

Daniel faced away from her and drew the jersey up over his hips.

Her heart physically hurt looking at the raw wound in his side and back. Taking his arm, she guided him to her bed in the middle of the room, the only room besides the bathroom.

"Pimisini. *Lay down.*" Anna ordered, pushing him a little when he hesitated. "Pimisini!"

Daniel tried to crawl up to the pillow but only made it half way, muttering, "Dad always said the reason he didn't marry you was that you were too bossy." The mattress muffled his words but she heard them.

"Kohtaawiy—sigos!" *Your father—weasel!*

"Poonihtaa! *Stop it!* Anna!" Daniel protested, "Please, just pull the glass out." He made it the rest of the way to the pillow and collapsed on his stomach.

Now that she had him safe, in a place where he could lie down, her strength and domineering attitude vanished. "Taaniyal, broken glass did not do this. I was afraid, for both of us, to tell you until I had you safe."

The bullet had entered his side mercifully shallow but it had deflected off at least one rib, shattering it, and continued on to plow through muscle until it erupted in a gaping hole in right side of his back. From there it must have gone on to explode the jars of sauce in the back pack. She could see small shards of bone driven to the surface at the exit wound.

Afraid and helpless, she dried his hair and then began pacing the small room. She had come down to this place without caring whether she lived or died. She had no means to get him to a hospital, no way to bring him help. Putting her hands against her face she cried softly, "Kirk, as we have chosen to live, I may kill your son as you have killed mine."

After a moment, her chanting ceased and her head became clear. The elderberries would still have leaves. She must gather them to draw the fever from his shattered bone, stop the bleeding.

Cautiously going down the back steps, where the generator and stores of wood were sheltered in an open area beneath, she found her way to the path. The elderberry lived near the brook. These were stubborn bushes, which liked to get their feet wet and thrived in spite of the minimal sunlight. Their powers to heal would be strong, for their fruit was still plump and their white, lacy flowers continued late into the season.

There was the sound of a kicked stone and footsteps coming down the path above her. Anna clenched her teeth and forced her eyes to acclimate to the growing darkness. She went quickly and quietly to the elderberries.

Peter would not have walked. He was the only other one who came here.

Anna filled her pockets with the leaves and gripping as many as she could in her hands, crept to the back steps. Quietly and slowly she ascended. At the top she closed the door softly and locked the bolt using the side of her leaf filled hand.

Dropping the leaves into a pot, she pulled the heavy muslin curtains shut with a single move. Without lighting a lamp Anna went to praying and the pounding of the poultice.

"Anna?" Daniel spoke as if in a dream.

"What my Taaniyal?"

"Tell Apisci-mosos, not to come."

"Tell the deer?"

"Apisci-mosos. There is danger. He is here. Tell her."

"Taaniyal, you are speaking of a deer? I don't understand."

He didn't reply. His lashes lay against his cheeks, looking like the little child his mother hadn't wanted, the little child she had loved as her own.

"You are dreaming, my son. Rest, God will help us. You must help us, Kisemato. Mother Merriyana, please send your son to help us. My heart can take no more pain."

"Mama, come!" A different voice whispered to her.

She felt Rusty near her. It had been this way, since he died, always around her. He came as a child, a child who did not want to be alone in this space between earth and heaven.

"You are so sad. Mama, come."

"No Rusty. You must go now! If I leave, your brother will die. Kiwii-itohtatahik kihci-kiisikohk. *Go now to heaven!* I need to be here for your brother." Anna wept, rocking slowly over the pot as she crushed the leaves.

CHAPTER 7

Emily was going down cellar steps. There were sticky spider webs against her cold face and hands. A single light bulb swung in its socket, moved by the fresher air pouring through the open basement door. It gave off a small amount of light, which moved across the dirt floor in an eerie sway. The stench was terrible. And there was the nurse— violated and dead.

"I've been waiting for you," the woman cried from, under the plastic. "My children are looking for me. You've got to help me get home. I can't move, please get my husband. I can't move. Help me, Emily! Help me!"

Emily sat up and grabbed her head shouting, "Stop, God, please stop!" Then she came fully awake and fearful of being heard. She listened, dreading the sound of footsteps. There were none. The garage was under the attic apartment. The temperature had dropped and she shut the window with a shiver.

A cloud of depression pressed in on her like a heavy, wet shroud. Her nightgown was stuck to her skin with perspiration. For a while, she just sat on the bed. Then, fully awake, shaking off the nightmare, she resumed reading Daniel's observation log on Richard Faidlee, picking up where she left off before falling asleep. His penmanship was crisp, legible, and more lengthy than the typed, official report, which she'd read earlier.

September 7—9:03 AM: Discharge of a firearm in a compact zone. Suspect: Richard Faidlee. Witness: Tom Lansfield, property owner. No damage, no observation of a weapon discharge. Suspect Faidlee was in the area with hunting dogs.

September 8—2:20 PM: Faidlee picking up bear hounds on South Worth Road with Bailey Wigman driving. Faidlee said he was training the dogs. Temperature in the 80's. Dogs dehydrated. No sign of a kill.

September 8—1:45 PM: On stopping at the post office, Faidlee's sister-in-law, Ila Brown, informed me that Faidlee had been drinking, abused his wife again.

September 9—9:15 AM: On a visit to Faidlee's residence, Teresa Faidlee said she didn't know where her husband was, but believed he engaged a client for bear hunting. No name for client. No timing for the hunt. No poaching location revealed. Mrs. Faidlee had bruises on her face but she would not press charges. She also mentioned her husband had given her a car, so she could pick him up, since he had lost his license. Refer: DUI accident—police profile. Mrs. Faidlee was given the name and phone number of a safe house.

September 10 3:43 PM: Josh Anderson, leaving Frenchie's with unsteady gait, said Faidlee was bragging earlier about making money by being a guide for "big paying clients". Faidlee joked that the new warden "Would find out just who ran the woods around here." Keys confiscated. Josh directed to walk home.

Emily thought about what Lisa had said and studied the rest of the log with concern.

September 11—7:40 AM: Pile of heads, tails and eviscerated remains found off South Worth Road by Rosella Thatcher while jogging. Miss Thatcher called it in on cell phone and waited until I arrived to show me the location.

September 11—8:03 AM: Baited Site visit: Tag in left ear of a sheep head, round, blue with numerical 108. Tag traced to Dennis Felton. He said he had sent sheep to slaughter house on September 8th. At Errol Slaughter House, Michael White said Richard Faidlee had asked for remains, "To trap coyotes."

September 12—1:15 PM: Completion of uninterrupted, 18 hour observation of the vicinity along South Worth Road produced no further evidence of hunting activities, dog pursuits or bait site custody. No sign of Faidlee. No evidence of poaching. Visit to Faidlee's home revealed evidence of renewed abuse toward Mrs. Faidlee.

This last entry was this afternoon and Emily put the report down. Ila, the postmistress, was Teresa's sister! Daniel gave Teresa the name of a safe house. Ila needed to talk to the warden. Was it to warn Daniel? Did Faidlee know Daniel was involved with his wife's leaving? Faidlee definitely said he wanted her to stop talking to Daniel.

"Emily, the people of Kaskitesiw have gotten on a long time without you," she said to herself, but instead of getting back into bed, she looked at her watch. It was not yet eight o'clock. "This is stupid," she told herself as she picked up her cell phone.

Teresa's sister's number was listed along with a few others. The phone rang twice and was picked up.

"Ila Brown?" Emily asked. "I met you today with the Constable. I'm Detective Harrigan. I am going to be standing in for Constable Hines while he is on vacation. Do you know if your sister is safe? No, you don't have to tell me where. Good!"

Now that her sister had escaped Ila was more talkative than at the post office.

Emily listened to her version of the story, and then concluded, "But Warden Claret had already gone to Anna's and you couldn't tell him Teresa got away. Why didn't you tell the Constable?"

Ila replied that she thought it was better that no one else knew about Teresa's escape.

"I understand that but—I'm sorry, what did you ask? Yes, he said he was going to Anna's before dark."

There was silence on the other end of the phone.

"Ila?"

Emily listened while Ila filled in the missing piece—where Faidlee had intended to hunt bear.

When Teresa called the post office, she told her sister that her husband was taking a client to Birch Hill and to tell the warden to be careful.

"Anna lives on Birch Hill and the warden was going there, off duty. Ila, do you think your brother-in-law would harm the warden?"

Emily didn't like Ila's passionate answer about being sure Richard Faidlee had killed Teresa's old boyfriend in a so-called accident at work, marrying the grief stricken sister soon afterwards. Her voice was guilt ridden about not telling Pete earlier.

"You did what you thought was best for Teresa, but I'm glad you told me now. Thank you. Please call me if you hear anything else."

Dressing quickly, Emily flipped the phone open again.

"Pete, this is Emily. You have to meet me at the office. I think Warden Claret may be in trouble." She pulled a sweater over her head and pressed the phone back to her ear. "You need to call him...why can't you call him?" She stopped and listened with a frown. "Call Anna! She may be in trouble, too." Emily jammed her Sig Sauer in the holster and slipped it over her arm. "You can't call her either? Then you need to go to Anna's."

At Pete's angry retort, Emily switched to a softer voice. "Please, Pete, you've got to trust me. I'll be at the station in twenty minutes. " She hung up, pinned her badge to her sweater pocket, slid her wallet next to it, pulled on her sneakers and put the cell phone in her other pocket. Then she was out the door and thundering down the wooden steps. The Wrights porch light came on, and she turned toward it. Her knock brought George to the door.

"George, do me a favor. What time do you get up?"

"Round 4:30." He looked at her curiously.

"If you don't see my car would you call the State Police and tell them to go to Birch Hill where a lady named Anna lives?"

"The old Indian woman? I know where she lives. Why?"

"I can't explain right now. Would you do it?"

"Sure. You need some help?"

"This would be a big help. If you see my car, don't bother calling anyone. Okay?"

"Okay." He watched, concerned, as Emily gunned the Mustang out of the drive and turned onto the main road to Kaskitesiw.

Emily burst through the police department door and Pete looked at his watch.

"Good God, girl! It's a good thing I wasn't out there tonight," the constable admonished.

"We've got to go."

"Just where do we gotta' go?"

"To Anna's. I'll explain on the way."

"You'll explain now!"

"Look, if you don't get us in a car and on our way I'll…"

"What?"

"I'll bring you up on charges that your breath smells like beer while you are in uniform. How many have you had?"

"Why you little… One!" he growled. "That's all I had time for."

"Pete, listen to me. After calling Ila, I believe Daniel is walking into an ambush."

"Daniel is cutting wood for Anna. He's going to be asleep on the porch when we get there. Why did you call Ila?"

"Give me the keys," she demanded, then snatched the keys off the desk.

"All right! All right!" He grabbed them back and started for the door. "I'm legal, damn it!"

"You'd better take a gun."

He looked at her angrily but unlocked the drawer and took out his holster. "This better be good," Pete grumbled, following her to the police cruiser. "First football game of the year and I'm out gallivanting around the countryside." He backed onto the road and headed in the direction of Birch Hill.

"Okay, now, Detective Harrigan, what's this all about?" He spoke with strained patience.

"I had this dream and couldn't sleep." The brakes came on so hard that Emily's seat belt tightened uncomfortably.

"You dreamed this all up?" Pete accused, and flicked on the interior light. He took a deep breath, trying to calm down. "Emmy, you need to see somebody. I know you have had some problems. I don't know how well I'd handle what…"

"I didn't dream this up, and I'm not crazy! Do you think I'd make a fool of myself? I'm supposed to be in your damn town for some R and R—a town that could run by itself this time of year. Isn't that what you said? All you wanted was a warm body to answer the phone. Damn it, I'm trying to get away from this shit!"

Pete sat there, hesitant to say anything else. She was staring out the front window. He could see her distraught face reflected in the windshield. Flicking off the light, he drove the cruiser slowly back onto the highway.

As he drove, Emily said quietly, "Warden Claret was going to Anna's and she lives on Birch Hill."

"Right, more like the bottom of it, but right," Pete cautiously agreed.

"Faidlee went hunting on Birch Hill today, because he had that paying client that wanted a bear."

"Emmy, Daniel and Faidlee have been at this since Daniel took over. It's like a cat and mouse game between the two of them," Pete said, trying to ease her mind.

"Ila thinks her brother-in-law killed Teresa's old boyfriend, that it wasn't an accident like everyone thought.

"That was years ago! I investigated it myself. Guy lost his footing and went down in the hot slurry at the paper mill. Nobody saw what happened."

"Apparently somebody did and was afraid to say anything. Didn't it seem strange to you, that within six months, Faidlee married that poor guy's girl? Pete, Faidlee knows Daniel had a hand in helping his wife leave."

"Daniel helped Teresa get away?"

"I read it in Daniel's report. He gave her the name of a safe house."

"Those Indians sure stick together," Pete shook his head in wonder.

"The woman was being beaten and he did what any good human being would do. I don't think it has anything to do with the fact one or both are Indians."

"I'm kidding, geezum." Pete tried to make light of what he had said to keep her from another tirade. "Look, poaching is one thing; killing a man is another. Everyone knows Richard Faidlee around here. He's a big mouth coward who beats up on his wife and dogs. He hasn't got the—well he hasn't got what it takes to kill another man. Ila never liked her brother-in-law, and I can't blame her, but there is no evidence that he steamed the Kirby boy on purpose."

Emily decided not to bring up the threats at the paper mill for it involved Pete's cousin, but her voice betrayed her concerns. "Look, these things happening at the same time could be coincidence, but I don't believe in coincidence."

"I just don't want you to get all worried about this. We'll take a look and say we're checking to see if the chili sauce was delivered. Okay?"

"Where are we?" she asked a few minutes later.

"We're heading to the town's namesake, Kaskiteway Swamp."

"Anna lives in the swamp?"

"She lives past it and down between Grave and Birch Hill. Anna and her husband, Russ, once owned twenty acres on the top of Birch Hill."

"Warden Claret isn't Anna's husband?"

He looked over, trying to read her, and she regretted the question.

"Nope," he said in a flat New England way. "Tell me, do you have these dreams about everyone or just people you care about?"

"I care about everyone, don't you? And I my dream didn't concern the warden." She pressed the button on her watch, glancing at the lit numbers. "How long is it going to take us to get there?" Her voice was businesslike.

"Another five minutes." Riffling around, Pete pulled a spark plug from the glove compartment.

She looked at him, questioning.

"ATV won't run without a new spark plug. It's a way to keep somebody from going off with it. I'm betting Daniel walked down, even with Susanne's sauce to carry. We can ride."

"What's that?" Emily jumped as something fluttered up in front of the windshield and another one flew in the headlights.

"Got me. Some people think they're moths, others swamp bats. They come around this time of the year. Mean to ask Daniel one of these days."

"Swamp bats?"

"Are you going to get spooked on me?"

"No, I like bats. They eat mosquitoes, the state bird."

He grinned. "We're almost there."

They were passing a dark house and Emily looked at him quizzically.

"That's where Anna used to live. Russ built the house, but soon after they were married, he died—lung cancer—never smoked a cigarette in his life! Anna moved into town with Rusty and Daniel. Now the house belongs to some down-country folks."

"Rusty?"

"Anna's son. She only moved out here again after Rusty was killed in Iraq. She's had a real hard time with it. Daniel and Rusty were best friends. He hasn't been the same since, either."

When Emily didn't say anything he went on, "Daniel's dad is a Marine. He was involved in that Bosnian mess but came out of it a hero for saving two of his fellow marines. He met a NATO secretary there, a French girl, married her. Folks say he had to. Daniel was born soon after."

Emily listened as she watched the headlights pick up glimpses of deep, forbidding forest.

"Everyone but Kirk, Daniel's father, expected she'd take off sooner or later. It wasn't all her fault though. Kirk stayed in the military, gone all the time. She couldn't take it, that and being alone here—that 'desolation' you mentioned." He looked over at her. "When Kirk came home for Russell's funeral, he found Daniel living with Anna and her baby, Rusty. Daniel was just a little kid at the time, one or two I guess. Anna was their neighbor."

"She left her son with a neighbor?" Emily asked in disbelief.

"Yep, but the arrangement seemed to suit everybody. Kirk was like a father to both boys, when he was around, which wasn't much. Rusty worshiped him, as if he was his own Dad. It was no surprise, when Rusty came of age, he joined the military. Daniel went to college, wild life biology, had a research job in Maine. When Rusty was killed, he came home to be near Anna. Ely Pike was slated to retire so Daniel went to the police academy and was assigned here under old Ely's tutorage. Ely never suspected Daniel was put here by the Fish and Game Department to get evidence of his poaching. Old Ely was padding his retirement by selling bear gall bladders to China, through a ring in Canada. Chinese think they're some sort of aphrodisiac and pay big bucks for them." Pete pulled to the side of the road.

"Daniel was a mole? Faidlee probably knows that too. This keeps getting worse, Pete."

"Daniel's Jeep should be about a half a mile down that way. I'm not going to take the cruiser down there." He handed her a flashlight, and zippered up his thick wool sweater. "I don't think Daniel took the ATV, so the next half mile, we'll ride."

Emily nodded and rubbed her arms, wishing she had grabbed the wool sweater instead of the cotton one. Outside the flashlight beam, the chilling darkness surrounded her, no street lights, no car lights, and quiet. The wind had died down and a hard cold was settling in. Pebbles rolled down the path in front of them. She felt like she was walking downhill forever, into an endless abyss. Maybe she was wrong. How awkward was this going to be if they did find Daniel asleep on the porch? She hoped there would be a big rock nearby to crawl under.

Above her, the moon was new, giving the stars their chance to light up the sky. Unlike the stars in Manchester, these looked close, almost as if they were hanging on the tree limbs. On the left, one seemed to have fallen to the ground. "What's that over there?"

Pete glanced briefly in that direction, "The swamp."

"Kaskitesiw Nipiy?"

"Great, now I got two of them correcting me. This time of the year it gets foggy like that," Pete said, turning a complete circle. "I don't see Daniel's Jeep or the ATV."

"Something is glimmering," Emily insisted.

"Probably the eye of a swamp bat."

She ignored him but kept the light trained on the round glow which continued to waver from small to large and then shrink again. "Can't you see it?"

"Emmy, I don't see…" He squinted hard in the direction she was pointing.

"Seems to get bigger and then smaller." Emily edged closer to the swamp.

His flashlight beam fused with hers. "Ah, no!" he started to run towards the water, yelling back at her, "It's a chrome bumper! It's Daniel's jeep!"

Heedless of the cold night air, they both plunged into the swamp, Pete submerged while Emily tried to find a door handle with the light.

Pete gasped coming to the surface. "There is someone in there."

Emily threw her flashlight back on shore and pulled on what she thought was a handle. It turned in her hand, and she pulled hard against the pressure of the water. However, the pressure had equalized. The act wasn't as strenuous as she thought it would be, and caused her to fall backward. The water went over her head, and she pushed herself to the surface coughing up the brackish slurry. Pete was half-way inside the Jeep. He gasped and struggled to his feet in the muck. "It's not Daniel. Throat's been cut." He coughed, shoving the flashlight into his belt.

"Who is it?"

"I don't know, but it's not Daniel." Pete found his floating cap and slammed it on his head. Grabbing her arm he helped her to her feet and led her out of the cold water.

She sat down on the bank, shivering, and pushed back her slimy hair.

The constable opened his .357 magnum revolver, flipped the cylinder over, rinsed it in the swamp and put the bullets back in. "I'm going to get you back to town. Call this in," Pete said.

"No!" she protested, pulling her cell phone out. "We can't do anything for this person. Daniel may still be alive." The phone was dead. She took her semi automatic out of the mud-filled holster, pulled out the slippery clip, rinsed it and hoped it wouldn't jam. "Does your radio work?"

"Not anymore and I needed the light to see inside the jeep. I'm sorry, Emmy."

"I'm not going back!" she said and then clenched her teeth to keep them from chattering.

"No, I'm sorry for not taking you serious. Come on." He pulled her to her feet. "We haven't had a murder in this town for as long as I've lived here."

"Lucky me!"

Only her flashlight worked, still glowing in the grass. They made their way down the steep grade, grasping at vague shadowy limbs to keep their balance.

"What's that smell?" She sniffed her arm. "Is it, us—the swamp water?"

Pete stopped. Surely, it was too soon for Daniel's body to smell of decay.

"It reeks like something left in a refrigerator too long." Emily wrinkled her nose and flashed the light around her. It rested on the heap of entrails. "Pete, what is that?"

"Bait pile." Pete stooped, then winced, his eyes watering. "Well, we know Daniel got this far alive. He put pepper foam on the pile to warn away the bears."

A crunching sound nearby made Pete stand quickly. He grabbed Emily and pulled her around to his back.

"Is that a bear?" Emily gasped.

"He's checking out the meat. Don't run. Stay behind me," Pete said quietly.

She aimed the flashlight at the bear's face. Small eyes squinted in the biggest head she had ever seen. The bear was obviously disappointed by this evening's snack quest and not in very good humor as he opened his mouth with a series of deep, yowling protests. Emily shuddered but stood still, removing the light from the angry animal's eyes and sweeping it over the rest of him. "He is so big!"

"We are going to move slowly down the path. Emmy, no matter what the bear does, don't run. If he starts towards us make yourself as big as possible, raise your arms, yell, don't scream but yell and clap your hands, lots of noise, okay? But don't run."

"We're going to scare him?" she asked doubtfully. "What's that popping sound?"

"Daniel says they do that with their jaws to warn us they're not comfortable with our presence."

"I'm not comfortable with his presence either."

"Just keep moving slowly, one step at a time. Keep your eye on him. Give me the flashlight."

They edged their way down the path a few feet, the bear taking a step to follow them.

Emily's foot tangled in something. It clinked like broken glass and dragged on her ankle to the point where she took a misstep. The bear rocked forward then surged upwards on his hind legs.

Pete lunged towards the animal. He waved his arms over his head. He swung his cap in the air and in the deepest, loudest voice possible yelled, "Get out of here, Bear! Scram, bear! Beat it!"

The bear dropped down on all fours and pawed the air with a forearm. He decided this other meal wasn't worth the encounter either. He turned and with a flat-footed gait, trotted away, his huge body cracking the underbrush.

When the sound faded, Emily let out her breath.

Pete turned back, hands shaking. "Well, that took care of him," he commented and inadvertently shone the flashlight in her eyes.

"Nice job," she spoke gratefully, squinting against the light. "I'm glad you didn't have to shoot him."

"Nine times out of ten—hold still," he said coming towards her, his hand held out towards her face.

"What?" She drew back a little, and he urged her to hold still. The light was directly in her eyes, and she closed them. She felt a stinging tug next to her ear and opened her eyes wide with accusation, just in time to see Pete tossing something small, black and worm-like into the brush.

"Was that what I think it was?"

"Swamp's still warm enough for leeches this time of year," he said matter-of-factly. "Resilient little buggers."

"Okay, leeches, as in, could be more of them," Emily hissed, shuddering with the thought and turned back to the trail.

Something was still pulling on her ankle and she tried to kick it away. "Give me the light. Swamp bats, bears, leeches, what has got my foot? You have pythons up here too?" Her voice was close to panic, and she kicked her leg hard. The strap came loose and the sodden backpack rolled away with the sound of broken glass and a sweet smell that, combined with the entrails, reminded Emily of old leftovers.

"Susanne's Chili Sauce," Pete said, turning the light onto the broken jars and chili sauce oozing from the backpack, "She's gonna' be ticked. This is what the bear wanted."

Other than picking at her sweater as if something might be crawling inside, Emily calmed. She lifted the pack.

Pete found the air horn and revolver which had fallen out, and stuck them in his vest pocket. "Whatever ever happened, Daniel didn't have time to get to his gun."

"Pete, bring the light over this way," she said, studying the outside of the pack.

"That's not the way a bear would rip into it. It'd be in shreds," he explained, fingering the melon size exit hole in the canvas. He turned the pack and looked at a fist size entrance hole. Holding up his hand in the light, Pete's face tightened. "It's not just sauce."

She released her breath raggedly, taking the flashlight from his hand. "Nylon's been melted on the edges. A bullet from a high powered rifle made these holes."

"If it hit Daniel first...," Pete stopped, not wanting to say what was on his mind. He watched her as she swept the ground with the light, wondering if the bear dragged Daniel's dead body off.

"Pete, look at this," Emily, who had walked a little way down the trail, called back to him.

"That's one of Anna's shawls! She uses that Indian design." His shoulders slumped as he looked closer. "There's blood on it. What the hell happened here?"

65

"There's more blood." Emily walked a few steps down the path pointing out spots of blood and drips of sauce with the light. Silently, they made their way down the path. Neither spoke, their eyes on the ground in front of them, their thoughts bleak.

A moment later, Pete covered her flashlight beam with his hand, whispering, "I thought I saw something on the porch." He took the light and switching it off.

"We're here?"

"I think somebody else is here too. See that shadow off to the right side?"

"Daniel? You said he camps on the porch." Emily strained her eyes.

"Daniel would be in his sleeping bag. There is someone or something sitting on the right. I can barely make it out."

Emily shuddered. "It's not the bear, is it?"

"I don't know but we've got to get you warmed up. Think you can run?"

"I'll fl-fly if I have to," she said, straining to see the unlit camp, and the figure Pete was talking about.

"Okay," he said, "We're going to make a run for the porch sounding like a Calvary charge. I'm going to shoot in the air. You use the horn. When you get to the door, shout Anna's and Daniel's name."

He didn't tell her that the huddled figure sitting on the porch was more likely a man, not a bear, but the charge to the door would make them a hard target and the pistol shots would throw whoever it was off balance. He would keep the flashlight trained on the figure, blinding him as much as possible. At the first sign of aggression, Pete's pistol would no longer be aimed in the air. If it was Daniel, he'd take cover, wondering if they had lost their minds.

Like two kids running down a street on Halloween bent on terrifying the neighborhood, they ran towards the camp. The figure on the porch threw off a covering and leapt into the trees.

CHAPTER 8

"Anna! Open the door! It's Pete Hines!"

"Anna, Daniel, please open the door!" Emily begged. Pete, she realized, was sheltering her with his body as he kept his revolver pointed towards the trees. "Anna!"

The door flew open and Pete pushed Emily inside. "Get her in the shower! She's been in the swamp."

"Turn on the generator," Anna yelled to Pete.

As they passed the bed, Emily tried to stop. They had made enough noise to wake up the dead but Daniel did not move.

In the makeshift bathroom, Anna roughly yanked Emily's sweater off. "Pete, the generator!" she yelled again.

"I'm trying! The switch won't work!"

"Start it by hand! It's down the back steps," Anna shouted impatiently. "The switch only works to stop it. Hurry up!"

"Daniel?" Emily asked, shuddering.

Anna did not answer her.

Drawing his gun, Pete maneuvered quietly down the steps to where the generator sat under the part of the camp built on stilts. The nearby stream was deafening. He felt the hair stand up on the back of his neck as he sensed someone watching him from the trees. Squatting down behind the generator, he pulled the starter cord.

Nothing.

Standing for the leverage, he pulled hard again, and the ancient machine rumbled into life. Figuring he would have been shot by now, he gathered an arm load of wood in the darkness then hurried up the steps and shut the door behind him. He dumped the wood in a heap by the stove and locked the door, breathing hard from the effort.

The noise of the generator did not arouse Daniel. Pete passed his hand in front of Daniel's mouth and nose and felt his breath, thin and feverish.

He unzipped his heavy wool sweater and removing his shirt and undershirt, hung them by the stove. Then he put the wool sweater back on. Even wet wool would keep him warm. They were stuck until morning, unless he could get his radio to work.

Anna tried to pry the buttons out of the holes in Emily's wet blouse with her thick deformed fingers. Emily took over. Her numb fingers weren't much better.

The walls rattled with the sound of the generator. Anna lit a candle in the windowless bathroom, turned on the water and tested it. "For you, warm enough."

The lukewarm water felt like scalding pins against her cold, bare skin. She tried to shake the muddy hair off her face and gasped, "It burns!"

"It is only a little warm. You are chilled to the bone, child. Just let the water warm you. The prickles will stop." Anna picked up the tiny gold medal of the Native American mother, Our Lady of Guadalupe, hanging from Emily's neck. She looked at Emily's coppery hair, frowning.

"Warden Claret, is he alive?" Emily sputtered.

"For now. Scrub yourself and I will get you something to wear."

She heard Anna's footsteps leave.

As Emily washed her face, her fingers touched the small welt by her ear. Remembering the leech, she visually and manually checked herself all over. A deep inner chill made her tremble as she toweled off with rough, aged terry-cloth.

As suddenly as it started, the rattling stopped in the walls. Her head was popped through the neck of a gray flannel nightgown. She stuck her arms through the sleeves and looked down at herself. The gown was short but wide enough to fit Anna's roundness. The neck line slipped off one of her shoulders.

"Do you have any antibiotics, like penicillin?" Emily asked, still shivering.

"I have nothing. The elderberry leaves have some ability to cool fever, stop bleeding, but the bullet pushed pieces of his shirt into the wound."

"We can call Dartmouth Hitchcock Hospital or is Colebrook closer?"

"We can't call out," Anna said, flatly.

Emily hiked up the slipping night gown. Anxiously, she followed the Cree woman. "You have no phone?"

Anna shook her head and opened a drawer. She took out a brush and pushed Emily's hair back from her face.

"How about a cell phone?" Emily looked at her hopefully.

"Those phones would not work between these hills."

"Maybe Pete can dry his radio out."

"It would not work down here."

"You have no communication at all?" Emily asked, stepping in front of the woman to study her face. Metal circles framed Anna's eyes, distorting them behind thick glass lenses. They were narrowly shaped and dark like Daniel's. Frown marks were cut raggedly into the corners of her mouth and on her upper lip, the cruel trick of nature, a fine but dark mustache. She wore her gray hair in two thin braids wound over her head.

"Not even smoke signals," Anna looked at the younger woman, bitterly defensive. Then realizing Emily's tone had not been confrontational, only concerned, she spoke more softly. "Come." Anna grabbed her wrist. She pointed to where Daniel lay. "Pimisini kinipewinihk ci-kisosiyan. *Lie down in the bed and keep warm.*"

Emily backed up as far as Anna's grip would let her. "What is she saying, Pete?"

"I think she wants you to get into the bed."

"I—I'm not going to do that!"

"He is burning up. You are freezing. You will be good for each other." Anna scowled.

"Pete?" Emily said anxiously, looking around for him.

"Better do as she says." The constable shrugged, as if he had lost battles with this woman before.

Emily stared at the ceiling. "I don't believe this!"

"I have only one bed. Get in. He has pants on," Anna huffed.

"Emmy, try to get a little shut-eye. It's close to midnight. I don't know when I'm going to need you to spell me." Pete's was a voice of reason in an otherwise crazy night. "We'll go for help in the morning. It's too dangerous to try in the dark."

"Hopefully we won't have to. I told George that if I wasn't at the apartment by four thirty in the morning, to send the State Troopers down here."

"You did?" Pete asked, with visible relief.

"My dad always told me to have a back-up plan."

Anna lifted the blanket and the candle. "Your father is a wise man and wiser is the daughter for listening to him. Now get into the bed."

Daniel lay on his stomach, his head partially on a pillow and his face turned towards them. Emily saw the green stained bandage wound under his right arm and around his back.

"Looks like you stopped the bleeding. Where is he hurt?" Emily asked quietly.

"The bullet broke a rib, maybe two here, I think," Anna said, lightly touching the bandage where she had packed the elderberry leaf poultice. "It passed under his arm and came through here, tearing much flesh. I found pieces of shattered bone there."

In spite of the bulky bandage Emily could tell something was severely wrong with Daniel's side. Where his ribs should be there was a depression. Dark bruising rose above the bandage, under his arm. She gently moved a lock of his hair and felt his temperature. "What happened here?" Her hand hovered over the gash on his forehead.

"He was unconscious when I found him. He must have fallen on a rock."

Emily took the candle and combed the hair away from Daniel's ear with her fingers, looking for signs of cerebral fluid as she had many time in forensic investigations. There was no indication of a fractured skull. "Have you tried to wake him or talk to him since?"

Anna nodded, her eyes glistening wet in spite of her stoic frown. "There have been brief moments. He does not seem right." She pointed to her head. "He talks strange things," Anna studied Emily and then said softly, "but maybe not so strange."

Emily glanced back at Anna, twice, then putting the candle on a chair seat, she put her arms around the older woman.

Anna stiffened at first, and then her arms slowly lifted to encircle the younger woman, tightening with desperation.

Emily could sense the terrible grief in Anna's body. One of her boys was dead. The other, perhaps, lay dying, and she could do nothing. She could feel it shake the older woman, a deep tremor from within, and yet Anna made no sound. Her clenched fists opened and her palms pressed into Emily's back holding her tight.

Feeling uncomfortable with the women's emotions, Pete submerged their guns in what looked like soapy water remaining in the sink, then searched for something to clean them with. He startled a mouse under the sink but came away with an old dish rag and vegetable oil.

Emily whispered to Anna, "The elderberry leaves were a good idea. They have stopped the bleeding. His lips are not blue, so he is getting enough oxygen. " She released the older woman and got into the bed.

"I will wash your clothes and hang them by the stove," Anna pulled the blanket over Emily and Daniel.

"Thank you." As close to the edge of the mattress as she could get, Emily curled her back towards the unconscious man.

"A lot of good you'll do each other that way!" With blatant annoyance, Anna walked away with the candle.

Emily turned on her other side.

In the dark, she could hardly see Daniel's face but his lips were parted and the breath that passed between them was warm with fever.

Slowly, she edged her chilled body close to his and laid her forehead against his arm. His warmth flowed into her, and she prayed her coolness would transfer to him. Gently, avoiding the injured area, she slid one arm beneath him and her other over him. The scent of him, the touch of him, seemed familiar, as though they had lain together from the beginning of time.

~~~~~

Anna brought Pete a cup of soup and a blanket, arranging it over his shoulders.

"Thanks."

"He knew she was coming," Anna said.

Pete stared up at the old woman. "I'll believe anything tonight."

"Hours ago he said to me, 'She is coming. Anna, tell her to go back. He is here!' I thought he was kiswewin, *not thinking straight.*"

"Faidlee was here!" Pete raised his voice then lowered it quickly. "He was on the porch. We chased him off but he could still be around."

"I know." She tilted her head to the rifle in the corner. "I am not afraid of death, but I will die by my own choosing if it is possible. Daniel may not bring a gun here, but I have that rifle, and I made sure that macatisowin, *evil one* knew I had it. I think he was waiting for me to fall asleep, and then would kill us both."

"I've been trying to dry out the radio, but it still doesn't work."

"Nothing works down here. I wanted it that way. I wanted to grieve for my son, in my own way. Doing so may cost my adopted son his life also."

"Thank God Emily sensed something was wrong and followed up on it." Pete glanced at the bed.

Anna nodded, "She is eka kawakew kisewasihk astehowew, the forbearer, the enduring healer who does not know how to heal herself. I felt it when she held me. She took my grief into her. I felt it leave me. Yet, she is not of our people."

"You know about her? What happened in Manchester?"

"No, but I sense she embraces the dead, and they embrace her." The Cree woman shook her head sadly. "Those, who are honored in my clan for this gift of themselves, usually die young."

Pete frowned and then dismissed the tribal lore. "Yeah, well, we've got about six hours until dawn. I'm not going to wake her up. Can you spell me in a couple of hours?"

"I'll watch all night," Anna replied.

"Try to get some rest. I don't know where." He looked around the one room cabin.

"I always snooze in my rocker. Make sure you call me," she ordered.

"Yes, ma'am. I'll add some more wood to the stove." Getting up he stoked the fire and tried to shut the metal door as softly as possible.

Anna was already snoring in the rocker. Pete pulled the blanket over his shoulders. In a few hours, Susanne would be leaving her parent's home, and they should be preparing for this vacation together. He hated to be selfish, but he wondered if that vacation was ever going to happen now?

CHAPTER 9

Emily was dreaming that a bear was growling and standing on its hind legs. With a sharp intake of breath, she woke up. The growling persisted though the bear had vanished. She couldn't think of where she was and lifted her head.

Anna sat in the rocker, arms folded against her bosom, snoring.

She looked over at Pete. A lit candle sat on the table next to him. She couldn't tell if he was awake or asleep, but he was resting, his head against his arm, his hand loosely holding a string.

The weight on her own numb arm made her lay her head back down. Slowly, and carefully she drew out her tingling appendage from under Daniel. He stirred but his eyes remained closed. Wriggling backwards on her stomach she found the floor with her bare toes.

"Pete?" She whispered close to the constable's ear.

A pencil pitched to the side and a small cardboard box thumped on the table.

"I almost had him," Pete whispered, grinning, but his eyes were bloodshot and in the candle light.

"What are you doing?" She smiled.

"Trying to catch a mouse, and," He rubbed his eyes and admitted in a tired voice, "trying to keep awake. I think Faidlee is gone. I haven't heard anything out there except an owl."

"You should have woken me. Close your eyes for awhile. I'm wide awake."

"How's Daniel?"

"I wish I knew. He is still sleeping."

"Did you sleep?"

"Actually, I did. Close your eyes. We still have an hour until the sun comes up."

Pete moved so quickly past her that he almost knocked the candle from her hand.

She turned to see him grab Daniel who was sitting on the edge of the bed, trying to stand.

"What the hell do you think you're doing?" Pete growled.

"Water?" Daniel tried to focus on the constable's face with confusion. "Pete? What you…?"

Emily went to the sink but the faucet failed to produce water. She found a plastic glass in the strainer and dipped it into a water bucket by the sink. Briefly, she wondered if she should boil it first. It looked clear and Daniel needed water now. She tasted it. It seemed fine. On her way back, she spied her clothes hanging from a drying rack near the stove.

"Angel…holding me." Daniel was gripping Pete's arm in an effort to remain sitting up.

"Here is water." Emily knelt down in front of him.

Daniel stared at her, the unruly waves of her hair glowing in the candle light.

"Is this your angel?" Pete asked, taking the glass from Emily and pressing it to Daniel's lips.

He took a small sip before coughing.

Pete laid him back down on the bed.

Daniel took a sharp intake of breath. His body went rigid from pain.

Emily took the pillow Anna had given her and wedged it above the injured area of his back, taking pressure off the wound. She tried not to show her concern that his moving may have caused him further damage.

"Thank you." Daniel's body relaxed a little, and he studied her face as if looking for answers.

"Shhh, don't talk." In the candlelight, his eyes were of deep blackness, their narrow shape distinctly outlined by the thick lashes. She combed the wet hair off his forehead with her fingers. "You're perspiring. That's good!"

"How did I…?" Daniel asked, angry at his helplessness

"Just stay with us." Pete said concerned.

He didn't respond and closed his eyes.

"Daniel?" She took his hand.

He opened his eyes but turned his face away as a painful cough wracked him. Afterward his breathing was shallow and distressed.

"I think his lung has been compromised. Look at me, Daniel. Try to breathe like this, like you're whistling." She glanced at Pete, unsure. "A man with emphysema once told me it helped."

Anna woke at the sound of Daniel's coughing. It took a moment and a few grunts for her to get out of the chair. "How is he?"

Emily looked up and showed, by expression alone, that all was not well. She pulled her sleeve up without letting go of his hand and looked at her watch. It was almost five o'clock and she prayed silently that George wouldn't let her down. She didn't know how close a friend he was to Faidlee. She didn't know how much of a role he might have played in planning the warden's demise. Lisa said George wasn't part of it, but Emily realized she may have asked a snake to look after the bird's nest.

Daniel gripped her hand and stiffened as an excruciating stab in his side took his breath and left him with the dread of trying to inhale again.

"I'm going to get dressed in case we need to go for help." She gently released his hand, grabbed her clothes and closed the screeching plywood door to the bathroom.

Anna rinsed a towel and wiped the perspiration from Daniel's face. As she did so, she spoke softly to him in her language.

Emily could hear Pete moving around, shutting the metal door to the stove. She dressed quickly. Daniel was not going to die, not like the rest of them.

From her forensic studies, she knew what might be going on with his lung and why he was coughing, but how to treat it? She wracked her brain for answers, praying for guidance.

"Emmy!" Pete called to her, his voice panicked.

She ran out of the bathroom, her arm half way in her damp sweater.

As Daniel shuddered with an involuntary deep breath, a shard of rib bone punctured the plural space of his right lung, collapsing it and triggering a spasm in the left side. His breathing became too shallow to bring life sustaining oxygen to his brain. His heart was rapid and irregular. How he hated to do this to Anna. His eyes pierced the ceiling and his lips moved in a silent plea for God to forgive him.

Pete grabbed his shoulders, as if by physical force, he could hold him on the earth, but Daniel's body slumped within his hands.

~~~~~

The Wright's alarm went off at 4:30 AM. Lisa rolled out of bed and went to make coffee for George. She came back a moment later and said anxiously, "I put the porch light on. She's not back. The car's not there. You gonna' call?"

George sat on the side of the bed, looking at the phone.

"After what you told me last night, I'm scared, George. Don't be mad but I told her what Faidlee said to you and those other guys at work."

"Lisa, why'd you tell her? She's a cop. What if that woman goes to Faidlee and asks him about it? He'll know it was Bailey or me that told her. Damn, I shoulda' never said nothin' to you."

"I was worried about her, since she was gonna be workin' with Claret. And, I was afraid Faidlee was going to drag you into doing something bad. After she left, you said he found a big bear on Birch Hill and he was going to shoot it through the warden if he had to. Maybe that's why she ran out of here, 'cause that's what Faidlee did!"

"Who knows," George said, unsure. "If Faidlee did half the things he said he was going to, he'd be in jail, and if you don't stop talking to cops, I'll be right there with him."

"I told her you weren't involved." She sat down next to him. "You aren't, are you?'

"There's got to be some law sayin' hearing it is as bad as doing it."

"George, I don't like how Claret is running things in the woods any better than you, but maybe he's right. We just don't see the big game like we used to. I don't want him killed 'cause we brought this on ourselves and don't have the sense to know it."

"You think I do?" He snapped at Lisa.

"Something bad has happened or she'd be back."

"What if Faidlee finds out? I've got you and Tracy and the baby to think about."

"One man makes you that scared?" Lisa frowned with surprise, putting her hand on his. "You think he might kill the warden, don't you?"

"He's killed before. Lisa, I think we ought to stay out of it."

~~~~~

"I think he's gone," Pete said desperately.

"No! Damn it—God—Not again!" Emily put her fingers on his throat and felt the weak pulse and his faint breath on the back of her hand. She felt the bandage encircling him. The poultice had hardened and she could tell his damaged side was swollen around it.

"I need a knife."

"What are you going to do?" Pete reached for his pocket knife, worried.

"The bandage has dried and it's too tight. Elastic—always use elastic on broken ribs! Somewhere I read—first aid?" Emily cut at the bandage and as soon as the heavy greenish wrap came free from Daniel's sides, he took a shallow breath with his quivering left lung.

"ABC, Airway, breathing, circulation." Pete shouted with renewed hope.

"I made his bandage too tight?" Anna cried with regret.

"The swelling and drying made it too tight," Emily said looking, at Daniel's discolored and deformed side with the raw gash plowing through it. "You stopped the fever and the bleeding, Anna."

"Maybe if we sit him up a little he can breathe better." Pete was encouraged by the rise and fall of the left side of Daniel's chest.

Emily said, "Moving may start the bleeding again but…" She looked at Pete for support.

"Circulation is last on the list." Pete agreed. "Anna, do you have any more pillows?"

"Daniel has one he keeps in his sleeping bag on the porch."

"I'll cover you." Pete picked up his gun and they opened the door. Anna looked up to where Daniel kept the sleeping bag hung away from mice over the rafter. It wasn't there. Faidlee had used it while he sat waiting for Anna to fall asleep. It was crumpled by the wooden bench and the pillow was discarded on the frosty ground. Pete ran down the steps and picked it up. Back inside, Pete put his arms as straight as possible under Daniel's back and Emily and Anna packed the pillows beneath him so that he could lay more upright. Blood became visible at the corner of Daniel's mouth as they settled him back down.

"I've never known George to not keep his word." Pete shouted angrily when he saw the blood. "Wait 'til I get my hands on that paper rat."

"His lung must be punctured." Emily turned her wrist to look at the watch again. "Six fourteen. Pete, I'm sorry to have to tell you but George has…"

Daniel regained consciousness, only to start to choking on his own blood.

Emily remembered that forward pressure on the lung could help with the pain. "Daniel, breathe like this." She whistled soundlessly and put her hand with some force, against his chest.

In a few minutes, as if hypnotized by her eyes, feeling her soft breath on his face, he began to follow the rhythm of her respiration. The torturous coughing eased and the sensation of drowning ceased.

When he started to drift away Emily urged, "You need to stay with me. Daniel, look at me!"

Emily smiled at his effort to come back to her and her voice quavered as she whispered. "That it. Look at me, lamb."

Anna wiped his face with a wet towel, nodding encouragement, convinced this woman could keep him alive if only by will power alone.

"Emmy, I'm going for help." Pete put his revolver in its holster. "The radio should work at the swamp, if it works at all. If not, I'll call from the cruiser."

"Be careful, Pete."

Pete turned to the door but stopped to look at Anna.

"Natohta! *Listen!*" Anna was staring down at the floor with her head tilted. She murmured, "I have been hearing engine sounds. It's getting louder."

"I hear it too," Pete said as he went to the window and looked up the hill as a droning sound grew louder. A second later he slapped his leg with a yell, "It's George, and it looks like he brought an army with him."

Three ATV's were heading down the trail in single file. One belonged to the State Police. The second ATV, ridden by an Emergency Medical Technician had a stretcher fixed on the back and the third was ridden by George Wright.

Emily smiled down at Daniel. "Hang on. Okay?"

Daniel blinked at the sound of her voice and focused on her eyes, holding onto them like a lifeline. He moved his left hand over the one she held against his chest.

She felt her heart quicken and her own breathing become painful. It was only physical empathy, she convinced herself. It happened to her all the time when involved with a victim.

George walked in and had to endure Pete's rough hugging and questions about being late and why all three were sopping wet.

"They had to get their ATV's loaded and we had to get that guy out of the swamp." George looked around the camp remembering when he and his brother came down here to hassle the two Indian kids building it. Rusty was ready to pitch a hammer at them but Daniel had invited them in to see the place, show them proudly how they had rigged up water for washing and a wood stove for warmth. Daniel taught him to snare a rabbit that day. George hadn't talked to either of the Indian boys since, but when he needed a rabbit, he knew how to get one. Until now he'd forgotten who taught him how.

His eyes rested guiltily on Daniel. What he saw sickened him. He might have been able to prevent this. "I'm sorry, warden. I'm sorry I didn't get here sooner."

Daniel tried to speak but no longer would his lungs allow words.

With dismay in his eyes, George backed out of the way of the EMT placing oxygen over Daniel's face. He glanced at the detective and sensed she knew of his conflict.

Together the EMT and a State Trooper strapped Daniel securely to the body board. The Trooper tried to help by fingering Daniel's clenched hand away from Emily's. Half conscious, Daniel resisted the move, and the young trooper smiled kindly, and said to him, "We'll give her hand back to you soon, sir."

"Anna and I are coming. We'll be there, I promise," Emily assured him. She turned to the EMT. "Where are you taking him?"

The EMT took out his radio. "I'm going to dispatch the Dartmouth-Hitchcock Advanced Response Team." After trying to call, he looked at them bewildered.

Pete looked from the EMT to the young trooper, "Son, take your ATV. Get up as far as the swamp and make that call to DHART. The helicopter should be able to land in that field up by the house on the left."

Pete addressed his cousin. "We'll walk up. George, can you take Anna?"

"I am not going on that noisy devil with wheels." Anna retorted.

"Anna, I'd like you to go with us just in case Faidlee doubles back." Pete said softly.

"Not on one of those things!" She picked up the rifle and unloaded it. "Peter, unplug the generator and open the water drain at the bottom of the steps. Apisci-mosos and I will get started."

"You're not coming back, Anna?" Pete asked, surprised.

"I'm not coming back," Anna replied. "I may have lost one son, but I have another to think of right now." Linking arms with Emily, she used the rifle's length as a walking stick. They started up the hill behind the Emergency ATV.

"Anything else you want to bring with you?" Pete called after her.

"Nothing, Peter. Leave the door open for the mice," Anna said without looking back.

"You take Anna up on the ATV." George said to Pete. "She'll listen to you. She'll never make it walkin'. Besides, I want to talk to Detective Harrigan."

Pete looked curiously at his cousin, but didn't argue. He convinced Anna to get on the ATV with the reasoning that her refusal could delay Daniel getting help. Pete, in spite of her protests, sat her in front of him and they drove up the hill. Emily and George each flanked the slower moving vehicle with Daniel on the back. They steadied the mounted stretcher from time to time when the ATV hit a rock or gully.

"Something you want to tell me, George?" Emily said seriously.

"What Lisa told you—I shoulda' done somethin' before now. I came alone here first, so as to not to stir up trouble 'less I had to. Top of the hill I found Pete's cruiser with the window stove in but I figured if that was all Faidlee did, I could stay out of it." He glanced at Daniel and his expression was grim.

"Go on." Emily ran forward to move a rock out of the path but George beat her to it, shoving it to one side.

"I unloaded the ATV and figured I'd better look around more. At the swamp I found the Jeep with the guy inside. I figured it was the warden. The other ATV was in the swamp too, in the cat tails. I went back to the top of the road, made the 911 call and waited for 'em, to show 'em the way down. They got the dead guy out and it wasn't the warden and then I figured we'd better get down here."

"And for that, I thank you." Emily smiled at him.

"I just never thought Faidlee had the guts to do it—stand up to the warden, much less shoot him like he said he would."

"He didn't have the guts. Warden Claret was off duty. He never had a chance to get his gun out. Faidlee ambushed him."

"You goin' ta arrest me for aidin' and abettin'—or something like that?"

"I don't think you ever approved of what Faidlee was planning. Granted, you liked the way things were before—when you could take game when you wanted. But I doubt you thought Faidlee's solution was the right one, am I correct?" Emily stopped and looked hard at George.

"No, gawd, no! I was just—I didn't know what he'd do to me if I went up against him. Last time somebody went up against Faidlee, he got bumped into the hot pulp bath."

"You certainly didn't aid or abet him."

George shook his head again but said with guilt, "I knew 'bout it. I didn't think he'd do it, but I knew." He looked again at the unconscious man slowly being driven up the rocky path. "Do you think he's goin' ta live?"

"If he does, it will be because of you. As far as Faidlee is concerned, I'll do everything I can to convict him."

"I'll help," George said sincerely. "He don't scare me no more."

"From what you said about the cruiser window, I think we're going to need a ride into town once DHART gets here," she said.

"You got it, Detective Harrigan, but I mean it, I'll tell 'em what Faidlec said in court if I have to. I'll tell 'em what he did to the Kirby boy. I saw him do it. "

"And, I promise you, I'll make it stick. Call me Emily, okay?"

CHAPTER 10

On reaching the police station in Kaskitesiw, Emily picked up the Mustang, and drove the two hours to the hospital in Lebanon with Anna. Pete stayed behind to put out an All Points Bulletin on Faidlee, phone in the insurance information for Daniel, and put the hospital in touch, on an overseas line, with Daniel's father.

When Emily and Anna arrived, Daniel had been taken to the operating room. No one would tell the two women a thing because they were not family, not even Anna. They sat in silence.

When Pete and Susanne arrived just after noon, Pete had better luck. He was the one whom the hospital staff had been in contact with. Kirk Claret, Daniel's father, had faxed the necessary paper work to the hospital, allowing Pete to make medical decisions on Daniel's behalf, including whether to terminate life support.

Pete told Anna and Emily what he learned from the surgeon; that they inserted a tube into Daniel's chest to remove the air and blood around the wall of the collapsed lung. They also removed the shattered bone fragments of his ribs.

"Can we see him?" Anna asked hopefully.

Pete looked back at the desk and said quietly, "He'll be in recovery for quite a while. We might as well head back to Kaskiteway, get a good night's sleep and come back in the morning."

Anna and Susanne got up to leave, but Emily remained seated. She was looking at the floor, wondering what she was doing.

They looked back at her and Anna said softly, "Ah, life is but the single breath of the buffalo in winter."

"What?" Susanne asked abruptly, as if the old woman had lost her mind.

Emily looked up at Susanne, maker of chili sauces and likely possessor of a gavel at Town Meetings. "I'm going to stick around for a little while, just until the warden is out of recovery. They know me around here, at least in the morgue. Maybe they'll let me know how he is, and I will call you." She added reasonably, "Plus, since I'm now investigating the case, I need check on the dead man's autopsy."

Pete walked over to the desk where a nurse was sitting. He said something to her and pointed to Emily. The nurse looked over at Emily, without smiling, and picked up the phone. Afterwards she wrote something down in a file. A few minutes later, Pete came back.

"They'll let you see him, for all of us, but they need to see your badge to confirm who you say you are."

Emily looked down at her sweater and for the first time noticed Daniel's blood on it. Her hand shook as she searched for her wallet. The wallet was not in the pocket of the sweater, but her badge was, thankfully, still pinned inside. She gave it to Pete, and he went back to the desk.

Anna took out a hanky and spitting on it washed a few flecks of blood from Emily's cheek.

"Anna, did you happen to take my wallet out of the sweater?" Emily asked, wincing at the motherly wiping, which left her skin red.

"No. I did not see a wallet," Anna replied, "There—you look better."

The constable's wife spoke again, her voice brusque, "She looks wretched. There is a gift store downstairs. I'll go get you a top to put on."

"That's okay. My wallet must have fallen into the swamp. Things are so expensive here," Emily protested as Susanne marched away.

"She's as soft as Pete underneath, but doesn't like to show it," Anna spoke affectionately and tried to comb back Emily's hair with her crooked fingers.

"Anna, what did you mean by a buffalo's breath?"

"As it was with my husband and me, life is only the single breath of the buffalo and time is not to be wasted for sometimes the buffalo takes a deep breath but sometimes there is only a hiccup."

"Anna, I am only concerned about Daniel as a fellow officer, nothing more. I told him I would be here. You'll go back with Pete and Susanne?"

"Ehe, I need to re-open my home in town."

"Here's your badge back. Where'd Susanne go?" Pete asked, looking around.

"Down to the gift shop," Anna said.

Pete grumbled, "I swear, you put a store anywhere near that woman…"

"She is buying something for me to wear. Pete, I need to cancel my credit and debit card. I lost my wallet in the swamp. It must have fallen out of my sweater pocket. What if Faidlee found it?"

"I've got to supervise pulling those vehicles out, and I'll look for it with a rake. If I don't find it, I'll call you. I don't think Faidlee could see it at night."

Emily nodded and shivered in spite of herself, remembering the cold, black water. "You probably won't find it. It's real thin, a couple of cards, my license, and forty dollars. Please let me know so I can cancel the cards."

"Here you go," Susanne dropped two bags beside her and handed her a cup of coffee saying, "I figured you were a cream and sugar type. Personally, I like mine black."

"Oh, thank you," Emily said, looking up gratefully, and took the warm beverage. "I'll pay you back."

"Receipts are in the bag. Get that horrid sweater off."

Anna smiled, kissed Emily's cheek and left with Pete and Susanne.

Gratefully, Emily sipped the warm coffee and opened one of the bags. A crusty cheese "Danish" eyed her with its lemony, yellow center. Emily gobbled it hungrily and blessed Susanne. There was no receipt in the first bag.

Motioning to the nurse who looked up and nodded, Emily picked up the other bag, and went to the bathroom. She washed her hands and face then took off her sweater and washed as best as she could at the sink with paper towels and hand soap. Groping inside the bag she pulled out a white Dartmouth sweatshirt with green lettering. It had a hood with ties and its newness felt soft against her skin. The bag also held a comb, lip balm, deodorant stick, tooth-paste and a tooth brush.

"Bless her, bless her." Emily felt for a paper at the bottom of the bag, thinking it was the receipt and pulled out a twenty dollar bill from a folded piece of note paper. On the paper was written simply, "For gas, phone or food." Emily smiled at the woman's thoughtfulness.

Coming out of the bathroom she took her seat again. The nurse paid no attention. Emily picked up a magazine with an elderly man playing with a child on the cover. It turned out to be a pharmaceutical ad for an arthritis pain medication.

"Emily Harrigan?"

She looked up to find an elderly Catholic priest standing in front of her, and dropped the magazine.

"Oh, no, no, no!" He helped her to pick up the advertisement. "He has not died. I have that effect on people. They think the worst when they see me."

She shook his hand. "Sorry about my reaction, Father."

"Not at all, not at all!" The priest looked eager to sit down for a minute. He took the chair next to her. "I'm used to it. I was here when they brought the young man in."

"Warden Claret?"

He nodded and murmured, "Terrible thing. Tell me, do you know if he is Christian?"

"I don't know. Why?"

"Well, because I gave him the Last Rites. No, no, don't be afraid," he said when she stiffened. "The sacrament is not just for the dying but to strengthen all those who are struggling to live. It is here for any Christians in need of comfort."

"I know. I'm Catholic, but brought up 'old school' Catholic. The sacrament of Extreme Unction meant the last curtain call," she said, shrugging apologetically.

"Last curtain call, I like that analogy." The white haired priest chuckled softly, like someone who had been around the dying so much, he had to find a bit of humor in it. "Well, I was just wondering," he said. "The sacrament will help him. I know it."

"Thank you for giving it to him."

"You look familiar to me," he said and tilted his head, blotchy with age spots. Then a shadow of recognition came over his face. "Ah, you were the detective at the Bow Park murder. I was there to try and offer some comfort to the parents of that poor little child. And I have seen you in the paper—the student suicide. How are you doing?" he said, putting his hand on hers.

She looked down at it. The hands of the priests she had known were always beautiful, even when marked by old age.

At first she was going give him polite rhetoric, but the old priest's eyes were so sincere the words tumbled out. "I am angry," she said, adamantly.

He nodded as if he understood and leaned towards her saying, "I take it you mean with God."

Emily looked around her but the waiting room was empty. "He lets things happen to the innocent. Maybe He doesn't do it, but He doesn't stop it either. How can He say He loves us when He allows His children be hurt, and worse?"

"Ah!" The priest nodded. "At times I have told Him, no wonder everyone is so mad at you."

"Honestly Father, I've heard it all—all the reasons, and not one of them convinces me of why He doesn't stop it."

"It is the evil in man, which does these horrible things."

"I don't mean to be disrespectful, but I've heard that too." Emily looked away.

"He tries to stop it." The old priest shrugged.

"Father, we're talking God here. God doesn't have to try—He does."

"He tries, Emily, through people like you and that young warden fighting for his life. The greatest evil begets the greatest good."

"He's God. He doesn't need us."

"Oh, yes He does. We are all He has to fight evil in this world."

"Are you saying that God is powerless to help us here?"

"His power comes into *us* when we pray. St. Augustine once said, 'Pray as though everything depended on God. Work as though everything depended on you.' '"

"We're 'it'?"

The priest nodded. "We're 'it'! Remember, we are the ones who chose to live without His worldly protection. But we have His divine power—prayer!"

"Then I have failed miserably."

"Why do you say that, my child?"

She said bitterly. "I'm always too late—the child, the nurse, the boy, and the warden could still die!"

He leaned back, knowing she would take anything he said further as merely comforting. Her pain went too deep. "I take it you did not see the morning paper?"

"No," Emily said softly.

"The reporters know that you're not in Manchester. The paper said that you may have some mental problems and may not be fit for your own trial—if the mother of that poor boy pursues this travesty."

Emily looked around. "How did they find out? I didn't chance going to a psychiatrist."

"The bullies of the world don't need the truth. They make up whatever they want." The priest peered over his glasses at her. "Your father made a statement that you are on vacation. It may keep those ink hounds off your scent for awhile."

"I doubt it." Emily stared down the hall as if she expected to see the press charge through the door. "Father, I didn't cause that child to commit suicide. I just couldn't reach him in time to stop him."

"You are very precious to God, Emily, for you suffer greatly in trying to be His hands. Evil uses people like that mother. She believes her pain will ease by gaining money."

Emily wiped a tear from her cheek and looked at it as if she had never seen one before.

"Needing God confuses and scatters evil." The priest said, desperate to get his point across as someone waved to him from a doorway. "Well,

I'd best be getting along. There is a lovely silver-haired lady close by who is timid about meeting Jesus. I must convince her that He won't bite." His smile was cheerful.

Emily looked up at him with glistening eyes. "Thank you. I'm still not sure but, thank you."

"One more thing, my child, God is not without mercy. When He created us with all the love in Him, He gave us the ability to shut off pain. No physician, since the beginning of time, can understand this. It is called 'shock'. He did not give this to His own son, but have faith that He would give it to one of His innocent children, and that He had His arms wrapped around that little girl you found at Bow Park, all the time." The old priest limped away, looking like he was near to exhaustion.

Two others joined her in the waiting room. So far no reporters had shown up to pick her bones but she expected the worst after what the priest had said. Then a nurse stood in front of her, her face serious.

"What is it?" Emily said anxiously.

"Officer Har…" She stopped and glanced around. "Father Michael thinks you should be in the recovery room, not out here."

Emily got to her feet quickly and followed the nurse through the large stainless steel doors which would protect her from the press. "Father must carry a lot of weight around here."

"You could say that."

The room was dim and people were lined up in beds, all in various stages of consciousness. The nurse nodded towards one of the beds and went to adjust the oxygen on another patient.

Tentatively Emily walked over to Daniel. He looked so drained of color, so sick. An oxygen cannula probed his straight nose. His firm lips were chapped and sore and his hair fell over his forehead, tangled and limp.

The nurse came back over. "Talk to him."

"Warden Claret?" Emily addressed him formally in front of the nurse.

"He has been slow to come out of it, but that is to be expected after what he has been through." The nurse flicked the saline bag with her forefinger, getting rid of a bubble. "It may be awhile longer before he wakes up."

Emily stared down at Daniel, feeling awkward and thinking, what if he wakes and doesn't recognize me?

The nurse slid a chair towards her and hurried off.

Emily sat down and picked up his left hand which was not tethered with needles and plastic lines. She looked at his face, remembering his resigned look when he thought he was dying. Her throat tightened and she put her hand over her mouth to stifle the sob. Father Michael had made her think too much, feel too much.

A startled scream came from beyond the curtain on the left. Daniel's eyes flew open and he searched his strange surroundings frantically.

Emily quickly wiped her tears. "Shhhh, it's okay. You're in the hospital. You're going to be fine."

He stared at her for a few seconds and closed his eyes.

"Sorry about that," the nurse said over her shoulder. "It's why we don't usually allow folks in here. People sometimes come out of anesthesia in strange ways."

"It woke him. He didn't know where he was."

"Then, I'm glad you were here. He'll be coming out of it soon." The nurse went off, again.

Emily looked once more at his dark hand in hers, and when her eyes rose to his face she took a quick breath. "There you are," she said, smiling, in spite of the fact he looked at her as if he didn't know who she was. "I just wanted to make sure you were okay before I went back to Kaskitesiw."

"You kept," he said, trying to clear his throat, swollen from the intubation tube, "your promise."

"I'm glad you remember that. You are at Dartmouth Hitchcock Hospital. You're going to be fine. It may take awhile but you're going to be all right now." She started to get up but before she could pull her hand away from his, he tightened his hold.

"Where are you going?" he asked, hoarsely.

"I'm going back to Kaskitesiw. I need to…" she hesitated and looked into his concerned eyes thinking she saw something more. "I,

I need to take over for Pete. He is going away tomorrow, remember? One of us has got to hold the fort and I don't think you're going to be in any time soon."

Regret darkened his eyes.

"You will be fine now, and I will be fine until you get back." She took the balm Susanne had bought her and smoothed it over his chapped lips. On an impulse she neither questioned nor fully understood, she moved the balm across her own lips.

A slight smile tugged at the corner of his mouth and he drifted back to sleep.

Slowly, gently, and with a strange longing, she pulled her hand free and went to the morgue to check on the autopsy.

CHAPTER 11

"Good morning, Detective Harrigan," Pete said cheerfully, "you're late for your first day on the job." He had on a Hawaiian shirt and his feet were crossed on the desk. He was holding a thin, muddy wallet. "Found it on the bank."

"Great!" Emily exclaimed. "My mom had a hundred questions about what happened, thanks to your phone call to them. The bear wasn't ten feet tall. Shame on you!"

"Hey, it was dark. He was a big bear." He eyed her blouse and khaki pants, and handed her a uniform catalogue. "Folks up here aren't used to plain-clothes detectives who run around in Mustangs. The Fish and Game truck is the only thing left running. Daniel isn't here, and bear season has started, so I suggest you lean to the green. I'll pick up the tab. All law enforcement officers share duties up here and have the same rights and jurisdictions. You can stop someone for speeding, as well as for poaching. I suggest you read up on the Fish and Game regulations. Raise your right hand. Do you solemnly swear...?"

Emily repeated every word after him seriously. As she put her hand down, he motioned for her to turn it over and put a deputy badge in it.

"Congratulations on your demotion, Detective!" A moment later he said, crestfallen, "Susanne and I don't need to go on this vacation."

"Pete, you have already booked your voyage. If I get into trouble, I'll just ask for State Police assistance. I contacted the Fish and Game Department in Concord this morning. I've worked with them on search and recovery. Not everyone is found alive and there has to be an investigation. With the help of the conservation officer in the district and Warden Despert in the next county over, I shouldn't have any difficulties."

"Sounds like you've got it covered. You know, you can call George too. He said he'd come from work if you needed him. I don't know what you said to him, but he says you're like family now. I don't suppose you know what that means up here."

"It is an honor," Emily said. She knew that among people of small New England towns, a person could remain a stranger, no matter how long he or she lived, worked or served there. A stranger becoming 'like family' was a rare occurrence.

Pete clapped his hands on his thighs as if that was the end of it, but then hesitated. "I'm not sure I should take off like this. The state police are convinced Faidlee is in Canada. They found Patterson's SUV near the border, but he could come back."

"If he comes back it will be with a Canadian escort. Stop worrying, Pete," Emily said with a smile. "At the risk of sounding like a stuck-up snob, I am really good at what I do. Besides," she added conspiratorially, handing him his cap, "I know you've tried to fool me the last forty-eight hours but Kaskitesiw isn't really a high crime area, now is it?"

"The last forty-eight hours ought to do us for a decade or two!" Pete put on his hat. "Gun's in the drawer. Here's the key to the office. I'm sure you'll find the rest. Okay then?" He was half way to the door. "Susanne and I are going to stop by and see Daniel on our way to Boston."

"Wait a minute! Pete, I just have to ask you. Where did you take your cruiser?"

"It's at Mac's Glass in Errol. Faidlee did quite a number on the windshield."

"Have they started work on it?"

"No, I just dropped it off this morning."

"I'm going to ask them to wait on fixing that windshield, if you don't mind."

"Sure. I'm not going to be using it."

"What about Daniel's Jeep and the ATV? Where are they?"

"We pulled them both out of the swamp yesterday. They're at the junk yard here—Andre's. He won't be doing anything with them until Daniel gets back. You think Faidlee might have left some clues in them?"

"You never know. I want an airtight case against that guy. Have a good vacation!" she said, waving him off.

Emily ordered two pairs of pants, shirts and a light jacket and then called to dispatch to say she would be out of the office and to reach her on the hand radio. She fastened the radio and badge on her shirt and slid the Sig Sauer's holster onto her belt.

She went outside and started to walk one way, turned, and walked the other, uncomfortable being the awkward stranger at an unfamiliar door. She'd go say hello to Joe. After all, he had deduced something suspicious about Faidlee, and he might have new information on him.

Joe's was crowded with men and women preparing for the hunt. She walked inside the small fortress with barred windows, and the conversation stopped.

Joe looked up from a gun he was oiling, and then stood. "Hey, Detective! Good to see you again. You're a deputy now!"

"You're busy today," she said, studying his narrow heart shaped face and stubby chin hair.

"Hey, no, don't worry about it. Most are just looking." His quick speech was emitted like the sharp tap of a snare drum.

One man left the store and another was on his way out. Joe didn't seem to care.

"Hey, how's Warden Claret?" he said in a low voice.

"He's going to be okay."

Joe dropped his voice even lower. "You got any leads on Faidlee?"

"We don't even know for sure if Richard Faidlee was the shooter."

"I know, innocent until proven guilty. That guy's guilty as sin," he said disgruntled, and then cocked his finger for her to lean closer. "Bailey Wigman was in here a little while ago." Joe's voice was just above a whisper. "He's good friends with Rich Faidlee, but I could tell he hasn't seen him lately. He's got Faidlee's hounds."

"So you think Faidlee has left the area?"

"I think he's gone across the border." Joe leaned back.

"The Canadian police are cooperating in the search."

"Hey, be careful, hear? That guy could slither out of a hangman's noose. And if his wife is still somewhere around here, he'll be back. Mark my words."

"I will," Emily replied. "Thank you. May I have some 9mm hollow points, please?"

"Hey, sure Officer. Appreciate you buyin' local." He reached under the counter and set two boxes before her.

She paid him. "Do you know where a woman named Anna lives? I don't know her last name. She said she would be moving back to her house in town."

"Hey, that's an easy one! Anna Miner, she's been here a long time. So she is moving back? Hey, that's good! It was a bad scene when Rusty was killed." He shook his head. "She took it real hard, though you couldn't tell by looking at her. But you knew, you just knew—first her husband, then her son." He straightened and pointed through the window. "You go up the street, this way. Turn at what used to be Martin's garage…"

"Wait, whoa, what is Martin's Garage, now?" Emily couldn't help smiling.

"Just a storage building, but it still says Martin's on it. Turn at the fork and go uphill. Her house is the third one you come to."

"Which side of the street?"

"There's only one side." He grinned.

How could you only have one side of a street? Emily let it go, thanked him and left.

She dropped the ammunition back at the office then walked past the Post Office, then the grocery store and made a mental note she'd have to stop in there before going back to Mica. The road turned to dirt. It was fretted like a washboard because of people putting their brakes on while coming down the hill. On the left sat a cement block building with faded blue paint boasting it had once been Martin's Garage. The windows were coated with cobwebs in which dangled fat fall spiders. Here she had a choice of whether to go right or left, but Joe had said up the hill, so she continued left.

96

The first house she came to was a chunky bungalow, square and painted white with red shutters. Joe was right. Across the street, the land dropped off drastically. She was now at the same height as the tree tops.

Next was a faded gray trailer still trimmed with Christmas lights. The third house, a small, yellow ranch with brown trim, had a dream catcher hanging from its porch.

Hesitantly, Emily knocked on the door.

The door opened and Anna grinned at her. "Pepitigwe! *Come in*! I am glad you came."

"I just thought I'd stop by and see if you needed any help moving in."

"Come in. Come in, Apisci-mosos! The house is much the way I left it except for the dust." Anna grabbed Emily's arm and pulled her inside.

"How are you doing?" Emily laughed at the little woman's assertiveness.

"Good, good! Api. *Sit down*," Anna urged and motioned towards a flowered sofa, so different than the austere furniture at the camp.

Emily took a seat on the edge, not knowing what to say next.

"Thank you for the call from the hospital. When Pete told me that my Taaniyal would be fine, I was so relieved. Would you like some ginseng tea?" Anna clasped her hands together.

"Sure, great," Emily replied. She'd never had ginseng tea.

On the table next to her were two framed pictures. One was of two dark, shaggy-haired little boys holding a fish between them. The fish was almost as big as they were. They were grinning at the camera, dressed in wrinkled swimming trunks, skinny legs bent in exaggeration of the great weight of the fish. The taller boy was missing his front teeth.

The other picture showed the two boys on another day, not of their faces, but of them walking away. They were older. The smaller child was in the front, his hair short, military style. He was pulling the taller child along, dragging him by the hand. Even without seeing their faces, they were cute in their sweat-shirts and long rumpled pants.

"Taaniyal caught the pike, but he wanted Rusty in the picture with him." Anna picked up the first picture.

"I am so sorry about your son." Emily looked up at her, sadly. "I understand he was killed in Iraq."

Anna wiped the dust from the frame against her skirt. "This is Taaniyal," she said pointing. "The younger boy is Rusty. My Rusty was so full of life, so happy, a—what is the saying?" she whispered thoughtfully, a crooked finger against her chin, "free spirit! He was good for my adopted son, Taaniyal, though the adoption of him is only in my heart," Anna confided with the same arthritic finger now at her lips.

"Taaniyal was always very quiet, very serious." Anna showed Emily just how serious with a frown. "Rusty got both of them in so much trouble. This is why I took this picture of Rusty pulling Taaniyal again into some mischief, always into some mischief, but so much fun." Her eyes behind the thick glasses smiled at the memory. "I know I scolded but…" Anna slid open the drawer of the table and took out another picture of Rusty, this one in his military uniform.

Looking at the picture, Emily's heart grew heavy at the loss of this young life. Dark like Daniel, Rusty had a smile which could have procured anything he wanted from anyone. There was an inner light shining through those brown eyes, impish, but devoid of any falseness or cruelty. Handsome did not fully describe him for he still had youthful beauty, even in the somber uniform.

Emily looked up at Anna and found tears running down the old woman's cheeks. "Maybe this wasn't the right time for a visit. I should have called."

"It is a very good time. I have been thinking about you," Anna said and went back into the small kitchen, wiping her face with her sleeve.

"Oh?" Emily opened the table drawer and reverently placed the picture back inside. She couldn't help but notice another picture. The man looked like an older version of Rusty—and strangely of Daniel too.

"I sweetened it with a little honey." Anna brought out two steaming mugs. "That is my husband Russell. I did not have him long. He came to my clan in Canada, wanted to marry me, so he joined my clan and took my name."

"He must have loved you very much." Emily reached for her cup.

"It was, the way they call it, love at first sight. Much like it is with you and Daniel."

Nearly spilling the tea, Emily stammered, "Anna, caring for someone is not the same as loving them."

Anna only smiled.

Emily took a sip. "Tasty!" She held the mug in her lap when she couldn't see a coaster or napkin on the table. In spite of dust, the wood was beautiful.

"I have a favor to ask of you," Anna said. "Will you go with me to fetch Taaniyal? Peter is not here and I can no longer drive with these eyes."

"When are they going to release him?"

"Probably, it will be tomorrow afternoon. He will be in Dr. Pomfret's care."

"I met the doctor. He seems nice," Emily said, but then asked seriously, "But is the warden ready to be released? It hasn't been two days."

"They say he can do the rest of his healing at home."

"You have to wonder if they are hospitals or assembly lines."

"He will be in good care with Dr. Pomfret. I worked with him many years when he was a dentist in Errol. Besides I know it is making Daniel kiskwewin to be in the hospital."

"Kees-kay-way-oon`?" Emily took another sip and set her cup on the counter.

Anna made a circle around the side of her head. "Crazy. Come with me to get Daniel some clothes to come home in." She picked up her shawl.

"Would you teach me more Cree?" Emily took her arm.

Anna pursed her lips in thought then nodded, saying as they walked, "Taaniyal, it is Daniel's name in Cree."

"Tan-ee-yell," Emily repeated.

"In our Cree, there is no D. We use a T. Almost same sound with tongue."

"Ah," Emily said curiously, "Is there a way to say Emily in Cree?"

"No, not 'Emily', except almost the way it is spelled, Emili, but your name is 'Apisci-mosos'."

"A-pees-tsee-mo-sos?"

Anna nodded, happily.

"But what does it mean?"

"Apisci, by itself, means to be small, but Apisci-mosos means," she arched her two fingers and made graceful leaps with her hands, "Deer! Before autumn, deer are colored like your hair."

"Apisci-mosos?" she asked brightly. "You gave me this name?"

"It was Taaniyal, who gave you this name."

"What, when?"

"When he was afraid for you in his sickness, he knew you would come! At first I thought the fever had him, but then I knew who he meant when I saw you."

"Anna, how do I say this—kiskwewin?"

"Ah, you are a good learner."

"I just met the warden. I'm only here a month. I have a job at home. I have a boyfriend at home. I don't mean to hurt your feelings but Daniel is just a nice person who was in trouble, and I'd do the same for anyone."

Anna pointed, "There is Taaniyal's house."

Emily shook her head and followed her up the dirt road. To the left, Emily could hear the sound of children laughing. "Is there a school up on that hill?"

"It is Father Paul's mission school. It must be morning recess," Anna explained.

"Anna, I'm curious. When they brought Daniel to the hospital, a priest gave him the Catholic Last Rites to help him, whether he was Catholic or not." Emily was listening to the children's laughter as if it were a symphony. "Is he Catholic?"

"Ehe, he is the same religion as you."

"How do you know I'm Catholic?" Emily frowned.

"The medal you wear about your neck. It is of Merryana, the mother of the first people."

"Our Lady of Guadalupe," Emily fingered the medal and said, "I feel this is how Mary really looks, as though she belongs to all races. I found it in a trunk in our attic when I was a little girl. My mother didn't like me wearing it, but she said it was my grandmother's way of giving it to me. I've never taken it off."

"You loved your grandmother?"

"I never knew my grandmother or grandfather on my mother's side. They died when my mother was still young. Her older sister raised her."

Anna changed the subject. "Taaniyal is very angry with God for taking Rusty. He does not say it, but I know."

"Then our anger with God is about all we have in common—not much to go on," Emily said, hoping to discourage Anna from further match-making.

The Cree woman grunted.

They reached the simple log ranch with a porch in the front. Humble in size and looks, it afforded a beautiful view of a marshland below. Snakes of water passed through the grasses, glistening in the sun. An unscreened window was wide open under the roof of the porch. There were still a few plants in a garden, wilted by the first frost. A pumpkin stood starkly against the brown leaves of its vine, and a few pale corn stalks rattling in the breeze. There was a huge pile of logs dumped on the left side and a little gray squirrel scurried in and out of them.

"What is that place down there?" Emily indicated the wetland below.

"Kaskitesiw Nipiy."

"The swamp? It looks so different from here."

"It has many faces. You were in its dark face the other night, the water without life, black with peat and rotting leaves.

"And leeches," Emily added.

Anna pointed down the steep hill. "If the old ones had seen this face of the swamp first, it would not have been called Kaskitesiw. It is the swamp's living face, bright water, in the open. It is a good place to catch fish for it has deep hollows where the fish can winter."

"My Dad would love that!"

"The swamp has a third face." Anna pointed to the north. "It is its ageless face where the water runs into the swamp, over bare rock. It is the most beautiful, I think. The song of the waterfall moves your heart."

"Can we go there sometime?"

"It must remain a memory for me but perhaps Daniel will take you when he has healed. The path is hard with many rocks to climb."

The same little gray squirrel chattered and flicked its tail from a nearby rock.

"It is all right, Nutmeg," Anna said softly. "Taaniyal will be home soon. We will not bother his things."

"Nutmeg?" Emily smiled.

"Taaniyal found her last year. The rest of her tipiyaw, *her litter mates,* had been taken by an owl. The mother had abandoned her. Her eyes weren't even open yet."

"And Daniel raised her?"

"Taaniyal's soul is one with animals," Anna stated.

"Ah!" Emily nodded.

"You say this as if you know this about him."

"Not really, I just mean, aren't most Native Americans one with nature?"

"My son, whose blood was pure, was allergic to dogs. He did not like animals or the woods."

"Oh."

"The only reason my adopted son is close to the animals is that he, like many children abandoned by both mother and father, needed to find a substitute, that which would make him comfortable on this earth. Taaniyal found acceptance among wild things."

"I apologize for stereotyping, Anna."

"It is a common error. Many of our people were close to the earth. Many more have forgotten how to be. I do know about medicinal plants because we had no doctor where I lived in Canada. And I have taught them to Taaniyal. Rusty wanted nothing to do with that either. All he wanted to be was a soldier like sigos, Taaniyal's father."

"I thought Daniel's father's name was Kirk. Is this how you say it in Cree?"

A mischievous little smile formed on Anna's face and she nodded. "Colonel Sigos, a respectful way to speak his name."

The squirrel's warning turned to high pitched clucks, ending in little growls. She ran up the tree to harass them still more.

Emily said, "She won't attack, will she?"

"Anigwacas, *the squirrel*, won't attack me," Anna informed her.

"That's comforting," Emily murmured, following closely behind the Cree woman. "A-ne-qua-tsace? Squirrel?"

"Ehe." Anna opened the door, which had no lock. Though the interior was chilly and the stove was cold, the walls gave off the scent of wood smoke and pine logs. She looked around the living space with its small kitchenette while Anna rummaged through Daniel's clothes in the sole bedroom and his toiletries in a small bathroom.

There were quite a few piles of loose-leaf ledgers and censuses on animals. On a home-made shelf, there were books on wasting and other diseases affecting game animals and books on deer, bear, moose, coyotes, wolves, every bird, mammal and amphibian you could think of.

Emily's eyes fell on a picture of two young men kayaking in foaming water. Even though they wore helmets, she could tell one was an older Daniel and the other was a grinning Rusty.

Anna came from the bedroom and caught Emily's perusal of the picture. "Look at the two of them! Again, Rusty dragged him off to try this," Anna explained. "They both came back excited. Even my Taaniyal was laughing. My Taaniyal, he is…" She searched for the words and not finding it, resorted to Cree and sign language, making a slow arch above her. "Pesohamew sakastew, *he takes small steps, slow like the sun.* Like the sun, he does not move fast, but when he moves, it is always with much thought, much caring, much warmth. My Rusty was kikway peyakwan acahkos, *like a shooting star!*" Anna opened her fingers and shot her arm to the ceiling.

Emily's eyes were shining at Anna's animation and the Cree woman studied her.

"For a year I have not spoken of him," Anna said solemnly, sure now that Emily was one of those who took the pain of the afflicted into herself. "It does not bother you for me to talk of a dead child?"

"He comes alive again when you talk of him," Emily said taking Anna's arm and leading her to the door. "I'm glad to know them both, and I hope you will tell me more of them and teach me more Cree. It is a beautiful language."

Anna nodded delighted.

"Taaniyal," Emily smiled and lifted her hand slowly in an arch. "He is more like the sun, sa-ka-ste-uw. He takes all day to do something but is always reliable."

Anna laughed, "Sakastew, the sun who rises and sets slowly, and…" She roughly pulled Emily's head towards her lips. "Apisci-mosos nestwasiw."

"What does that mean?" Emily pulled away giggling.

Anna pulled her head towards her face again and whispered, "Hot for you!"

"Anna!" Emily looked at the little Cree woman, shocked. "Shame on you! There is no reason for you to say that! Really Anna! What are you—where are you getting this stuff?"

Anna tilted her head back and laughed uproariously.

"Really, shame on you," Emily scolded.

"Mihkwaw," Anna said laughing and patting her face. She pointed to Emily.

Emily felt the heat in her cheeks and tried to look aghast at the woman. "I'll 'mee-he-qua' you. Come on. Enough Cree lessons for today."

As Emily was shutting the door behind them, she looked back and felt a sense of sadness and loss. The only warmth here came from Nutmeg, chattering on the open window sill, a fur ball with a hot temper.

CHAPTER 12

After leaving Anna's, Emily parked the Fish and Game truck at the top of Birch Hill and walked down to the swamp. The sky had darkened, and a drizzle began. She remembered the bear and felt the automatic at her side. If he showed up, hopefully, it would be enough to scare him off.

The air moved with slow, sweeping fingers of fog. Her hair and clothes were damp in a short while. The forest, on both sides of the path, looked ominous in the sodden, quiet atmosphere. If she didn't find what she was looking for now, the rain would wash it away.

A quarter of a mile past the swamp, the decaying stench of the meat made Emily gag as she reached the bait pile. She'd have to work fast.

A pair of ravens cart-wheeled in the air above her. They were screaming at each other in what seemed to be a variety of profanities.

"They're birds, Emily, just birds." She shook off the foreboding. Carefully she searched around the pile. Anna said Daniel had fallen on a rock. There were thousands rocks around the site, all glistening wet. How was she going to find old blood on a wet rock? But as the fine rain moistened a granite ledge outcrop, the water turned the dried dark blood into a reddish pool once more. She bent over it, studied it and estimated the angle of Daniel's fall. Daniel was shot in the side, front to back. The shooters intent would have been to place a bullet directly in his chest. Daniel must have turned at the last minute. A bullet hitting him at that angle would have spun him around, like putting English on a cue ball. She worked her geometry in the dirt and then turned, gazing at possible trajectory points from both hills and tried to imagine the scene. Frustrated at finding nothing, in the mist, she picked up a long straight stick and put it under her right arm at the angle which the bullet had entered Daniel. She let the stick protrude in front.

Emily rotated slowly, directing her vision to where the stick pointed. Recalculating for an estimate of Daniel's height, she placed the stick against her neck in what she hoped was the same angle and sighted up the stick. Halfway around, she saw a large rock on Grave Hill. After studying it for a few seconds, she twisted quickly and her eyes fell on the ledge now cleansing itself of Daniel's blood.

Dropping the stick, she made her way through the brush then began to climb. Tree branches snagged her hair and clothes. The knees of her pants were dark with soil. Finally, she was at the granite bolder which an ancient glacier must have deposited as it receded up the valley.

Emily circumvented the huge rock and found herself on a fairly flat place. The soil was much higher on this uphill side. She was actually tall enough to see over the rock to the place where she had been on the trail.

Emily put on her latex gloves and got on her hands and knees. Gently, she raked through the wet forest debris. Faidlee may have picked up his shell casing, but maybe not. There was a sound, a small 'tink' against the rock. Carefully she turned the leaves over until she saw the brass-colored casing. She lifted the .30-06 with her pen and looked at it closely. Opening a small baggie, she dropped the casing inside. "I suppose you could have been left here by anybody but let's go see if your buddies are at Joe's."

Alarmed by the human voice, a grouse flew out of the brush and disappeared instantly within the fog. Emily caught her breath and looked around. Nothing moved except for a piece of birch bark hanging from its pale tree. In spite of the stillness, once in a while the curled bark would move, like the broken wing of a bird, silently trying to refold its detachment.

She strained her eyes to see any other movement in the mist-darkened trees. The image of the bear rose before her again in the form of a decayed stump. A warbler scratched at the dead leaves on the forest floor, bent on uncovering insects. Emily put her hand on her gun. She spied the little culprit and was glad no one was around to see her reaction to the tiny bird.

Once back in town, she pulled the truck in front of the gun shop and went inside. She was glad there were no other patrons around to see her filthy clothes.

"Hey, Detective Harrigan! Geezum! Looks like you got dragged under a horse!" Joe exclaimed looking curiously at her soiled attire.

"Joe, would you pull the ammunitions log on what you sold to Faidlee and his client, Patterson."

As was his nature, he thought of a joke to tell her as he flipped through the pages, "Here's a funny one for you, Detective, since you're from the city and all. I sell a lot of whistles and pepper spray to people for protection against bears. Do you know how to tell from scat whether there is a black bear or a grizzly around?"

"Got me there, Joe," Emily said, trying to remember what scat was.

"The Grizzly's got pepper spray and whistles in it," Joe snickered nasally.

"Good one!" Emily said, enthusiastically.

"Here it is," Joe said, as his fingers opened to a page in the log. He handed it to her.

"Can you show me a box of those?" she asked, pointing to the page, "And a list of all rifles you sell that they're used in."

"Sure, but they are pretty common," he replied, digging under the counter, "but they would go with Faidlee's flea-market rifle, if that's what you're lookin' to compare."

She took a bullet from the box then produced the casing from her pocket and turned it over within the plastic bag. "We have matching brands," she announced quietly, hoping there was a finger print on the casing. The bullet casing she found was still shiny and most likely came from Joe's recently. It would be even better if she had the rifle to match to the casing. Looking back at Joe she asked, "What did you say about his flea-market rifle?"

"It wasn't one I'd sell him."

"Why's that?" Emily murmured, still studying the cartridge.

"He got it cheap, a year back. He bragged about it in the store, that I was charging too much. I don't know where he got it, but it was a Springfield 1903 with a case-hardened bolt. Their bolts are prone to failing under pressure, like when a bullet jams. They can fly back and can kill the shooter. Faidlee said I was full of crap and gloated every single time he walked in here, 'cause his hadn't misfired. But I studied military rifles. Ones like his all have serial numbers under 800,000. The military stopped producing them—too dangerous. No reputable gun shops will sell them 'cause of that. Ones over 800,000 were double heat treated, much safer."

"Are there still many of the old ones in circulation?" Emily asked, putting the bullet down, listening intently.

"Not many. But they're out there. Scary thing is the grandkid, who inherits his grandfather's old rifle, may get the bolt right in the face. Not all of them do that for sure, but it's enough to make them guns non-gratis."

"I'll send this casing down to ballistics, so if we get a hold of the rifle we can compare it. You have really helped. I'll buy this box of shells and then I'll have a date and proof of purchase to compare with the copy of Patterson's purchase. Can you make me copies of that sales slip to Patterson and the bullet log, please?"

"Appreciate you buying it. Ely Pike was always taking my stuff for what he called 'evidence'. You're like Claret that way."

Emily was still studying the casing as if trying to imprint the firing pin mark in her mind. She looked up. "Joe, what is scat?"

Joe looked at her for a minute as if trying to find out if she was serious, and then burst out laughing. "You didn't even get the joke!"

"No, well, sort of. Is it—poop?"

"Yep, you could say that," he said, trying to hold back his mirth.

"I might need to know that since I'm standing in for the warden too." She raised her brows with a funny expression of being out of place. "This is much different than Manchester."

Joe grinned. "Wait 'til I tell this to Ike. Welcome to Kaskitesiw, Detective Harrigan. When a bear comes in, I'll close the store and come help weigh it."

"I appreciate that Joe. I may need some help," she said, thankfully. She noticed he said the name of the town the way Daniel did, and wondered if he too was Native American.

Emily drove to Mac's Glass in Errol. She could find little evidence on the broken windshield, except that the blows were done by a blunt object, probably metal, maybe a flash light. The impact strikes were large and web-like. There was a small speck of what looked like blood, and she worked the shard of glass loose and stabilized it. She would send it off to the lab when she got back to the office.

Emily asked them to wait another day to fix the windshield and went back to Kaskitesiw to look at Daniel's Jeep and the ATV at Andre's. They were caked with black slime, and decaying weeds.

She went over every inch of the two vehicles, glad she had not bothered to change clothes.

Daniel's mud-encrusted rifle was still secured in the door rack with the trigger lock engaged. There were soaked papers in the glove compartment, including a copy of the Fish and Game Laws. A flashlight was mounted near the hinge of the door. A set of chains and a jack were under the seats.

She went over to the ATV and lifted the wobbly plastic hood. The spark plug looked old and corroded. It hadn't been replaced by a newer one, similar to what Pete had in his glove compartment. Though Faidlee could have rigged the ignition on the jeep, he must have pushed this vehicle into the swamp. They found it only a few yards from the Jeep but nearer to shore in a wide area of puffy cat tails. Her eyes rested on an empty circular holder. Taking out her pen, she pushed at the clip and found it broken at the seam.

She went back to the jeep and looked at the flashlight clip. It was the same as in the ATV but with the flashlight still in it. She was about to stand up when a big drooling face got into her line of vision. Emily jumped slightly and then rubbed the mastiff's ears. Andre had introduced her to the dog saying he wouldn't hurt a fly, but folks didn't know that because of the way he looked. His name was Uggh, Andre explained, because people were always saying that when he drooled on them. After a while, the dog just thought that was his name.

"Uggh, you've got to get out of the way," she said, pushing the big dog to the side as a line of drool went from the corner of his mouth to her sleeve. That action only triggered a playful response. He galloped around her then targeted the wonderful smells of the swamp clinging to the Jeep.

Emily looked once more at the flashlight. It was twisted slightly in its clip. She pushed Uggh away again, put a glove on, and moved the flashlight. There was play in the metal clip, but no break. Suppose Faidlee had tried to take this flashlight but it wouldn't come free? Emily bent her head upwards, and then shouted, "Andre, would you come get Uggh?"

Andre, toothless and lame, hobbled up and spoke to her legs protruding from the jeep. "Pardon, Mademoiselle Warden. Was he bozering you?"

"No, just hold him for a second, please." She opened a small case and took out a pair of tweezers and a baggie from her pocket. Lying on her back on the muddy floor, she reached up to a sharp edge of the dashboard, just above the flashlight. Carefully, she picked off a small piece of skin containing a few hairs. "Gotcha!" she exclaimed softly and dropped the evidence and tweezers into the bag. She wiggled out of the Jeep.

"Did you find somezing?" Andre` asked with expectation.

"Maybe," Emily replied. "Andre, I don't want anyone touching these vehicles. Keep Uggh away too."

"Yes, Mademoiselle."

Emily stooped, looking back at the jeep, thinking out loud and patting Uggh at the same time. "The dead man was in the passenger seat. He could have been slumped over, under the steering wheel and scraped his hand when the rush of water swept him back up. But I don't remember a cut on Patterson." She said to the dog, thinking of her visit to the morgue yesterday. It would be easy enough to check out. Even if the body was gone, the wound inventory would be there.

Uggh gave her a lick of agreement with a tongue so big it covered half her face. She stood up laughing.

Andre grinned. "You like dogs?"

Emily wiped her mouth. "I like dogs—never had one though."

"He is ze fader of Madam Gendolyn's puppies."

"Oh my! They'll be big puppies, but I bet they'll be as cute as teddy bears."

"Would you like me to have Joe save one for you?"

"I can't have a puppy in my apartment." She apologized to Uggh.

"I had to try. Ze least I can do for Joe." He gave Uggh an exasperated look.

CHAPTER 13

Emily looked up from the chain of custody form she was writing for the new evidence and stared at her watch—ten thirty in the morning. It would take them two hours to get down to the hospital. And she still wanted to stop by and talk to Ila. At the post office she discovered this was Ila's day off. Again, by asking Joe at the gun store for directions, Emily found Teresa's sister's trailer.

"Hello, Ila," she greeted softly, "I'm Emily Harrigan. I talked to you the other night."

"Oh, ayuh!" Ila said, coming out to greet her. "Teresa's still hidden good. I heard from her, again. She is real sorry about Warden Claret though. So am I."

"He's going to be all right," Emily reassured her. "You helped save his life by telling me what you knew."

"My brother-in-law is a miserable hound."

"Ila, has Teresa asked you to clean her house while she is away?" Emily asked.

"She asked me to pick up a few things. She left in such a hurry, you know."

"Have you done it yet?"

"Just haven't found the time with the post office work. This is my day off."

"Do you think you might have a little time—say, right now?"

"You need something from in there to catch Richard?" Ila's eyes lit up.

112

"I'm not asking you to get me anything from the house. But if you were to be throwing some things away, like beer cans, old tooth brush, cigarette butts, or hair from the shower, you probably wouldn't mind me picking through the garbage—outside."

"This is like that TV show."

"Sort of."

"I got you, Officer Emily." Ila shut the door behind her, without locking it.

They walked to a ramshackle trailer, which sat far from the others, alone in an overgrown field. There were no footprints in the waist-high grass. Emily walked around the outside, peering in the windows. The pungent odor of a skunk emanated from under the trailer.

"If you think it smells bad out here, it's worse inside. You know he's got a hook in the ceiling where he dresses deer."

"Dresses deer?"

"You know—guts 'em out. He does it right there in her living room. Hauls 'em up by that hook. Teresa's tried but she can't get the smell out, 'specially when he nicks a gland. He does it in there so nobody sees him poach, the bastard. But the smell gets in the floor boards. He don't care."

When Emily was sure Faidlee hadn't entered the trailer recently, she nodded for Ila to go inside. "I need this fairly quick, okay?"

Emily walked around the wind-peeled aluminum frame of the trailer to the garbage cans. One can stood on a wood pallet, under a window, and the other was tumbled onto its side, the probable target of the skunk. She heard the vacuum going and looked at her watch hoping Ila would reappear before she did the whole house.

It wasn't long before the window opened and a hand extended with a white bag which held the vacuumed collections. Emily lifted the trash can lid and with a flourish, Ila opened her fingers and let the bag drop in.

"Thank you, Ila." Emily whistled, like she just happened by. She lifted off the lid again and picked out the white bag. "My, what do we have here? Guess nobody wants these," Emily commented.

"You get him, Officer Emily! He won't be beatin' up my sister again!" Ila shouted through the window as Emily hurried off.

She should have been at Anna's by now. At the office she carefully sifted through the hairs in the vacuum bag and placed the ones she picked out in a moisture-resistant envelope. In separate bags, she put the bloodied shard of glass from Pete's windshield and the piece of skin she'd found in the jeep. Then she made up the package, added a note, and addressed it to the New Hampshire Crime Laboratory. Lastly, she called dispatch and made arrangements for her coverage by the State Police and enlisted a state trooper in Lebanon to be a protective currier for the evidence until it arrived in Manchester.

~~~~~

Anna was standing outside her door with her arms folded and a surly look on her face. Grabbing her arm and the paper bag on the porch, Emily led her down to the Mustang.

Anna was quiet as they drove to Lebanon. An hour into the drive, Emily asked, "Are you feeling all right?"

"Yes."

Another half hour passed.

"Are you mad at me for being late?"

No answer.

"Anna, trust me! I can't discuss facts, which I may need in court. I just want you to know that there was a good reason I was late. It concerns the man who shot Daniel."

"You got that macatisowin, *evil one*?" She rearranged her arms over her bosom, with contentment.

"Maybe," Emily said. "What is ma-ca-ta-eeso-way-o?"

"It means same as the devil."

"Faidlee certainly fits the description. Try as I might, I can't find anything good about him."

"You are trying to find something good in him?" Anna said, incredulously.

"It was my father's way of never being judgmental before he had all the facts, a different slant on 'innocent until proven guilty'. Every case we ever studied together he would pull up a history on the suspect.

114

It would ruin my 'cut-and-dry' opinion, confuse me, until I could see more definitively what all the facts were, without tainting them with emotions."

"Your father taught you well, as if you were his first son." Anna remarked.

"He taught me well as his daughter who would someday work with him."

"The main entrance is this way," Anna pointed when Emily did not slow down.

"I know," Emily said. "I just have to meet with the state police and run into the morgue for a minute." She passed the entrance and went around to the side of the building. "I'll be right back," she said before Anna could protest. A few minutes later she returned, and with a smile, suggested, "Let's go get Daniel. We're late!"

Anna, a bag of Daniel's clothes in her arms, walked up to the desk and asked for directions to Daniel's room. They found the door open, and to their surprise, Daniel was fully dressed in a pair of jeans and a light blue shirt. He stood, unable to straighten his right side. His lips were a little pale, his face sallow, but otherwise, he looked good. Emily swallowed hard.

Anna grunted disapprovingly at his appearance. "I said I would bring clothes! Who got you clothes?"

"Tanisi, Anna? *How are you, Anna?*" someone said from behind the door.

Anna swung around. Her eyes flew wide and she hissed, "Kohtawiy! *Your father!*"

"Ekaawiya kikiwaasi, Anna. *Don't be angry, Anna.*"

Emily looked back at a tall, handsome man with crew-cut hair and a military uniform. He looked like Daniel, but his face was fuller, hiding the high cheek bones and angular jaw of his son. He was smiling contritely. It had no effect on Anna. When he glanced Emily's way, she said politely, remembering her Cree, "How do you do, Colonel Sigos?"

The man frowned at Emily, quickly judged her innocence and turned to Anna, rendering her culpable.

"Matika nema! Sigos! Namoya! Awin siihkos mostosomiya. Awas! *There it is! The weasel! No! You are the dung of a weasel. Get out of here!*" Anna screamed at him, flinging her arm at him, "Awas! *Leave!*"

"Asay mina kwantaw kiwi—ati ayamin! *There you go, starting an argument!*" The man shouted back.

"Wayawe! *Take this outside!*" Daniel commanded in a low voice.

Anna gave the dignified man a not so dignified push and they both went out of the hospital room. You could hear them all the way down the hall.

Emily lifted her brows. "Okay, I'll just go down to the waiting room until you and whoever—whatever are ready to go."

"I apologize for my parents," Daniel said in a quiet voice.

"All families have their ups and downs. I know mine does," she commented, starting to leave.

"Detective, wait. I'd like to explain," Daniel called to her.

"You don't have to. It's okay, really."

"Emily."

She stopped when he used her first name and turned back.

"Please," he said sitting back down on the bed, as if he had to, breathing as if he had run a mile.

She walked back into the room and sat on the edge of a chair next to the bed. "You don't have to explain. Obviously, they are angry with each other over something."

"In our custom, when one dies, the person crossing over must have medicines made—a ceremony—to be released from this earth within four days. It is an old belief but a strong one among many tribes. When Anna's son died, my father could not come. He was the one who should have performed the ceremony, but he was in the hills of Afghanistan."

"Four days isn't much time. What if the ceremony doesn't happen in four days?"

He watched her, hoping she might be able to grasp even a part of his reasoning. "Then those who love the one who died must send him away. It is not an easy thing to do. Many times, the spirit wants to stay and those who cannot find comfort and courage by ceremony, keep him here, unable to enter heaven, unable to re-enter earth. It is the belief that the kisatinam—the detained spirit—eventually may take those grieving to the other side with him. My father says it is just an old and superstitious custom."

"No wonder Anna is angry." Emily shifted her eyes, pleased he confided in her, but unsure how to respond. "Anger can be therapeutic. And in your language, it sounds very therapeutic—if not fatal."

"I'm afraid those were not our finest words. Her son, Rusty, loved my father. His own father died very early. I shouldn't bother you with this. I appreciate that you brought Anna here."

"Rusty was like a brother to you," Emily said.

Daniel searched her face.

"Pete told me," she said shrugging, "and Anna told me a little."

"Ah, then you know the whole story?"

"Some! Why don't you lie back down until they get this straightened out?" She put her hand on his shoulder, and he raised his left hand to cover hers. Her heart bound so she thought it must be audible.

"Come on," she urged. "Lie back. I can't believe how quickly hospitals release people."

As he lay back, gratefully, she took his hand which was on hers, turned it, looking at his palm, back and forearm. Then she pushed his shirt cuff up his right arm, lifted it gently, and studied both sides of his hand.

Daniel's eyes were curious.

"All you have been through and no cuts on your hands or forearms," she smiled triumphantly.

He put the left hand under his head and studied her face. "What am I missing now?"

"I found some evidence that Faidlee may have been in your Jeep near the time of the shooting," she said. "He scraped the back of his hand on a bolt at the bottom of the dash board. I found enough flesh to test for DNA. The dead man had no such scrape wounds and neither do you. Faidlee must have been trying to yank your flashlight out of the jeep." She took a breath, and continued, "I think Faidlee used the flashlight from the ATV to smash in the cruiser's window, either to prevent us from leaving or just to show his displeasure. There was a small drop of blood on the windshield. I am betting it is Faidlee's also, hopefully matching some of his hair in a discarded vacuum bag which came from his trailer. I'm going to look around the…" Aware that she was being loquacious, she stopped mid-sentence.

"You have done this already? Pete said it was you who put all the pieces together to save my life." Daniel said, pushing himself up on his elbow.

"It's my job. Lie back," Emily said, pleased and embarrassed.

There was an awkward moment of silence.

"How are you feel…" She began.

"I want to thank…" He started to speak also, stepping on her sentence.

They both grew quiet, not wanting to chance a second collision of words.

"It was great your Dad came home to see you," Emily broke the silence.

"He came because Pete called him about operating. Pete thought they might need permission from next of kin," Daniel said, his voice was flat and his face expressionless.

"Sounds like maybe you and your father don't get along too well?"

He rolled his head against his left hand slowly and explained, "No, it's not that." He didn't seem to mind her prying. "He is a good man. He serves our country. He does what has to be done for all of us."

"It doesn't sound like Anna understands this."

"No, she blames my father for Rusty's death." Daniel wasn't sure he should tell her the rest. "Anna is a good woman but be careful of the things she tells you in Cree. She can be…" He hesitated, trying to choose a polite word.

"Naughty," Emily said quickly, remembering Anna's interpretation of Daniel as the sun being hot for her.

His look was both sympathetic and amused. "Sigos means weasel."

Emily looked horrified and exclaimed, "I called your father a weasel!"

"He knew that you were deceived." Daniel smiled. "No harm done."

"Your father has explained!"

118

Emily turned at the sound of Anna's voice.

Kirk Claret stood beside Anna whose thick arms were folded obstinately, but it looked to Emily like there were tears in her eyes.

"Only have a twenty-four hour leave. Need to shove off. Glad you're doing better," the colonel commented without coming near his son. "Glad the clothes fit. Stay away from speeding bullets."

"Yes, sir." Daniel didn't smile. "Thank you for the clothes."

"We'll see you at Thanksgiving," Kirk added crisply, replacing his cap. "Get a haircut."

"Yes, sir."

Kirk Claret nodded to Emily in acknowledgement, but without smiling.

"Kiseyaya iyapiw," Anna snarled as he passed her.

"Kiseyaya mayatan posis," He grumbled back and was gone.

Daniel's eyes were on the empty doorway. Emily wanted to hold him so bad that her arms ached.

"What did they say?" she asked, leaning towards him.

Her breath tickled his ear, sending a rush through his body so that he no longer thought of his father's hasty retreat.

With the same effect on her, he whispered back, "She called him a buck goat, and he said she was an old, ugly cat."

"I'll go bring the car around." Emily bit her lip to keep from laughing. She went past Anna, giving her a look of admonishment, and then glanced back at Daniel.

He was grinning at her.

Astonished, Anna whirled to look at Emily.

~~~~~

During the trip home, she knew Daniel must be hurting because of his silence. Mustangs were built for speed, not for comfort. She stayed on the Vermont Interstate most of the way because it was faster and smoother than cutting across Ragged Mountain.

Anna said nothing but around Fairlee, she fell asleep, her snores reverberated off the windows.

Emily smiled and looked at Daniel. He was either staring out the side window or fell asleep that way. It made for a long trip and the sun had set when she dropped Daniel at his cabin. He would not hear of staying with Anna. Emily hated leaving him alone at the dark house but this was not her call to make.

Before she had left for the hospital, she put a note on the police station door saying she would be back by 6:00 PM or to call the State police in an emergency. It was 5:53 and someone was huddling by the front door. She made out the features of a slight woman. "Teresa?" she wondered aloud. Emily parked the car quickly and got out.

The girl watched her coming, eyes puffy and red. She took in a ragged breath and started crying, "I didn't know what else to do," she managed to say, looking at her dented car as if it was the culprit alone. "I didn't mean to hit it."

Emily comforted the young girl, who had been on her way to college and convinced her to take her back to where she hit the deer. Leaving the girl inside the Fish and Game truck, Emily got out and searched the highway. She found the doe still alive, but badly injured in a ditch.

"Sweetheart, you don't want the animal to suffer any more than I do."

The girl shook her head. "Do what you have to." She gulped back her tears.

"Okay," Emily put the blue flashing lights on and turned on the radio. "You like this kind of music? Turn it up as loud as you want."

The girl turned up the rap music until it was blaring but still covered her ears.

Feeling as upset as the girl after shooting the deer, Emily figured out the Fish and Game winch system and pulled the animal into the truck bed. Trying not to show her feelings, Emily drove back into town and not sure of what to do with the meat, called George who came gratefully. Emily waited with the girl until her parents arrived. They vowed to return the next day for the dented car.

Driving back to Mica, Emily crawled into bed, exhausted, but the nightmares came around three o'clock in the morning.

"Mommy!" A little pale hand rose from the pile of leaves. "He's hurting me." Emily grabbed the child's cold hand frantically digging

in the leaves of a ditch to find her. Instead she found the deer. Emily lifted the doe's head out of the leaves, understanding the fear in the soft brown eyes.

Tears of regret and guilt tormented her the rest of the night.

CHAPTER 14

Bear season had been underway since the first of September. Bow season started today, the fifteenth of September. People were coming in for licenses and deer checks. These hunters spoke and acted with responsibility. Emily saw no reason to be concerned about them, and began to relax with the job. She did have two people quibbling about survey stakes but the forester convinced them to wait until Pete returned before cutting any trees.

A bear was brought to the station to be registered. In the dark, Emily did not realize how extraordinary these animals were. Its black coat glistened. She was fascinated by its paws, so huge and dangerous with long curved claws. Its teeth were white and terrifying and the body was formidable, even in death. Had she seen this bear before seeing the one on the trail, she would have been far more frightened.

The bear had been shot by a hunter, a man about thirty, accompanied by his father. He was proud of his marksmanship, and his happiness was contagious. Joe and a couple of others helped Emily weigh the animal in at 320 pounds. Some of the townspeople gathered, curious over the second 'bear baggin' of the season.

Though Emily didn't appreciate the killing of this great beast, she tried to make conversation as she filled out the out-of-state registration, "So are you coming back to Kaskitesiw for another bear next year?"

Without the crowd around them now, both the father and son shook their heads in unison. The son spoke, "This is the only bear I will ever shoot."

"Do you mind me asking why?" She studied their suddenly serious faces.

"You're a game warden. You've heard them die, right?" the son asked, looking to her for understanding.

"No," she replied, putting down the pen. "No, I haven't."

"I don't think I'm ever going to get that sound out of my mind."

"I wasn't prepared for it either," the father said.

"What did it sound like?" Emily was almost afraid to hear the answer.

"It sounded like I was killing a person, a human being. I mean, the moan was so human."

His father nodded in agreement. "I never heard anything like it, except in the war."

Disturbed by what they said, Emily quietly went back to filling out the registration. Finishing, she said, "I was talking to this lady the other day. She is Cree Indian. Maskwa, the bear, is closest to man in the Cree way of thinking. That doesn't mean they don't kill bears, but when they do they honor the animal. They tell their children who lie in the bear skin all about the animal, how it gave its life so they could be warm and fed. Maybe, if you do that, the sound of its death will go away. It won't be what you remember when you talk about the bear."

They both stared at her silently. Did they think she was nuts? Then the father stepped forward to shake her hand. "That makes a lot of sense, Officer. Thank you."

The son smiled also, saying, "We will do just that. My kids will lie on its fur and I'll get books about bears. I'll read to them on it. We will eat the meat, thankfully, even though I've heard it's greasy."

They left. Emily sat down at the desk, smiling to herself. "You're not so bad at this job."

Emily was feeling closer to the people of this town every day, but since Daniel had come home, she had not gone to visit him. She wasn't sure why. She had stopped in at Anna's, daily, sharing a cup of tea with her and asked about him, but she couldn't make herself go up the road to his log house. The realization that she loved him had a strange affect on her. She still had no idea how he felt. So far their relationship had been based on care-giving and gratitude, more conducive to obligation than to love.

Emily rubbed her eyes and looked at the clock. Writing reports was the same whether she was in Kaskitesiw or Manchester. She wanted to get back into the truck and travel the country side. The leaves of the sugar maples were just beginning to turn a beautiful orange. She knew most of the back roads now, and when she would wave at someone, they would likely wave back. At times, she would stop and talk. It made her smile when a person would motion an oncoming car around the Fish and Game truck, while they chatted in the road. She'd like to see anybody try that on Brown Avenue. Most people seemed respectful of her position but she gathered from their conversation, that Daniel hadn't been one to socialize much since taking the job.

Before she left, she decided to call the Lab and see if it there had been any progress on Faidlee's DNA. She started to reach for the phone when it rang.

"Officer Claret! Okay, Daniel then. How are you?" She tried to make her voice business like. "Everything is going pretty well. Checked my first bear in, issued a lot of bow licenses, checked in two deer. Just run of the mill stuff."

She replied to his question, "The bear weighed 320 pounds. It looked good. Coat was healthy. Male. Its teeth were in good shape, no periodontal disease." she reported, squinting at her "to do" list in registering a kill. "Ticks? What about ticks? Oh," Emily winced and said, "I'll check closer on both the deer and bears from now on, but I didn't see any obvious ones. The animals seemed healthy—well, up until then, of course. Joe helped me with the weigh-in. The people here have been great."

She put the phone to her other ear and began flipping through the directory for the NH Lab. "No, I was just going to get in touch with the lab about the DNA when you called. The state police believe he is still over the border. But the report on the bullet casing came back."

"Oh, sorry! I didn't tell you about that? 30.06.—trajectory was right to have been from your shooter's vantage point. The print was solid. Faidlee is our man, even without a rifle to compare it to. He'd been fingerprinted before for DUI." She smiled at something he said and found the number of the lab.

"Stop by?" She flipped the rolodex shut. "I think I have time. I'll stop on my lunch break and bring you the reports. No, no problem. I'll bring lunch! Nonsense, I don't mind, really. You like turkey? Well, if you eat and rest, the sooner you'll be back here to help me. There is meaning in my madness. Okay, be there about noon."

She hung up the phone and sat there smiling. Finally, looking at her watch, she decided she had enough time to make those calls, drive around the northern edge of the town roads, grab two grinders at the diner and get to Daniel's cabin by noon.

Shortly after twelve o'clock, she went up the path to the porch door and the 'chew-chew' chattering started. The little gray squirrel, tail twitching like it had an electrified life of its own, stared at her from the fence post.

"Hi, Nutmeg!" Emily wondered if the squirrel might decide to hurl her small body onto a trespasser. She figured anything that could break open nuts had pretty sharp teeth.

"Meggy!" Daniel's voice came hoarsely through the open window.

The little squirrel bound onto the window sill, disappearing within the cabin as Emily knocked.

A moment later, there was a sound of hurried movements, a series of quiet oaths and Nutmeg shot back out the window and straight up the oak. Emily didn't know whether to wait or open the door. Hesitantly she knocked again and called, "Daniel? You okay?"

"Wait, wait a second—where'd I?" Daniel said in a rushed voice, "just a minute, I'll be right there."

Another crash and Emily flinched.

There was a rapid padding of feet across the wood floor, and then a door slammed. Did he have someone in there with him—perhaps a woman?

"I can come back another time," Emily called.

"No!" he said as if his mouth was full, "Justsa' secon'."

Emily shifted the bag to the other arm and raised her brows.

There was a thump, an "Ow!" and the sound of hopping.

"I'm coming in there!" Emily threatened.

Daniel opened the door, his right side slouched, a two-day growth of beard on his face. She remembered him so fit, tall and trim in his uniform on the first day they met

"I'm sorry," he apologized in a raspy voice. "I was going to clean up, but I fell asleep again. I shouldn't have asked you to come. When I called it seemed like I had a lot more energy. I can't believe I fell back to sleep."

"This is why you are home and not at the office," she said guiding him back to an old, worn sofa. "Your body needs time to heal. If you had met me at the door all spruced up and raring to go, I would have been offended that you weren't helping me at work. You have toothpaste on your chin," she added, looking at a chair tipped on its side. "What were you doing in here? You want to wind up back in the hospital?"

He rubbed his chin. "Just let me go shave. It'll only take a minute."

Emily looked down at his right arm hanging limp, the torn muscles in his side and back making it too painful to lift. Then she said, while staring at his right hand. "I have determined, by the pencil callous on your middle finger, that you're right handed. You would have to shave with your left hand. Don't you think you have lost enough blood for one week?" She put the lunch bag on the counter.

"This morning I thought I could do it and I wanted to see you."

Emily felt her heart take off like a bird, but she kept her face expressionless, "Worried I wasn't minding the store?"

"No, not at all but Anna said I should call, that you had some questions and—and I wanted to thank you for all you did to help me."

"Anna said so? You're welcome. Here, I brought you a sandwich." Her tone was flat, hiding her disappointment.

"I knew this would happen!" Daniel said angrily. "I'm not doing this right!" He looked down at his folded hands. "Rusty said it over and over. I have no skill when it comes to—you have been kind and I will ruin…"

Emily sat down slowly next to him saying, "What will you ruin?"

He laid his head back against the sofa, his lips pressed tight.

126

Emily couldn't take the suspense any longer. She got up and dug into the lunch bag. "Here, eat this." She handed him three fourths of the two grinders.

"Thank you." He looked exhausted. "I am sorry I cannot help you."

"At work?"

He nodded with a defeated look. "You have no idea, how sorry I am."

"I'm doing okay. Eat!"

He took a bite, and closed his eyes, relishing it.

While going over the reports, Emily ate her part of the sandwich in the time it took him to eat the three.

She paused in her chewing and looked at him. "I thought that maybe Anna was bringing you something."

"Anna has so little," he said, wiping his mouth, "I told her I had plenty, but I haven't gotten to the store."

"Good grief," Emily said, looking at him squarely, "you know you could have picked up the phone before now. I thought people took care of each other in a small town."

"Ila brought me a rabbit stew the first day. I've been away from town for quite awhile, and I am new at being a warden here," he stated without complaint.

"And being an officer of the law can set you apart. My dad has always been a police officer. All our friends are police officers, and we stick together, help each other. But this is such a small town. It's just you and Pete."

"We don't enjoy the fraternity as in bigger towns but Pete has become a good friend." He took the last bite of the grinder and murmured a heart-felt thank you.

"But Pete's not here." She huffed, "Well, take it or leave it, you got me. Your hair needs a good washing. I'll help you shave and wash your hair after work tonight. You'll feel better."

"You would do this?"

"Would you rather have Anna do it?"

"No! I mean I was going to have Anna cut it when—I still don't remember much of that day. But I remember I thought I was seeing an angel."

"You almost did." She quickly changed the subject. "I may be stereotyping again, but I thought American Indians didn't have beards."

"It is from my mother. I mean, some tribes have very little facial hair but many have crossed blood. And some always had hair from the beginning."

"Interesting." Emily gathered up the sandwich wrappers.

"I don't want you to feel obligated to come back."

"I won't come back if you don't want me to." Emily wasn't sure what he wanted. "Either way, I won't feel obligated."

"Tomorrow?" Daniel didn't want her to see him like this, didn't want her to feel like she had to help him. She was already doing his job. "Tomorrow, could you come? You don't have to bring lunch but maybe you could stop by and fill me in on what is going on—you might have a question I could—help *you* with."

Emily could sense his pride. Here she was, telling him that he needed his hair washed. Could she be any more forward, insensitive? Well, she had her pride too and the last thing she wanted was to have this man think she was throwing herself at him. "I can stop by tomorrow if there are any new reports, but on the condition that you let me bring you something to eat."

"I should give you some money."

"Oh please, I'll keep a tab if you like." Emily smiled but rolled her eyes. She left with the unhappy feeling she hadn't handled this right. A few feet away from the cabin, she softly mimicked her own naivety with disgust. "I thought American Indian's didn't have beards."

"Apisci-mosos." Daniel called from behind her.

Emily stopped and tried to get rid of her smile as she turned back to him. "Anna said this was the name you gave me; that you wanted to warn someone named Apisci-mosos."

His eyes were thoughtful for a moment as he slouched in the doorway. "I don't remember. I only know the name has always been yours. There is a lot I don't remember," Daniel admitted, ruefully.

"That's probably best. I remember enough for both of us." Then she asked, shading her eyes, "By the way, what are swamp bats?"

He grinned. "They are a baseball team in Keene, New Hampshire."

"You mean there is no such thing as a flying animal called a swamp bat? There was this big thing in the headlights."

"Well, you might hear different from someone in Keene, but no species like that lives around here. You probably saw an owl moth, Thysania Zenobia, they grow quite large—owl moths—please, come tomorrow."

"I'll bring lunch around noon. You sure you're okay until then?"

Looking like a bent, shaggy, misfit holding up a door frame, Daniel nodded.

~~~~~

That afternoon, a second bear was brought in. The story was different than with the first bear, and Emily didn't like it one bit.

It was a sow, a female bear. Emily found mammary glands which, still, in death, exuded a small amount of milk. The bear must have had a cub. She had been run up a tree by dogs. Josh Anderson had arrived to simply shoot her out of the tree.

Emily found herself clenching her teeth as she examined the bear for ticks and parasites as Daniel had specified. The hunting dogs, caged in the back of the truck kept up such an incessant din of barking, she could hardly think.

"I don't know how to thank you for your help, Joe. Is this going to be an everyday occurrence now?" Emily asked, clicking her pen irritably.

"Hey, no, you might not get another bear all season. Just the way it works sometimes. I can't stomach those kinds of hunters, though," Joe said.

"I think she had a cub. I can't help thinking about her little cub out there, alone."

"It won't last long, Detective. It will be crying and something will get drawn to it, kill it."

She knew Joe meant well, in spite of the new image he created in her mind. "Thanks again, Joe."

Before sunset, Emily drove the back roads near where the hunter had reported getting the bear. As darkness settled in, she had to give up looking for the cub and headed back to town with a heavy heart. She knew it shouldn't, but not finding the cub weighed heavily on her. It was one more time she wasn't able to fix the injustice in this world.

CHAPTER 15

Emily's endeavor to—get away and all her problems would be solved—wasn't working. The old truck she drove by a half a mile ago would never have passed inspection. She did a U-turn thinking that if she didn't get some sleep soon, she wouldn't be able to do her job efficiently or testify on her own behalf at the trial—if it came to that. She met up with the vehicle with its roped and drooping bumper once again. The driver looked like he figured he had been too lucky the first time the Fish and Game truck went by. The license number didn't match the vehicle, but the man was honest, telling her that he took the plate from his car just to deliver the truck to Andre who had offered him money for parts. She left it as a warning, telling him that this afternoon she would be looking for that truck in Andre's junk yard.

A call came over the radio. It was Ike, Joe's friend.

"Detective—deputy—what the hell is she?" He asked someone.

"Deputy will do." She said though the question was not addressed to her.

"Well, deputy, what we got is two juvenile delinquents hanging out in Pop Malhoit's corn patch, smashing pumpkins, drunk and disturbin' the peace."

"I'll be right there." She knew where Malhoit lived because he was the one who always stopped her on the road, wanting to chit chat. He was a nice old guy who just seemed a little lonely. His place wasn't far from where she was. She just hoped one of those delinquents wasn't Tommy, the cyber junkie at the gas station. He was the same age as the boy who committed suicide and for some reason she felt it was her place to keep Tommy from the same fate.

Pulling up to the house she saw Joe, Ike and Mr. Malhoit standing near the corn patch.

"They won't come out?" She asked walking up to them and noticed the smashed remains of several pumpkins.

Joe shook his head. "Nope, them two are in there causing all sorts of havoc, breaking down the corn stalks, throwing pumpkins at each other."

"And you believe they are underage drinkers?" All Emily could see was the occasional waving of a dried corn stalk.

"Got to be. Puking all over the place."

"You know who they are?"

"Got an idea but don't know for sure." Joe wiped his mouth. Ike and Mr. Malhoit were looking off into the patch. They had offered no information, nor had they even looked at her.

"Okay." Emily sighed and stepped confidently into the corn field, walking with measured ease until she stepped into a pile of corn riddled vomit. These kids were consuming a dangerous volume of alcohol on top of raw corn and needed to be brought in for their own good. When she had gone far enough to feel hemmed in by the tall stalks, there was movement on her right. One of the suspects, in dark clothing stumbled through the stalks. Emily grimaced at the sound of vomiting and then a dark face lifted from the rows of bent corn. It smacked it lips with eyes pressed together in satisfaction. One furry ear was cocked forward on the small black bear.

Emily took a step back as another small bear tackled the first, and they both tumbled to the ground. One, standing on unsteady hind legs, was getting ready to pounce on the other again when they smelled her. With a resounding burp, he looked in her direction, and made an almost human gesture of pointing. His brother stood on his hind legs, gazed at her with squinting eyes then fell over backwards. Rolling over, his four legs unsteadily beneath him, he started to run away. Glancing over his shoulder, the brother, tripping and falling, followed behind him.

She could hear laughter behind her and knew she had been set up by practical joker, Joe. As much as she would like to stay with a stern, official face, she knew she wasn't going to manage her smile.

"Officer, you let them get away!" Ike spoke with forced concern, though grinning.

"Wouldn't a let you go in there if mama was around, or they were older and had their wits about em." Joe said quickly. "You weren't in any danger."

"They really were drunk and disorderly." Emily laughed. "Ike, you want to cuff them, be my guest. What made them intoxicated?"

"Sweet corn." The three men said in unison.

"Pop here always leaves some of his corn for the wildlife. Puts a little bulk in them for the winter." Joe explained.

"Trouble is they eat so much at one time they puke it up." Pop said. "The fermenting sugar in it makes them drunk. Eventually they'll digest what they need. Deer eat it too but they know what their stomachs can take."

"Thanks for setting me up guys but it was great. I'll never forget it."

"They were last year's cubs. Mom probably dropped them off at the bar so she could make her escape." Joe explained. "She wanted to be loose and fancy free again. But I think these are the cubs of that sow brought in yesterday so you don't have to be thinking that the little thing lost out there, crying for it mamma." His voice was sarcastic to hide his real feelings in front of the others.

"Thanks Joe." Emily said warmly. "They're old enough to take care of themselves?"

He nodded, glad that she appreciated his way of making her comfortable here.

"That's if they stay off the whisky." She grinned. "You want to press charges Mr. Malhoit?"

"Naw, they'll be hibernating soon." The older man laughed.

"They sure have made a mess out of your corn field."

"Do every year after I pick. Nothing goes to waste. Deer and turkeys will feed on it next."

"So if scat is bear poop, what is bear regurgitation?" she scraped her boot in the dried grass.

"I believe the scientific word is vomit." Joe chuckled.

"Gaining wisdom every day," She nodded solemnly and walked back to the truck.

~~~~~~~~~

After patrolling the roads on the east side of the swamp, she picked up some sandwiches at the Bear Bones Diner and went to the cabin at noon. Emily was about to turn the door knob when she heard someone talking inside, though no other car was parked nearby.

A stern voice bellowed from within, "Look, I don't want you taking aspirin or any of Anna's concoctions to reduce fever—too much danger of hemorrhaging. I just don't want to fool around with this, Daniel! If your temperature goes up any more, you could be in real trouble. If you start coughing you could wind up back in the hospital." There was a slight pause, and then a shout, "It's damn cold in here!"

Emily thought of the wood stove. Yesterday had been warm but today was ten degrees colder. Autumn in the northland was unpredictable.

The voice came again, a bit calmer, "Daniel, I think you should go to the rehab in Colebrook. It's obvious you can't take care of yourself in this condition and I don't want you lifting wood. What's a simple cold, for anyone else, could be very dangerous for you. It would be so easy for pneumonia to set in and you could lose that lung and maybe your life."

Emily pushed open the door and Daniel met her eyes. Doctor Pomfret, who was listening to Daniel's chest with a stethoscope, wondered what caused his patient's heart to suddenly beat so rapidly. Catching the direction of Daniel's stare, he turned and looked at Emily over his glasses.

"I'm sorry but I just came to the door and heard what you said," Emily apologized.

"Hello, Detective, nice to see you again," the Doctor greeted her. He looked back at Daniel knowingly.

Emily stepped into the room. It was cold in here, to the point of being able to see your breath. She put the bag on the counter and looked at Daniel. With effort he sat upright on the old sofa.

"Is he all right?" she asked the doctor.

Doc Pomfret swabbed off the old mercury thermometer. "He's picked up an infection."

"Nosocomal?"

"Maybe, but it didn't help that he caught a chill sleeping in a cold house with a wet bandage around him. It's probably a simple rhino virus, but for him, it could be dangerous if he gets a lot of congestion." Doc said seriously, "I think he'd be better off in a warmer more supervised environment until he can do for himself again."

Emily looked at Daniel and cursed under her breath. He had showered, his hair was clean and it was obvious that he'd made a clumsy effort to shave himself. She knew he had done this for her. She should have come back last night.

"Doc, it's just a cold!" Daniel appealed to the old doctor to reconsider.

Emily thought of what Anna said about Daniel going kiskwewin, *crazy*, stuck in a hospital doing puzzles all day and impulsively said, "Doctor, Anna and I can take care of him. We'll keep the stove lit, and make sure he does what he needs to in order to recover. If one of us has to leave the other will be here. I know Anna will agree to it. I know she would like to help—just hasn't been asked. It's something I would do for any fellow officer."

"At least I could help Officer Harrigan with any questions she might have if I stay here." For a moment, Daniel's eyes brightened then clouded again as he realized if he didn't do as the doctor said, he would be a burden to her and Anna.

Dr. Pomfret looked up at Emily. "You sure you want to do this? You look pretty tired yourself."

"Being physically tired at the end of the day would be a good thing for me." She flushed at his observation but smiled cheerfully.

"I want to get him on some cough medicine." Doc Pomfret said and took out a prescription pad.

"I'll drive over to Errol Pharmacy after I get a fire going." Emily tried to make it sound like she actually knew how to make fire in that little metal box.

"What does a detective know about nosocomals?" The doctor asked while writing.

"I've studied a case or two in forensic medicine." Emily's tone was measured. "Occasionally people die from germs they pick up at the hospital.

"Ah, forensics!" Dr. Pomfret laughed good-naturedly. "Not a great track record for patient recovery."

"True, but my patients don't complain," she quipped back.

Dr. Pomfret chuckled, and then addressed Daniel. "I've removed the staples but now I have to take that drain out." He took out a syringe and vial.

"What is that, Doc?" Daniel asked.

"Morphine. It's going to hurt pulling the tube out of your chest."

"No morphine—I'll be okay."

"Daniel, when I say something is going to hurt, I mean it's going to hurt."

"No morphine. Emily, maybe you'd better go."

"I'm not going anywhere. He is going to pull a tube out of your chest. Daniel, take the morphine! What, are you afraid you'll be addicted after one dose? That's not going to happen."

"Smart girl! What's it going to be? You take the morphine or I send you back to the hospital to have it done. I am not going pull that drain out while I know that you're hurting," Doc Pomfret said. "It must be the dentist in me."

"I'm outnumbered," Daniel relented.

Doc gave him the shot. After a few minutes he removed the tube. Daniel was drowsy and the pain was minimal.

"Call me if his fever gets higher or if he starts coughing too much. I've written this cough syrup prescription for him and I'll call in a renewal for the antibiotics. The codeine will make him sleep."

"No codeine." Daniel murmured.

"Has he always been this stubborn?" Emily smiled at the doctor.

"You will take codeine to keep from coughing. If you don't, I'm going to slam your ass back in the hospital and they'll give it to you in a drip. Do you understand? You can't cough. You could rupture that lung. This is reality, son. Your body is damaged and it has to heal!"

"I'll make sure he takes the codeine." Emily said softly.

Doc Pomfret took his coat from the chair. "And keep in mind that the healing is going to take a while. I'm going to leave you some morphine tablets. Broken ribs and lung injuries are debilitating and painful. You listen to the good detective here."

"How long, Doc?" Feeling no pain at the moment, Daniel made a clumsy effort to sit up but found Emily's hand forcefully restraining him.

"The cold should be gone in a few days, but as far as your overall condition, at least a month of complete rest. Then we'll see. This is not some fairy tale. You've lost bone, a lot of muscle and injured a lung. We'll just have to wait."

"A month!" Daniel protested, his voice slurred. "Doc, I have things I have to do."

"Detective, do you think you will be able to get through to him that if he pushes it now, he'll be in a lot worse trouble?"

"Please, call me Emily. I'll make sure he follows your orders."

"And for that month, absolutely no lifting!" the Doctor continued to advised. You're not going to be able to fire a rifle, so keep that in mind, and don't do anything that would put pressure on your chest. Don't exert yourself enough to cause heavy or rapid breathing. I mean it! I even want you to be careful breathing in cold air. Wrap a muffler around your mouth and nose if you go out. No plane trips either, not that you've ever been on one. Hear me? You've got to take it easy for at least four more weeks."

Daniel scowled but said nothing, awkwardly trying to find his shirt buttons with his left hand.

"He hears you," Emily said, smiling at Daniel. She lifted her eyes to find Dr. Pomfret watching her.

"Goodbye, Daniel." He handed the prescription to Emily.

"'Bye, Doc." Daniel, studying the button, looked like a little kid who was just told he couldn't go fishing with the rest of the gang.

Dr. Pomfret said in a low, sad voice to Emily, as if she were family. "I don't think he's going to be able to stand straight much less have full lung capacity."

She had noticed two of the doctor's fingers were swollen and bent from arthritis. She helped him on with his coat and buttoning it for him. "We have to keep hope."

He winked, "You're right." Then he closed the door.

Emily took the blanket off the bed and wrapped it around Daniel. "Before I go to Errol, I'll bring Anna here. She can teach me how to light a fire."

"You are going to be so sick of me!" He squinted at her.

"No feeling sorry for yourself. Do what you're supposed to and you'll be fine in a month."

"But you'll be gone in a month!"

Emily tilted her head unsure that it wasn't only the morphine talking.

"You'll be happy to be gone! No wonder. This isn't fair. I can't believe—I can't believe I was so stupid that I walked into that trap."

"You hush now before you get coughing." Emily said seriously, "The only one to blame for what happened to you is Richard Faidlee. Daniel, I want to help you. I want to be your friend." She knelt down beside the couch, "But you have to help yourself. You have to do everything you can to get well. Okay?"

He lifted his left hand unsteadily, to touch her cheek. "Just a friend?"

Apparently it was the morphine talking. She grabbed it playfully and tucked it back under the cover. "Are you listening to me?"

Daniel grinned. "I am going to heal so quickly that you'll be amazed."

"Good. Stay put, I'm going to go get Anna."

~~~~~~

As Emily suspected, Anna was happy to fuss over Daniel during the day. Emily took care of things at the office and in the field. She

138

used her radio and cell phone, posting its number on the office door at lunch and in the evening. People seemed to accept the fact she and Anna were staying with the warden. He was sick. He needed some help. When someone in town asked, she updated them on his progress, and in turn, people asked more often, caring about their new warden as he had not let them do before. Having lived here his whole life, she surmised that Daniel had stayed a stranger, keeping to his self and to the forest.

After dinner Emily would walk Anna home; then, she kept the fire going through the night. Making her bed on the sofa, she read Daniel's books and notes as he slept. When he was awake, they would spend hours talking about wildlife diseases, parasites, habitats, and environmental issues. They were growing easy with each other, teasing and mischievous at times. Neither could remember enjoying another person's company more. But those things which caused them anguish still separated them. Emily sensed this separation most; in the growing lack of confidence in her work and in the confusion with which she perceived her once efficient and sufficient world. Emily's victims, and the perverted creatures responsible for their horrendous deaths, visited her nightly. Though they were locked away during the daylight hours, they left her drained, her thoughts fractured, and her future unsure.

The fact that she slept only a few hours a night, fearful that her nightmares would come and disturb Daniel's sleep, was a secret which she kept from both Anna and Daniel. But tonight, exhausted, she let down her guard.

Anna had gone home and Daniel had gone to bed after taking the codeine. She sat up reading a book on bears until her eyes grew tired. Emily didn't miss television at all. At home in the city, as soon as she walked in the apartment and kicked her shoes off, she turned on the TV to watch the news. Here she was alone with just the symphony of the crickets, the crackling of the fire, and books. She had grown familiar with the coyote's yipping and the owl's hoot. The occasional bobcat's scream no longer made her feel like she had been doused with ice cold water.

Emily loaded the wood stove, pulled the covers up around her and settled on the sofa in her jersey pants and top. She immediately fell asleep but in a very short while there was a crash. Another explosion, sharp like a bullet and the scene of the boy in the school hallway played again. The burst of hot light followed and a small child's face looked up at her from the leaves, twisted forever in agony.

Emily did what she lost hours of sleep trying to avoid, she cried out.

Cupping her hand to her mouth, she sat up quickly, praying Daniel hadn't heard her.

But Daniel was at her side in an instant, holding her damp, trembling body. "Acorns," he whispered into her hair. "It is just acorns falling on the metal roof."

"Acorns?" she wiped the perspiration off her face with her sleeve.

Another one hit the roof and she jumped involuntarily.

He pulled her to him protectively. "The wind is causing them to fall. A cold front is coming in. You filled the stove up to keep me warm, but it is too hot for you out here."

"I'm sorry I woke you up," she said and began to pull away. Her head was pounding from being overheated.

Daniel got up and went to the sink. He rinsed a towel in cool water and came back. Sitting down next to her, he tried to wipe her face.

"I'm okay." Emily withdrew from his hand. Embarrassed and feeling the effects of the dream, she shut him off. "Go back to bed. You need your sleep. I'm sorry."

Daniel looked at her with a puzzled frown.

"I'm fine, really. Acorns! Nutmeg should be happy tomorrow." Emily brushed off the incident with a smile, and said, "Scoot!"

Daniel's troubled face was lit by the stove's air vents as he slid them shut, damping down the fire. She was excluding him from what bothered her. He shut the door to the bedroom and spent the night sleepless also.

Emily kicked the covers off and stared at the ceiling in the dark. Another acorn fell but this time she did not jump at the sound. Around midnight a new sound was added to the percussions. Rain fell, steady and hard against the roof. The sound against the metal was soothing, but sleep still evaded her.

The next morning, she stoked the fire and left for Mica before Daniel appeared. She showered and changed and then went to the office. At noon she was too busy with check-ins and issuing licenses to stop at the cabin for lunch. At dinner time, she opened the screen door hearing music. There was a pot of moose chili on the stove but Anna was nowhere in sight. Daniel sat on one of the bar stools, doing a monthly comparison to last year's bear kill census. The music came from a small, portable CD player on top of the counter. A woman sang beautifully in a language Emily did not understand. Daniel was caught up in what he was writing but occasionally followed along in the repetitious chant, unaware Emily was there. She shut the door softly and stood behind him, smiling when he sang part of the verse while turning the pages. Though she had not moved, within a moment he stopped writing, shut off the music and turned to her.

"Don't stop it. Her voice is beautiful and you sing pretty nice yourself."

"We Indians are a harmonious bunch." Daniel smiled with embarrassment. "It is Joanne Shenandoah, an Iroquois woman."

"May I hear more?"

"It is sung in Haudenosaunne Iroquois."

"So, tell me what it means."

"This one is about friendship, trust and wanting to be near someone."

"Play it, please." Emily took the stool next to him.

He clicked the player back on and she closed her eyes, tilting her head while listening. "She is a mother."

"How do you know?"

"She sings it like a lullaby."

The third song came on and he suddenly flipped the player off again.

"Why did you do that?"

"It is a song for dancing."

"I like to dance."

"It is a traditional dance."

"So that means that I can't do it?"

"No, but it is not a safe dance. Things can happen."

"Oh, it might be too strenuous for you."

"No, that is not what I mean. The dance itself is simple and slow. You do not touch each other."

Her eyes teased. "Do you know how to do it?"

"I have been to ceremonies where it is done. It is a dance between a man and woman."

"Most are."

"Many Native American dances are not."

"You just don't want to teach me." Emily shrugged and started for the wood pile.

"Not true. You have no idea of how much I would like to teach this dance to you."

"Then why not?" she laughed. "Is there is some tribal law that says I can't learn it?"

"All right, Apisci-mosos. You keep your hands at your sides and you only look at each other while you do the steps."

"Hands at sides—just look at each other—it sounds pretty harmless to me." She pressed the button on the player.

His arms straight at his sides, he moved to the dance, coming up on the balls of his feet then back down on his heels. She looked up at him playfully at first, and then her eyes grew somber in awe. In spite of his flannel shirt, jeans and sneakers, he looked truly native at this moment and she could imagine him doing this dance in firelight. She tried to match his step to the Iroquois rhythm until both their bodies moved as one. With their eyes locked on each other, their movements were mesmerizing. She no longer needed thought to control her steps. Emily began to feel as if there was no one in the world, but him. The dark beauty of his eyes drew her into his soul, where she longed to be forever. His face bent over hers, his hair hung forward, shutting out all else but the two of them. Suddenly a great, black bird hovered above her. She blinked but it remained. It was suspended in a wind which lifted its feathers as it watched her from above the earth. Emily pushed herself up on her toes, wanting to fly up to it. She rose! The bird lowered its great black wings and caressed her face. She kept her hands at her sides and let the soft feathers envelope her bare shoulders, take her breath from her. She felt the pounding of the bird's great heart, the beating of its wings as it lifted skyward with her. Emily let her head fall back, her lips parted. Daniel's mouth caressed hers.

The music ended; their breath mingled as his face became familiar once more.

"What just happened?" Emily whispered, visibly shaken.

"Are you all right?" he asked.

"Yes," she said breathlessly, "You became a bird—a very big, a very—seductive bird."

He pulled her to him and kissed her hard. Fighting off the temptation of her body, she pushed him back after a moment, saying, "Daniel, no, we shouldn't."

"I am fine," he said huskily

"No, you're not." She breathed out and gently touched his damaged chest saying, "Are the other songs that dangerous?"

"They are beautiful, like you," he said, bending to kiss her.

She pulled away from the kiss quickly, lest she lose herself once more and said firmly, "Daniel, I'm not ready. You saw what happened the other night. I don't know my own mind right now, much less my heart."

"Do you have any idea of what you have done to *my* heart?" He kissed her neck.

"About the same thing you have done to mine, but no more with the bird or I'll start wondering if I can handle the indigenous you." She pulled away, knowing a second more of the sensation of his lips against her skin would mean complete surrender.

He left her standing there and went back to his deer census.

"You are not ready. Are you angry because I'm not ready?" Her voice was accusing more than questioning.

"No," he answered simply.

"You sound angry." She picked up a piece of wood and opened the stove door with it to keep from burning her hand, and then shut it with her foot.

"Do you have another?" He watched her.

Emily stared through the vent to see if the wood ignited. "Even though I feel like I've known you all my life, I haven't. It has only been two weeks." The fire caught and she slammed the vent shut.

"This is true." He turned the page. "You did not answer my question.

Is there someone else?"

Emily shrugged. "A friend, someone I have known all my life."

"Is he your mate?"

"No, I don't have a mate." She turned and looked at him, amused at his choice of word.

"I have no right to say this because I can offer you little, but I love you."

Emily's heart soared with the raven once more, but her face did not show happiness.

Daniel let the book close. "It troubles you to say the truth—that you do not love me."

She stayed where she was, saying sadly, "I know now, that have to leave as soon as Pete comes back."

"Your job." He sounded resolute, accepting.

"My mind. I can't sleep; I can't think straight anymore." Her hands clenched and she looked at the ceiling to keep the tears from spilling. "But it will be so hard to leave you because I love you so much."

Daniel came up out of his chair so fast that pain seared through his side, making him stumble. He ignored it, taking her in his arms.

The misstep wasn't lost on her. "Aren't we a pair?" Emily laid her cheek against his chest, and melted into his body.

"Peyakwayihk—One—pair."

~~~~~

Emily thought that her dream the night before was forgotten by Daniel. Tonight, he retired at about ten o'clock. But at midnight he came into the living room and found her reading. He stood before her with a James Bay blanket around his shoulders.

"How long has it been this way?" he asked seriously.

"Two years," she answered, as if it were merely a fact of life. "It came with the job. Daniel, I'm a mess. I'll leave. I'm no good for you. I've gotten you up when you need to sleep."

"Shhh." He sat down next to her, put the blanket over her shoulders and pulled her into his arms. She stiffened.

"No," he whispered and put his lips against her forehead. "Don't do that."

"I never wanted to disturb anyone," she said, her body still taut.

"So you stay awake?" he asked sadly, smoothing her hair back.

"It's like, I need to stand guard over my own mind," she tried to explain.

"Tonight I will stand guard," he murmured and kissed her gently on the top of her head. "Just relax. If you have a bad dream, I will be right here."

"Daniel, go to bed. I'll be okay."

"Emily, I will ask nothing from you!" he sternly admonished her. "I only want to hold you. I want you to sleep."

"You need your rest."

"Come lie against me."

"Daniel, please, I don't—you shouldn't..." She pushed the blanket away.

"I want you to get some sleep!" he said in a firm tone she had not heard before. "Emily, come here," he demanded and eased her against him, pulling the blanket over them both.

"I need to put some wood in the stove," she remembered, stretching forward but he pulled her back.

"We won't freeze. There is plenty wood. No more excuses," he gently wrapped his arms around her upper body and laid her against his left side.

She was quiet, but her eyes were on the ceiling, the wall, the stove, anywhere but on him. He closed his own eyes, hoping she would follow his example.

"Daniel?"

"Shhhh."

"Are you all right? Are you comfortable?"

"I am fine. Go to sleep. For once, Emily, just let someone hold you. For once, don't be the healer. Let someone else stand guard." His strong young face was soft in the dim light. She forced her body to relax against him.

"Daniel?"

"What is it now, Apisci-mosos?"

"Do you ever have bad dreams?"

He sighed, knowing it wouldn't be easy to get her to sleep. "I dream of my brother, Rusty, though it is not a bad dream."

"What do you dream?"

He laid his head back against the couch and opened his eyes looking at the ceiling, and then said. "We are children again, walking through the forest but I know in my heart that Rusty is dead. He wants to bring me to this great bear, which is very strange because Rusty always ignored the power of animals. The maskwa is huge, but Rusty is not afraid of him. He takes my hand but doesn't really take it—you know when people are in spirit form?"

Emily looked up at him and tried to fathom what he meant, never having felt a 'spirit form'. He was talking as if was the most natural of all things to encounter a ghost.

"He leads me to maskwa, telling me to come with him. He says the great bear will protect us. For some reason I pull away—and then I wake up."

"Do you think he wants you to die with him?" Emily asked.

"Look, no more talking. I want you to sleep."

Emily did not want to take her eyes from his face, but compliance meant closing them. With a sigh, she nestled in his arms and felt the rise and fall of his breath, that precious breath which he had almost lost forever. It was like rhythmic waves on her shore. His heart was a soothing drum, softly beating out a message that her nightmares must vanish. He was here and would protect her. Emily fell asleep, a sleep without dreams. In the gray of morning, she jumped slightly, waking him.

"Was it the bad dream?" he asked and tightened his arms, afraid he had not succeeded in keeping her torment away.

"So many bears," she murmured sleepily, "I'm not afraid. They're good bears."

"It is still early. Enjoy your dreaming." His lips brushed her temple.

They fell back to sleep and did not notice Anna's arrival. The old Cree woman opened the door and shuffled in. Her eyes went to the

146

sofa and a smile crept across her lined face in the dim morning light. She started to back out the door. Suddenly, on the counter, Emily's cell phone began to vibrate. Anna hissed and, putting her cane in her other hand, grabbed it in her crooked fingers. Glancing at Emily and Daniel again, she crept out the door cursing quietly in Cree about an amo, *a bee,* in her hand. Outside she studied the face of the phone and pressed talk. She held it up to her ear. "Ehe!

The caller identified herself.

"Ah, Mrs. Harrigan! Tanisi. *Hello.* How are you? " Anna said, smiling into the phone. She put it back to her ear then pulled it away to speak into it again.

"I am so glad to speak with you. You have a fine daughter." Anna added brightly, "No, she cannot talk now. She is sleeping with Taaniyal."

Anna placed the phone to her ear then pulled it away, scowling. "Namoya tapahteyihtakosiw! *Not love making!* Wehpehtowak! Wehpehtowak! *Sleeping!*"

CHAPTER 16

Emily thought that Daniel would have been proud of her today. A simple acknowledgement of her efforts wasn't undue flattery. She didn't need praise but a small gesture of approval would have been nice. Yet Daniel acted like she had done something wrong and she was getting tired of it.

Her whole body ached from her attempt to stand in for him on a search and rescue call. As a city cop, she wasn't used to crashing through the forest. Granted, she worked out at the police gym at home but it had been almost three weeks since she'd done any real exercise. What was his problem? She picked up a piece of wood and stuffed it inside the stove and then, balancing with a wince, shut the stove door with her boot.

Maybe his feelings for her had cooled. When his cold was over she went back to her apartment in Mica, returning to his cabin for meals and to stoke the fire. At night she left him small pieces of wood, easy to lift into the stove. She was doing everything she could to help him. She certainly hadn't signed on for this extra work, especially when it seemed so unappreciated.

Emily pushed back her snarled hair and looked at Daniel. Her cheeks were still burning from the cold of her wilderness pursuit. Emily had joined up with Knoll Despert, the warden in the next county, and his dog, Bohden. They needed to find a child who had wandered away from his parents in the White Mountains. And they needed to find him before nightfall when the temperatures would drop below freezing.

Knoll and Bohden, both ancient looking, went bounding through the forest like a couple of deer, leaving her stumbling and panting in their wake. She kept up though, close enough to see the dog find the child in the rotted hollow of a giant sugar maple. The little boy hugged and kissed the old smelly shepherd, and that dog just looked at them, so proud of himself that she and Knoll both had to laugh. At the road, once again, the dog received the same hero's treatment from the child's family.

Not only was she mentally spent from worry over the missing child, but was physically exhausted from the rapid full-day trek through the woods. She noisily tossed the broom back into the corner, but Daniel didn't seem to notice, scraping a plate in silence.

Emily tried once more to get him to converse. "Knoll said that Bohden had a wicked swelled head now, and he wasn't going be able to live with him. It was only the second sentence Knoll said to me all day. But he did say that if you had been there, you would have found the child sooner. I tried hard and didn't slow him up, but I could imagine the three of you in the woods, searching…"

Daniel took his foot off the pedal of the garbage can so quickly, the lid slammed shut. He went over to sit on the tattered couch, and stared vacantly, hands folded. His people believed that a person's soul rode upon the breath. His lips were pressed hard and tight, barring her from his soul, his heart and mind.

Emily went over to him and sat down. She didn't touch him and remained silent, waiting for him to speak.

"This is taking too long," he said finally.

"Any day now, Doc will tell you can return to work."

"For some stupid reason, I thought I would be normal again, like this never happened."

"It takes time to heal." She didn't say he could never be the same as he was.

"Too much time! After you left, I tried to run."

"Daniel, you can't! Not yet! Why would you do that?"

"I can't, period!" he shouted viciously to the rafters. "I was wheezing like an old Indian too fond of his pipe."

"Daniel, you have done so well in such a short time."

"I can't erase this ugliness for you." Daniel said bitterly, looking down at his side as if his repulsive wound would materialize on top of his shirt. "I see how you look away."

"Damn it! It's only because I can't stand to see you hurt. I love you." She shouted back. "You think so little of me that you feel I can't be satisfied with less than an unblemished hero?"

"Hero?" He turned on her angrily. "I am nothing but a green game warden; one who got in the way of a poacher's gun. What did my father say? Stay away from speeding bullets—like I was some dumb, wide-eyed creature which didn't have the sense to know what was coming and get out of the way."

"Daniel, you're not being fair to yourself." She was tired of fighting and tried a calmer tact. "Your discipline is paying off. Every day you are better. "

"Ah! Discipline—the main rule!" His voice was uncharacteristically sarcastic. "We must hold ourselves to a higher standard—no room for foolishness. Give them no excuses to call us Indian!"

"Look, I don't know where you're coming from with this rant— maybe your father. All I know is, this isn't easy for either of us, but self pity isn't—."

"You think that is what I feel, self pity?" he asked furiously.

"Yes, I do!" She said with anger, but her eyes filled with tears. She could not believe what was happening.

"Then leave! Awas!"

Emily got up and went to the door. Her heart was beating fast and her stomach felt knotted. With forced calmness, she swung the door open.

Daniel grabbed her wrist.

"Let go." Her voice was like ice.

He released her with instant regret.

At the sound of her car driving away, Daniel put his hands over his face. He had hit a wall, a wall of hopelessness. Coming off the codeine had made him sick and sluggish. In spite of the pain, he hadn't taken the morphine tablets Doc Pomfret had left, but lately he was thinking that if he took them, maybe he could do more, be less of a burden. Temptation was working on his tired, frustrated mind—the temptation to give up. What could she want with a deformed, useless man? His concave right side looked like it had been gnawed away by an animal. He couldn't stand up straight anymore because of the taught re-attachment of muscle. And his body, which once propelled him through the forest like a deer, wouldn't respond to his bidding.

~~~~~

Anna asked her to walk up to the mission church on Sunday. Emily had not been there but had heard the children playing at the school. Sunday morning she dressed in her uniform. Being the only one at the office, she had to work afterwards. Her heart broken, Emily didn't feel much like going to church but Anna had asked for her physical assistance.

She met Anna on her porch. Emily's eyes were tired and red but Anna did not seem to notice. As they climbed the hill, she remembered Anna saying this was where Daniel and Rusty had gone to school and the sight of a lone grave near the embankment made her stop and work at a knot in her throat. She knew whose resting place it was.

The old Cree woman nodded, agreeing with her unspoken thoughts and bent to straighten the American flag.

From Anna, she had learned of Rusty's spirit. Anna kept him alive. Now she was seeing him in reality. His grave shook her with the realization he was indeed dead.

"They will put a monument here when they get the money," Anna said. "He is the only war hero our town has had."

"What about Daniel's father?" Emily cleared the lump in her throat. "Pete said he saved his men."

"He is not a hero to me and he is not dead yet," Anna responded bitterly and taking Emily's arm, leaned on her as they ascended the path to the church.

Anna dipped her fingers into a ceramic bowl and made the sign of the cross. Knowing the ritual well, Emily did the same, blessing herself with holy water.

Though her heart wasn't in this, as she looked up at the crucifix, she felt at home. Made of logs and plaster, the little church had a chalet roof, half logs for a small number of benches and only the floor for kneelers. The altar was a simple linen covered table. Beside it, graced with beautiful Indian carvings, was a polished granite tabernacle.

Emily was so busy looking around, that she almost ran into Anna's behind when the woman stopped to semi-genuflect. Emily knelt on one knee and Anna stepped back, ushering her into the row. She started in and found Daniel waiting for them. His hair was shorter, regulation length. He was looking quite fit in his uniform, quite handsome. As she stepped into the pew, he stood straight. Only she knew the difficulty of that. She acknowledged his presence with a nod.

As Emily sat down, she saw a man in line at the right side of the church and asked Anna what time Mass started. Anna said it would begin at 9:00. Her watch showed it was twelve minutes of.

"I'm going to go to confession. I'd like to receive the Holy Eucharist," she whispered to Anna. Getting up and without looking at Daniel, she stepped in front of Anna and went to stand in the confessional line. If the man before her didn't have any major sins to get off his chest, she would be in and out of there by the time Mass started, and could receive Communion. He went in, and then it was her turn. She opened the door and found herself face to face with a smiling priest instead of the dark, enclosed confessional at the cathedral back home.

She said softly, "Hi, Father. I mean, bless me Father, for I have sinned. It has been over a year since I've been to church. I would really like to receive Jesus today."

"Is that all, my child?" he asked, smiling.

She blushed, and then said, "It was a whole year!"

"You are here now. Is there anything else?"

"I was very angry with God. I still am. I don't know—maybe not as much."

"Anger is good; staying away is not good. Nothing is accomplished. But you are here now," he repeated. "Is there anything else, my child?"

"I've had some thoughts about loving someone, and I did lie to my mother about where I was one night."

He nodded and asked once more, "Is that all?"

"I, well I…" she stammered looking at her watch. The last thing she wanted was to hold up Mass.

"We have time, my child," the kind priest urged.

"Father, I am ready to give up my job, everything I have, everything I am, for a man I have only known a few weeks. I may even be giving up my mother because I know she won't approve of him."

"This man you love, is he a good man?"

"I'm not sure he loves me, but I believe he is good and honorable and I have waited a long time to find someone like him."

"How old are you?"

"Twenty-four."

"Have you prayed on this?"

"I—not really. But recently, I have started to pray again."

"Pray and ask the Dear Lord what He wants from you and Daniel." Emily sat up straight, eyes wide in shock.

"Pardon me child, it is a small town. You are right! Daniel is an honorable man, even though he rejected the Lord when his step-brother died. I have known him since he was a child. His heart is good. He and the Lord will win your mother over. Have faith. Now say an Act of Contrition!"

"He came to church today," she whispered conspiratorially.

"He came to confession, first, and I'm not going to tell you what he said about you." he whispered back and Emily blushed.

The rotund priest laughed so loud, she was sure the others heard.

"Heaven is rejoicing today. Two lost lambs are back in the fold! Now! An Act of Contrition!" He clasped his hands together and bowed his head.

Emily prayed and as she was absolved her of sin, he made the sign of the cross, and Emily did the same.

"For your penance say one Hail Mary for courage, and one for patience. Then call your mother to assure her that you love her. Love conquers all."

"Thank you, Father. I hope I haven't made you late for Mass."

"Five minutes of," he said, looking down at his watch and got up. "The nicest thing you can do for yourself today is to let Jesus come to you, give you His strength and grace, Emily."

"Thank you," she whispered again, surprised at the time but not at the fact he knew her name. She walked quietly back to her seat in the pew. No one seemed to be watching her. Anna was reading the bulletin. Daniel looked up and saw the smile in her eyes.

During the service, Father Paul was filled with obvious love of God and his parishioners. He poured out his joy of the good news to everyone, and the people sang *Hosea* by Gregory Norbet, *"The Wilderness, will lead you, to your heart, where I will speak."*

Though the nightmares followed her, this wilderness had led her to a love she thought she would never have; led her to question herself, who she was and what she needed. She had the questions but still no answers.

At the sign of peace, she kissed Anna on the cheek and extended her hand to Daniel who took it amicably. Their eyes on each other told another story and a woman behind them giggled and whispered, "Saakihew." Emily turned and shook the woman's hand and the hand of the grinning gas station attendant, Tommy, who stood beside her. Emily smiled, and thought: So this is what it is like to live in a small town where people know more about you than you do.

When Mass concluded, Father Paul stopped the three of them as they left the church. He blessed Emily and Daniel for the work they did. Then he engaged Anna in a request for a woven shawl for the Church raffle, as two little children ran around him, trying to hide from one another behind his robe.

Emily and Daniel walked a little way down the hill to wait until Anna's conversation with the priest was over.

"I will never tell you to go again," Daniel said in a low but earnest voice.

Emily bent and picked a piece of dried Timothy grass, stroking the seed head absently, keeping a discreet distance between them, since they were both in uniform.

"I will never touch you with anything but love," Daniel said louder.

"We were both in a bad place the other night." Emily whispered as a couple approached and passed them. "You were disappointed and depressed and I felt like I'd been beaten up by an evergreen. As soon as I used the words 'self pity' I wanted to swallow my tongue." She snapped the seed head off the grass and waited until a group passed in happy conversation. "But as much as I love you, Daniel, I will leave you if I feel threatened."

"I know that. My family speaks roughly to one another. Sometimes Anna and my father can be physically pushy. But that is no excuse."

Emily twirled the stem between her lips. "Why are you in uniform?

"Doc cleared me for light duty."

"Great! What does light duty mean?"

"It means that I can drive *you* around for a change."

"Hey, it's a start," Emily said, smiling. "I'd like to be the passenger. I assume you haven't been cleared for running a marathon."

"Apisci-mosos, I'm sorry. Since our argument, I haven't been able to eat or sleep." He stepped aside to let two children race by him.

"That is what you get for 'awassing' me." She smiled cordially at a couple walking up the hill and waited for them to pass. "Do you have any idea how much I want to hold you right now?"

Daniel stopped short and gazed at her longingly over the terrible, foot-long distance between them. "I'll be in the office today after I run over to the Littleton Clinic for one last chest X-ray. Doc called and got a technician to do it on a Sunday so I could start with a full week and he could go to his hunting camp. Everything sounds fine. They just want a healed base to go on for the future."

"Another X-ray!" Her face, once delighted by the news he was coming to the office, fell with concern, "You've had so many you'd probably click if I held a Geiger counter to your chest."

"I'll see you in a little while," he said with an official nod and left her standing there as a crowd divided around her.

"What is the matter, Apisci-mosos?"

Emily looked from Daniel to Anna limping down the hill with her cane and said, without a smile, "Daniel can return to work."

"This does not make you happy?"

"Oh, it does, it's just that—never mind. If you look for trouble, trouble finds you."

"You are wise, my little deer. Trouble always finds us. No sense looking for it. Can I teach you of the humble lambs quarter which gives good food and blessings to us?"

"I'd love to learn about that plant, Anna but I've got to get back to work. What does sauky...?"

"Sah-key-hey-oo?" Anna had apparently heard the woman's word from behind them.

"That sounds more like it."

"It means she loves him." Anna chuckled. "You may walk apart but the people know you are in love with each other."

"We have been so careful." Emily frowned.

Anna only laughed. "You can fool your kind of people for they only look to their own path, but not our people."

"Are there many American Indians here—in town?"

"Not enough to cause trouble. That too is the way Europeans think."

Emily sensed the separation between them and wondered why Anna seemed so accepting of her and Daniel being together.

CHAPTER 17

After walking Anna home, Emily went back to the office. The impending rifle season was picking up momentum with moose lottery winners checking in as well.

There was excitement in the air. The town buzzed in preparation for the coming season. Shots continually echoed in the outlying areas, as hunters sighted in their guns. Though she was cordial as each person came in for a license and rule book, she was relieved that Daniel would be in today and hoped that was him coming now.

A truck pulled in carrying wooden dog crates in the back. One of the two scruffy-looking men yelled at the dogs to be quiet as he pulled open the tail—gate.

Another bear carcass lay in the back of the pickup. Emily moaned, picked up the record book and went outside. She couldn't believe that these magnificent beasts were hunted relentlessly though out autumn. When they weren't hunted, they were being legally harried by dogs "in training"—chased—along with every other creature the dogs came in contact with.

Emily held out her hand for the hunting license. "Which one shot the bear?" Bailey Wigman and Josh Anderson looked at each other. She had met the man, Josh, when he brought the female bear in.

"Let's see, you shot the last one, so this one is mine." Bailey snickered, punching Josh on the arm.

"Where is the tag?" she asked, impatiently. "I can't seal it without a tag."

"Go get it," Bailey ordered the younger man. Josh, in spite of his extra weight, jumped up in the truck, dug it out his gun case and fastened the tag on the bear.

"Where did you get it?"

"Birch Hill," Bailey said.

Emily's heart sank as she looked at the bear. The animal was big. From nose tip to tail it was a little over six feet. She studied its face, blood dripping from its mouth. She wondered if this was the bear that she and Pete had seen that night they searched for Daniel.

"You said the dogs treed it?" she asked squinting at the panting canines as they stuck their heads through the chewed wooden holes in their boxes.

"Sure did." Josh said proudly. "He managed to climb pretty high for an old bear 'fore we shot him."

Emily looked at the bear's yellow teeth for an estimate of its age. She got in the truck and the dogs started barking at her, still looking frenzied from the kill.

"Shut up!" Bailey screamed at them.

Emily studied the dogs, their tongues hanging out the sides of their mouths, and asked, "Have you given these dogs any water?"

"Will when we're done," Josh said.

"Give it to them now!" Emily ordered. "There is a hose on the left side of the building."

Emily checked for parasites. The animal had been healthy over all. An image of it standing on its hind legs in front of her and Pete confirmed in her mind that this was the same bear.

"Weigh it," Emily said coldly.

Joe wasn't around so these two would just have to handle it themselves.

"Take a picture of us?" Josh asked, shoving a camera in her face, once the bear was hauled upward.

"Not my job," she replied, writing down the weight. Finishing up the record—keeping on the bear, she went back inside the office and sat down, emotionally spent at seeing the great bear rendered to a pile of meat and fur in the back of a dog-slobbered pick up.

After the two men left with their prize, she pulled herself together and was getting ready to drive the back roads, when a man stepped inside the door. He came in holding a sack in his hand. She got up, alarmed, when she saw the sack was moving about on its own. A strange, almost human cry came from inside.

"Is the warden around?" he asked, looking about the room anxiously.

"I'm the deputy warden. What do you have there?" She confronted the man, her voice harsh, concerned for what he held in his hand.

"My wife was trying to rear it. Its mother was killed in the spring 'cause she was getting into my grain bins. But it's getting too much to handle, getting too big. We just want to do the right thing," he said, dropping the bag with a thump, and hurrying out the door.

"Wait a minute!" Emily yelled and started after him, "What's your name?"

The man vanished around the building.

Another child-like cry drew her back inside. There was squabbling and squirming coming from the sack.

What was in there? She knelt down next to the bag.

The squirming and bawling continued and in spite of her trepidation at what might lie within, she reached out her hands to the string which cinched the sack and loosened it. No sooner had she done so, than a furry head popped out. It was a bear cub. She held her breath as it came towards her and with painful pin pricks climbed up her legs until she had to support it round furry bottom in her arms to keep it from making her chest a pincushion. It sucked on her ear till it hurt and she pried the elastic lips off with her fingers.

"Oh, my gosh!" Emily cried, "Look at you! You are so cute." She sat on the floor holding the clumsy flatfooted little bear with a mother's ease. "Are you hungry? What do you eat? Must be more than ears," she said, looking at the door, angry that she hadn't gotten the name of the man who tossed it into the room.

"What in the world am I going to do with you?" Emily asked, pointing at his nose, and he took that finger into his mouth. The cub made a "wub wub" sound as if trying to talk.

"You haven't been weaned? I expect your real mother would have weaned you by now. Those teeth hurt." Emily picked him up as his round bottom started to slide off her lap, saying, "You're a heavy little guy."

Bouncing him like a baby she tried to detach his wiry mouth from her ear again and saw Daniel standing in the doorway.

"Actually he is small for a spring cub." Daniel shut the door behind him.

"Hi," Emily smiled. "I've got a little problem here." She was trying to pull the cub's lips from her ear lobe, again.

Daniel lifted the bear under its forelegs, while Emily detached the lip-lock, and then he sat it on the floor. "Hey, little guy." Daniel gave the cub a rub on the head. The baby bear rolled over on its back and swatted at his hand like a kitten, a kitten with very big claws.

Emily, who still sat on the floor, was the cub's next target and he rolled over to crawl in her lap once more, and right up her chest. "Oops. I don't know why he has this thing about ears," she said wincing at the tug.

"It's a suckling action, like a child sucking its thumb. They do it when they feel insecure," Daniel said.

"Here, suck your own thumb," she said and put its paw in its mouth, playfully. The cub rolled off her lap again and began to roam about, sniffing noisily.

"A man had him in that sack. He tossed the sack in here and got away before I could stop him, but from what he said, I think he killed the mother this spring for getting into his feed." Emily looked from the bear to Daniel.

"Last spring the snow stayed late; there was not much early forage. It would have been better if the cub had died too," Daniel said, glumly.

The coat rack crashed to the floor as the bear tried to hang on Emily's jacket.

"That's a nice thing to say," Emily frowned at Daniel and went to set the rack back up but one of three wooden legs had broken.

"I'm sorry but he is too old to try to acclimate to the wild," he said with apology in his voice.

Emily asked hopefully, "A zoo, how about the trading post?"

Daniel shook his head. "They have all they can handle and anything less would be a cage."

"But can't we try to teach him how to live wild?" she asked sadly.

"Apisci-mosos, that is a big commitment and he is too old. He is too used to people. It would take years to assimilate him with his own. He's probably been treated like a toy but now he's getting too big to play with. You can tell he hasn't received the lessons his own mother would give him."

"I can be his mother. I can teach him," she affirmed, her eyes childlike, hopeful.

Daniel stared at the ceiling. How was he going to tell her that this was impossible, without breaking her heart? Looking back at her, with the cub, he loved her more at that moment than he could possibly love anyone on this earth. Still, he tried to be rational as he said, "You'd have to acquire a license to work with wild animals. That takes training."

"You have a license. I saw it," she interjected, "and you trained Nutmeg."

He encircled her in his arms, "He is too old, too domesticated. From the time Nutmeg could open her eyes, I was training her to get her own food. And a bear is not a squirrel. A bear, not properly acclimated to the wild, can cause a lot of damage, even turn on people."

She breathed the masculine scent of his sleeve and relaxed into his body. "I'll come back. I'll take care of what I have to do in Manchester and come right back."

"What am I saying?" Daniel asked, astonished. "Of course we will try."

A chair crashed in the room.

"You little bugger!" Emily said, laughing at the cub's antics.

"Reality check," Daniel straightened up, "Emily, you have a job in Manchester, a job you do very well. I'm praying that somehow that job extends to Kaskitesiw in the future, the near future. But we haven't talked about that yet. We haven't talked about anything yet."

"Just give me the remainder of the week. We'll figure out something after that—that is, if you want me to come back."

"You know I want you," he whispered, cupping her cheek in his hand and kissed her gently on the lips.

Suddenly, the office printer was pulled off the counter by the curious marauder.

"It's probably not a good idea to be kissing in the office anyway," Emily said, disappointed, tucking her shirt in tighter and eyeing the destruction.

"I'll go find the transfer cage downstairs," Daniel said, resigned, and went to the basement door.

"When you do, let me help you bring it up," Emily called after him and knelt down, trying to pick up plastic shards of the printer and a cracked ink cartridge. She managed to smear its contents across her hand as the cub decided her back was a hobby horse. She knew she shouldn't be rough with him, because he could be rougher, so she let him sit on her back and paw at her hair until she was blinded by her own tresses. If she tilted upward he would slide and she didn't like the idea of claw marks down her back.

Emily decided his lessons should start immediately and made a very deep growl. The cub scrambled off her back and crawled under a chair. She had tried to pretend she was an irritated mother bear and it worked. She smiled and pushed her hair back, unaware of the ink on her hand.

Whether it was her growl, or the fact two other people had entered the room, the cub ran into the corner, arching its back. Emily saw the man and woman's shoes from her kneeling position and prayed it wasn't Pete and Susanne. This was not the time to set an example of how well she kept the office.

Kneeling amongst the ravages of equipment, she couldn't decide whether to look up and face the music or stay where she was. Then Emily heard Daniel coming back up the stairs. She saw the edge of a large cage protrude through the opening and stood to find her parents standing before her.

"Oh, Daddy, help him with that. It's too heavy!"

Emily's father went immediately to help Daniel.

Emily's mother stared at her daughter as if she were looking at a stranger. This disheveled, ink-smeared girl could not be the sophisticated young woman who had left Manchester almost three weeks ago. And of all things—she was picking up a growling little bear under its forearms and dragging it toward a cage with its claws still around the arm of a chair!

"Come on, you little wart. I wish you had called first, Mom. There were some things I needed in Manchester, some maternity tops and ginseng tea," Emily said as she pried loose a paw.

The cage hit the floor a little harder than it should have and she looked up to see her father and Daniel staring at her with open mouths.

"What? Oh for pity sake!" she rolled her eyes. "The tops are for Lisa, my landlord, and the tea is for Anna." She gave her attention back to the cub. "Okay, you little bugger, let go of the chair."

The bear was not happy with its confinement. It stood on its hind legs and pushed at the side of the cage in a rhythmic motion. But the cage was large enough to keep from tumbling over with its furry contents.

"Hi, Mom!" Emily brushed her hair off her cheek, leaving an ink stain. "I've got an apple in my lunch." Emily pulled open the drawer to the desk, opened the cage door, and gave the little bear the fruit. The cub took it, mouthing it with its rubbery lips. It sat on its round bottom and chewed eagerly, ignoring everyone in the room.

Emily stepped back satisfied, pushing her hair off her forehead. Ink smeared there too. Remembering her parents were there, she kissed her father and then her mother, who still looked as if she was in shock. "Mom, nice to see you too," Emily said at her mother's wide-eyed expression of dismay.

Emily's father was grinning. "You look great, sweetheart."

Emily looked at Daniel, who pointed to his own face.

She gave him another quizzical look, then wiped at her cheek, making an ink smear worse.

Daniel, trying not to laugh, pointed to his own hand.

She looked at hers. "Oh, dear, I'll be right back," Emily excused herself and hurried off to the bathroom.

Emily's father was chuckling. Aghast, Maureen Harrigan turned to look at her husband and then accused Daniel, "What have you done to her?"

"I'm not sure what you mean," Daniel stammered. He couldn't tell if she was being serious or not.

Henry extended his hand. "You must be Daniel. It's nice to meet you, son."

Daniel shook it, saying politely, "You too, Detective Harrigan."

"How are you feeling?"

"Fine, sir. I apologize for all this." He indicated the topsy-turvy room.

"Nonsense! You had your hands full with that ruffian," Henry said mirthfully and went over and scratched the top of the bear's head through the cage with his finger tip. "This is as close as I have ever been to a bear. Maureen, look at this little guy!"

"I'll look at him from here," she said flatly and took off her coat. "That is not my daughter who left home three weeks ago."

Daniel opened his mouth but said nothing. He took her coat to hang it up. Realizing the coat rack was broken, he laid it on Pete's desk.

"Maureen!" Henry turned to his wife jubilantly. "Emmy looks happy, wonderful!"

"Mom!" Emily emerged cleaned up though there were now red marks where the ink had been. "What are you doing here? Why didn't you call me, tell me you were coming?"

"Your mother was worried," her father said.

"I heard the foliage was turning early up here. I just thought a Sunday drive might be nice." Maureen tilted her head up in that stubborn look that Daniel was beginning to know very well in her daughter. "Can we have lunch?"

"I can call dispatch." Emily looked at Daniel. Her superior officer was back.

"You go ahead, Officer Harrigan," Daniel offered quickly.

"Oh, can't you come too?" Maureen pouted at Daniel.

There was silence. Emily wished she had been abandoned and brought up by orangutans. Her mother was too old for that persuasive expression.

"The bear is fine for a half-hour, I'm sure! Henry's buying," Maureen insisted, smiling coquettishly.

"Mom, Warden Claret has a lot to do. He's very busy," Emily said, trying to get Daniel off this unexpected hook.

"Nonsense!" Maureen took Daniel's arm and led him to the door. "You are quite handsome." The emphasis was on the 'are', as if she was confirming something that Emily had said. Her glance back at her daughter was one of keeping your enemies close.

Emily could tell by that look that she disapproved of Daniel. "I'll call dispatch," Emily said morosely to her father. She finished calling and her dad put his arm around her and said, "You look alive again, baby."

"I think I just died," she whispered exasperated, inclining her head to the door where Maureen and Daniel had walked out. "I love you, Daddy. I love Mom, too, but why does she have to act this way?" Her shoulders slumped as she attached the radio to her uniform.

"I'm sure your game warden understands." He excused his wife.

"He's not *my* game warden—yet," she said softly and lifted her eyes. They spoke worlds to her father.

Henry held her back and studied her seriously. "You sure, honey?"

Emily nodded. Her eyes were full of love as she confided in her father. "I've never been so sure of anything in my life."

"Oh, baby," he said, hugging her tight. "I will curb your mother. Don't worry. He's a good man?" He took her arm and led her to the door.

"Like you are, Dad."

CHAPTER 18

The Bear Bones Diner was not what Maureen Harrigan had in mind, but it was the only eatery in town, "That's not how you spell bare," she remarked.

"It's a play on words, Mother," Emily said, having taken her mother's arm from Daniel, rescuing him so he could drop back and talk with her father.

"What a name for a place to eat," Maureen's voice was sarcastic as she looked around the town with displeasure.

Everyone had to sit at the lunch counter on bar stools. This stifled conversation from including all four, and obviously irritated Emily's mother. The talk which did filter down the row, thanks to Henry, was light. Emily's father had parked himself next to Daniel, putting the warden at the end of the line. He kept the conversation on police work. Maureen was as far from Daniel as Emily could get her.

"Hi Kevin," Emily smiled at the proprietor. "I didn't know you ran the diner too."

"Usually my wife runs it, but she's got a cold. Warden! Welcome back. This calls for a celebration. These folks with you?" He looked back at Emily.

"Kevin, this is my mom and dad, Henry and Maureen."

"Please to meet you," he said, shaking Henry's hand. Maureen didn't offer hers. "Hey, I've still got some of Emily's 'road-kill' back in the freezer. How'd you folks like a nice venison steak? George won't mind. I've been keeping his meat in my locker. It's sliced thin, so it won't take a minute to thaw."

166

Emily was wincing, refraining from looking at her mother's reaction and said, "I think my mom and I will just have one of your great turkey sandwiches."

"How about you guys," Kevin wanted to impress them, "smothered in onion gravy?"

"Sounds good to me," Daniel said and Henry agreed.

"Road-kill?" Maureen gasped, looking wide eyed at Emily.

"It's deer meat. I didn't want it to go to waste," Emily said simply.

"You scraped a dead animal off a road?"

"Mom, it wasn't like that. I didn't scrape it—yes, iced tea, please, Kevin. The meat is fresh. Anyway, how are things in Manchester?"

"I didn't raise my daughter to eat road-kill."

"How is Aunt Marge? Has her cancer spread?"

"No," Maureen reluctantly followed the new subject. "She says she is curing the cancer with cigarette smoke."

"Your sister is one tough lady," Emily commented, shaking her head.

"Tough as she is, I bet she never ate road-kill."

Emily looked at the door as two men came in and sat at the other end of the counter. She whispered, "Mother, get off the road-kill! You're not going to eat it either. Thanks, Kevin. Here! Kevin makes good sandwiches," Emily said, shoving the plate towards her mother.

Pausing before taking a bite out of her sandwich she leaned toward her daughter saying in a low voice, "He *is* Indian!"

"I told you he was part Cree." Emily bit down on a pickle.

"Please tell me that you're just friends. Oh, that smells awful!" Maureen exclaimed loud enough for the other patrons to hear, watching as Kevin placed two steaming plates in front of Daniel and Henry.

Emily sighed.

"Emily, you can't be serious." Maureen whispered, swinging back to her daughter.

"Not now, Mom," Emily said, glancing over to see if her father liked the venison. "Good, huh?" she asked her dad.

"Excellent! I should take up hunting."

"Oh please, Henry!" Maureen looked down the counter at her husband. "You get lost in our own backyard."

Emily closed her eyes.

"If you would like to hunt, sir, I would be happy to partner with you. Good hunting can be as exhilarating as fishing," Daniel said cutting his meat.

"I'd like that!" Henry agreed.

"You'll be the only one eating it, or cooking it," Maureen commented and then turned back to Emily and in a low voice said, "They beat their wives, you know."

Emily stared at her mother long and hard then stuck a chip in her mouth.

Maureen fingered a piece of lettuce back into her rye bread and accused quietly, "They're pagans. Besides, he's crippled. He'll lose his job, then what?"

Emily put her sandwich down and waved to Daniel at the end of the counter like everything was fine. "He is not crippled. He slouches a little."

"Think what your children will look like."

"They would be beautiful and you would be 'ga ga' over them." She glared back at her mother.

"They steee-al," Maureen sang in an undertone, pulling out a piece of turkey, rolling it between red-nailed fingers and put it into her mouth. Then she flicked her fingers, as if flicking more than crumbs away.

Emily moaned and looked to heaven for that conquering love Father Paul said she should have. Wheeling towards Maureen she hissed as quietly as she could, "Mother, you are so wrong! You are so prejudiced and so wrong! Instead of trying to figure out what he is, why don't you get to know who he is? He is a good and kind person, very worthy of your love."

Maureen raising her brows with superiority spat back, "I know these things. You won't be happy with him. You have so much more intelligence, a career! You'd be throwing that all away."

Emily pinched chips in half and chewed them slowly, refusing to say anymore after her mother had raised her tone enough so that one of the men at the end of the counter looked towards them.

After the stressful meal, they walked outside. Maureen Harrigan scowled at the wind for mussing her hair.

"It was nice meeting you, sir," Daniel said, extending his hand to her father. "I've got some rounds to make. Your daughter has been doing my job ever since she arrived in Kaskitesiw. I think I'd better start pulling my own weight."

"Oh, Warden, couldn't you take an old police officer with you this afternoon? Henry would just love to go…"

"Maureen, the man is busy," Henry remarked, frowning at his wife.

"It's just that Emily and I have so much to talk about," she demurred.

"Sir, it would be an honor to have you as my partner this afternoon. Your experience would be of benefit to me," Daniel offered.

Henry motioned for Daniel to lead the way.

Emily could have kissed Daniel right then. She hoped her eyes conveyed that, as she looked at him.

It certainly was conveyed to her mother. "Yes, well," Maureen said, linking arms with her daughter, "you guys have fun. Come on, it's freezing out here. Where shall we go?"

"We'll go back to the office. I want to see how my little charge is doing."

"Tell me you're not serious about keeping that bear."

"No, I don't want to keep it. I want to try to help him acclimate to the wild. I'm hoping we can release him." She tucked her mother's cold hand into her pocket. "In spite of your aggravating ways, it is good to see you. I've missed you."

"I've missed you too, sweetheart." Maureen leaned into her daughter. "I'll be so glad when you're home safe and sound. How can you stand this place?"

"I like it here!" Emily looked around her, smiling.

Maureen Harrigan stopped, and said with a frown, "You're joking. There is nothing here but little poverty row houses and that horrid diner. I mean the whole town is one shack after another."

"They're not shacks. Most are nice little houses that are easy to heat. And they're actually some houses which would meet your approval on the outskirts of town."

"Sweetheart, I didn't raise you to live in a shack," Maureen pleaded.

"I don't live in a shack. I live in a nice apartment in the next town." She opened the office door and found the little bear had shuffled his cage half way across the room until it lodged against the desk where he was now trying to pull a telephone cord inside it with a claw.

"No, no, no!" Emily cried and pulled the cage out of harm's way.

"What is that smell?" Maureen asked from beneath her hand.

"Most animals don't soil their own cages but this little guy must have been left alone too much of his young life," Emily said, opening the door of the cage. The cub wandered out.

"Emily, don't let that thing loose!"

"Mom, I've got to clean out his cage. You'll be okay," she insisted and grabbed some paper towels from the bathroom.

"He's coming towards me. Emily!"

"He just wants to smell you."

"He is trying to climb up my leg. Oh, my good pants! He's pulling the threads!"

Emily backed out of the cage and threw the paper in the trash. "Come here, you terror," she said, scooping up the cub and sat down with him on her lap. He tried to chew her pony tail and Emily swung it to the back.

"My daughter, the finest detective in New Hampshire, is picking up bear poop."

Emily rocked the little bear as she would an infant. "It's called scat, not poop."

"So, when are you coming home?"

Emily leveled her eyes on her mother, "I'm only telling you this because I love you, but you're taking the red-head thing to a whole new level. And the lipstick doesn't need to go over the edge of your lips."

"Gloria says it makes my lips look fuller," Maureen said, pouting at her reflection in a cosmetic mirror.

"You don't need to make your lips look bigger. Ow, stop that! That's too hard," Emily said firmly, and then extracted a finger from the cub's mouth. She addressed her mother once more, "Your hairdresser can't be trusted."

Maureen looked miffed for a minute but then decided maybe the lipstick was a little much. She watched Emily playing with the cub, circling her finger down to its furry tummy. "What's its name?"

"I don't know that he has one," Emily whispered and jiggled the little head as the cub dosed off with her reclaimed fingers still in his mouth.

"Who was that bear in the Irish fairy tale I used to read you?" Maureen asked, crossing her legs.

Emily smiled remembering. *"Galen, Noble Bear of the Forest."* I loved that story. That's a good name for you, Galen. Thanks, Mom."

Maureen watched the cub's face with a slight smile, saying softly. "He's going to sleep."

"Tired little boy," soothed Emily, "He had a big day. First he was abandoned, then he had to wreck a police station." She nuzzled him behind the ear with her nose.

"Don't do that, you might get lice," Maureen commanded, but then she was forced to smile again at the cub, slumped, so relaxed, in her daughter's arms, "You're going to make a good mother."

"I'd like to be somebody's mother, someday. Be a good mom like you."

"Okay, we're not used to this." Maureen repositioned her crossed legs more comfortably.

Emily giggled softly so she wouldn't rouse the bear and whispered, "Best get back to walking on egg shells."

"And speaking of which, you didn't answer my question."

"Which one?"

"When are you coming home?"

"The job ends in another week. I'm going to see the police psychiatrist in Manchester. Wrap things up at work—hope that mother has decided not to sue me for the death of her son. Then I'm coming back here—continue work on the Faidlee case and help train the cub. "

"You can't be serious!"

"I really like it here. I'd like to help train this little guy and I am in love, Mom." Her eyes searched her mother's face for a reaction. She didn't get the one she wanted.

"Honey, it's all this wildness; it's affected you," Maureen moaned.

"I have never felt more alive," Emily said, easing the sleeping bear into the cage. "The wilderness—it's like every breath is full of life. And the people—they are so down to earth and caring. They try to hide it but..."

"No, Honey, Sweetheart. It's like when Daddy and I took you to the rodeo when you were a little girl. You wanted to be a rodeo rider, a cowgirl, for months afterwards. It will pass as soon as you get back home. This Cowgirl and Indian thing—it's just a passing fancy."

"I'm not a little girl anymore, Mom."

"Emily, what are you thinking—being with a man like that?"

"A man like what, Mom?"

"Honey, you have a very prestigious career."

"And you are very prejudiced!" Emily snapped. "How can you judge Daniel? You don't even know him."

"Emily, there is a reason there aren't more Indians in New Hampshire. They're either in jail, or have run away to Canada for beating their wives, or—or drank themselves to death."

"I don't believe what I'm hearing! The reason there aren't more Indians around is because we either killed them with disease or bullets, or drove them away because we wanted their land!" Emily shouted, waking the bear.

Maureen slapped her glove on the arm of the chair. "Don't yell at me like that, Miss Smarty Pants!"

Emily closed her eyes and took a deep breath. When her mother was convinced of something, no matter what beauty shop or market rag she got it from, she would argue all night to prove her point.

There was silence, except for the cub shuffling around its cage.

"I want more for you than I had." Maureen changed tactics and pleaded with her daughter.

"But you married the most wonderful man in the world!"

"Your father is a good man, but there were things that I would have liked to have had. We were always hand to mouth. You have the chance to do so much better than me, with Seth."

"Answer me honestly, is it because Daniel is Indian that you don't like him? Or is it because he is a police man, like Dad, and doesn't make the money Seth Horan does?"

"Honey, it is common knowledge that these people don't want to make themselves better. At least your father tried to make something of himself. I'm still waiting for him to succeed but…"

"Stop it, Mother!" Emily cried, "Please don't make me choose between you and Daniel, because if I have to, I will choose Daniel."

Maureen Harrigan looked stunned. She got up and walked to the window and then turned back. "Oh, dear, this is more serious than I thought."

Emily was visibly shaken. She had never asserted herself so vehemently to her mother before.

"It's all right, sweetheart. I know you have been under a lot of stress. I should never have agreed to let you come up here. You're confused. I would never make you choose. We are a family. Whatever makes you happy!"

Emily scowled, unsure her mother's words were genuine.

Maureen hurried towards Emily and embraced her, "I can't lose you—I love you so much."

"I love you too, Mom." Emily hugged her back, relieved the strain was over. "I will always love you and Dad. Come on. I need to go to the store to get Galen some supper."

"I have to go back out in the cold?" Maureen complained.

"You have to go back out in the cold. Button your coat up. There." Emily drew her mother's collar together.

"It's warmer in Manchester. Remember that sailboat Seth has, and how he loves to take you to the theater?"

"I'm not in love with Seth's sailboat or him," Emily said with good natured exasperation. "On our way back, there is someone I want you to meet."

"Not another Indian, I hope."

"How did you guess?"

Emily bought lettuce, apples, pears, baby formula, dog bowl, large collar and a dog leash. The wind was getting stronger, knocking leaves off maples as they went further up the street.

"Don't people drive around here?" Maureen spoke from inside her collar.

"It's not far," Emily reassured her, "We're going to see Anna. She is Daniel's 'almost' mother."

"Almost mother?" Maureen questioned with irritation. "You mean she's a step-mother."

"Not quite. It's a long story."

"Spare me. Shouldn't you call first? Emily, I'm not dressed to meet future in-laws, even if I don't believe that will ever come about," Maureen complained, hanging back.

"Believe me, you're just fine."

They walked up the one-sided street, past the trailer and bungalow until they reached Anna's ranch style house.

Maureen looked over the modest dwelling with the dream-catcher hanging outside. "No, I'm *not* fine, I'm overdressed," Maureen said curtly.

"Mother, be nice! She is a wonderful lady. Okay, here's a quick briefing. She lives alone, her husband died many years ago and not long ago she lost her son in Iraq. Daniel and Rusty were like brothers."

"Oh, Lord! Emily, this is awkward."

Emily knocked softly and called, "Anna?"

She could hear the television being turned off and footsteps coming to the door.

"Waciye, *hello!*" Anna greeted, her round face beaming. "And who is this?"

"Waciye! Tanisis? *How are you*? This is my mother, Maureen. Mom, this is Anna."

"Hello," Maureen responded, smiling a little too brightly. "How nice to finally meet you."

Emily looked back at her mother curiously.

"Pepitigwe! Api! Api! *Come in! Sit down! Sit down!*" Anna extended her hand to the flowered sofa and chair. "Can I fix you some Lemon Balm tea?"

"Oh, no, don't go to any trouble," Maureen replied, waving her glove in her hand, remembering this woman's voice on the phone, telling her happily that Emily was sleeping with that Indian.

"It's good. I'll make it. You sit down, Anna," Emily urged and went into the kitchen.

"Apisci-mosos, would you also bring a piece or two of wood in from the porch?"

Emily opened the back door and went out.

"Well…" Maureen smiled, "You are not what I expected from our phone conversation."

"You either." Anna squinted through her thick round glasses. "You are much more sophisticated than you sounded. Have you met my Taaniyal?"

"Who?"

"The man Emily was sleeping with." Anna chuckled.

"Oh, yes I did. We had lunch together." Maureen was going to kill Emily if she didn't get back here.

Emily came back with two pieces of wood, loaded them into the stove and then put the kettle on top.

Maureen watched her daughter, so familiar with this woman's house. "Apisci-mosos?"

Emily looked at Anna.

"Use that new tea at the left of the cabinet."

"Apy, what?" Maureen asked.

"That is what we call your Emily. Her hair is the color of a deer in summer."

"Is it really?" Maureen pretended to smile.

"Your daughter is very smart, like you."

"Well, you are just too kind." Maureen smiled up at Emily, her eyes saying she wanted out of here.

"Sophisticated!" Anna said again.

"Word for the day!" Maureen said, looking around for her daughter. She found Emily had gone into the kitchenette.

"I will give you the name, Otehimin mestagay."

"Here is tea," Emily announced, bringing in the cups and casting a hopeful glance at her mother.

"Anna has just given me the name 'oteh…'".

"Mestagay…otehimin mestagay," Anna repeated with a nod of emphasis.

"That's nice." Emily looked at Anna suspiciously, but the Cree woman took her cup from Emily, without meeting her eyes.

"It means sophisticated," Maureen fallaciously chortled.

"Ah, huh," Emily said, and shifted warning eyes to Anna, again.

Anna was beaming, sipping her tea.

"I have a bear cub, Anna!" Emily said as if announcing the birth of her first baby.

Anna frowned. "How did you get a bear cub?"

"A man dropped it off in a sack. His wife tried to raise it."

"How old?" Anna asked with grave concern.

"Daniel thinks it's about five or six months old. He thinks the mother had it late or was sickly or injured. That is why she searched for food on a farm rather than foraging. The farmer killed her in the spring."

"Then the bear knows nothing of being wild." Anna put the cup and saucer on the table.

"No, but I will teach him," Emily said confidently.

"Better if you kill him now."

"That's horrible!" Maureen was appalled.

"That's what Daniel said. Well, maybe not quite so bluntly." Emily's shoulders drooped.

"The little thing deserves a chance," Maureen chimed in, defending her daughter.

"The bear must be killed or it will kill you, in many ways, Apiscimosos," Anna said more gently. "I can see by your eyes you are fond of it already."

"I really think I can make Galen wild again." Emily's affirmation sounded more like a plea.

"Ah, you have named him," Anna groaned, shaking her head. "You cannot make the winter stay away, and you cannot make this bear wild again. Soon, he will be a danger to all those around him. It is a sin to cage him, better to let Daniel shoot him. No one can hold the spirit of maskwa."

"Well, Emily, I think the boys will be returning," Maureen Harrigan said, having heard just about enough of this kind of talk. "It was very nice to meet you, Anna."

"Come, have your tea. We will talk no more of the bear," Anna said quickly. She did not want to upset Emily.

Maureen sat back down. Emily smiled at her mother with encouragement.

"Your Emily, she is very special," Anna said, and took a sip of tea. "The spirits are very close to her."

"I know that she is special," Maureen said and tasted the tea, "I don't know about spirits."

"She is what our people call a…"

"Okay, let try this one more time. We're not going to talk about Emily, either," Emily said. She rose and moved to the table. "Mom, come look at these beautiful shawls. Anna wove and crocheted them."

"Oh, those are lovely," Maureen commented and fondled a shawl woven of different colored strands of yarn. The end tassels were threaded into small glass beads. "Do you sell these?"

"No, but I will make you one," Anna offered, and flashed her wide smile. "Christmas, I will make you one. I am almost finished this white one here." She carefully folded back tissue paper to reveal a finely woven shawl, made with soft, thin, merino wool yarn and delicate mother of pearl beads which were cupped by tiny white feathers.

Emily caught her breath, "Anna, it's so beautiful!"

Maureen was impressed also. "I have never seen anything so lovely. One thinks of wool as being heavy but this is really quite gossamer. And you made it?"

"Yes, it will be finished for a bride."

"So it is an Indian wedding shawl?" Emily smiled, learning one more element of Anna's rich culture.

177

Maureen caressed it with her red painted fingertips. "It is so soft." Then she drew back as if touching a snake.

"Merino is the finest of sheep wool," Anna went on, enjoying the attention. Her smiling eyes rested on Emily. "It will be for my adopted son's wiikimaakan, *wife*."

"Wiikimaakan?" Maureen's voice was strained. "How nice."

"You know what? You're right, Mom," Emily said quickly, reading her mother's thoughts. "Dad and Daniel will be back." She stood up, picked up her grocery bag, and grabbed her mother's hand.

"Thank you for the tea, Anna," Emily called back.

From a distance, they could tell the lights were on in the office, so Daniel and her father had to be back.

"Let me guess—wiikimaakan—wife," Maureen asked, "and that adopted son is Daniel? Does everyone know something I don't?"

"Hi Daddy," Emily said, kissing her father, as they came inside. "Did you enjoy your patrol?"

"Sure did," Henry said enthusiastically. "Got a drunk off the road, and was asked permission by this fine young man to court my daughter."

"What did you say?" Maureen demanded, unable to hide her desperate look.

"Well, of course I said yes!" Henry Harrigan looked happy, satisfied.

Maureen asked Daniel in a sweet voice, her memory and articulation of the words meticulous, "What does 'o-tay-hee-mi-nay mes—tay-gay' mean?"

"Otehimin means strawberry and mestagay means ha…" Daniel looked up from his report. His eyes went to Maureen's hair and his face fell. It was evident he did not want to say the rest of the word.

Emily closed her eyes, thinking of a means to murder Anna.

"Come on, Henry. It's late. We're leaving!" Maureen brushed Emily's cheek with a kiss and strode to the door. Then she turned back, took an envelope out of her purse and handed it to Emily. "Here, this came for you."

"What is that?" Henry asked, catching an embossed 'Lady Justice' on the return address. "When did that come?"

178

Maureen threw her hands in the air. "How should I know? I just signed for it."

Henry hesitated, concerned about the letter, but at Emily's encouraging smile, he followed his wife out.

"Bye. Love you," Emily said after them and looked down at the letter. She opened it and her face showed the bad news.

"What is it?" Daniel came to her.

Putting her hand on her forehead, she handed it to Daniel. It was from a lawyer requesting that she appear in court the twelfth of November to answer charges of wrongful death brought by a Cathleen Droger concerning her son, Alex Droger.

Daniel put the letter down and watched Emily feeding the cub formula from a bottle. She was smiling as he drank, rocking him in her lap. Daniel knew her; knew she felt deeply, loved deeply and hurt deeply. This last emotion, she tried to conceal from everyone. She should be angry. He was. He'd like to take the letter and shove it down that ambulance-chasing lawyer's throat. Instead he watched her as a man who tries to keep his eye on a jewel tossed in tide washed sands, each new wave threatening to take her from his sight.

CHAPTER 19

"We have time at lunch to take Galen out," Daniel said finishing up the morning log of Moose lottery winners.

"Good," she said, writing up her own report on a dog complaint. "I'd like to work on his tree-climbing abilities."

"What tree-climbing abilities?" Daniel teased.

"He'll get it. I don't know why he can't use his front legs to hold himself onto a tree."

"He just hasn't used those muscles in his domesticated life. Hopefully, they will develop, in time."

"That is the first encouraging word you have said about Galen." She looked up happily.

The fact that Galen didn't have the desire or instinct to become wild had Daniel secretly making phone calls in hopes that one of the better parks would take him. So far he'd had no luck. For Emily's sake, he would explore every avenue but the permanent cage. To cage maskwa would be to kill his spirit. Not even for Emily could he do that. He prayed that she would understand.

Emily clipped the leash on Galen's collar. Today, Daniel showed her a trail leading down into the marsh area from his cabin.

She thought that the land behind the house dropped off severely and never noticed the path hemmed in by bushes. Emily balked at first. Though it promised seclusion for training the bear, the way down was steep and narrow.

"Daniel, we may get down there, but how do we get back up?"

"You mean, how do I get back up? I have been walking every day and I am stronger. There is an old orchard down there, Symonds Orchard. If you want the bear to forage for himself, it is an ideal place with many raspberries growing wild. Besides it is not as steep as it looks."

"Maybe not for a mountain goat! If we take our time coming back up, it might be alright."

"Yes, Mother," he teased.

On the way down, Daniel, on his hands and knees, searched for the tasty ants under the rocks while Galen nosed his ear. At first, the cub wouldn't pay attention to the way Daniel turned the rocks over, too happy to slurp up the insects once uncovered, but now he was turning the stones over himself. He seemed to be enjoying yanking on the rocks to lick up ants, a sign that Daniel admitted was encouraging. They both marveled at the dexterity of his paws.

At the bottom the trail they came to an old road which was not visible from above. Daniel said it was only used by fishermen and hunters and eventually led through the orchard and pasture beyond. It came out three miles from the camp where Anna had stayed. If they were to go left, they would come to what Anna had called, 'the ageless face of the swamp' with its waterfalls. At Emily's urging, Daniel promised to take her but admitted he wasn't ready to climb the boulders yet.

They turned right on the grass-covered road and soon it opened up into a vast field with a few gnarled apple trees still standing. Around them was a sea of raspberries, once domesticated, now wild, but still juicer than their native cousins. Emily picked some raspberries and tempted Galen to come to the bushes and find the fruit. Grinning, she gave Daniel the thumbs up sign when clumsy cub, obviously happy with his new find, pounced onto the vines, crushing them and the berries. Soon his lips, with finger-like agility, managed to pull the fruit away from the sharp thorny stems.

"Admit it," Emily said, tilting her head up at Daniel.

"Admit what?"

"Galen is learning how to feed himself."

Without warning, Daniel took an air horn from the pocket of his jacket and pressed the button. Emily jumped and so did the cub.

"Run to that apple tree and climb it." Daniel pressed the button again.

Not understanding, but trusting Daniel, who had said don't run with the bear, she headed for the old tree.

"Call the bear!"

"Galen, come on. Galen come, come on." She called and clapped her hands as she ran.

The cub started to follow her but the loud noise was forgotten when a clump of ripe berries came into reach.

Daniel walked up behind the cub, pulled out his revolver and fired it in the air. It started to run towards Emily who was calling it. She had a foot up in the crook of a branch and was pulling herself up on another higher branch. "Galen, come on. Come on, baby. Climb the tree."

The cub sat at the base of the tree, frightened, looking up at her, unsure of what to do.

Emily awkwardly tried to get her foot off of the branch. She climbed back down and realizing what Daniel was doing now, tried to lift and push the cub up the tree. Daniel fired again and the bear "short treed" took a couple of lunges upward on its own, not high enough for protection but off the ground. Emily and Galen both looked around at Daniel as if asking if this was okay and please don't shoot the gun again. The chubby cub pushed himself over Emily's protective arms and dropped to the ground.

"There is still a very long way to go." Daniel said and holstered the gun.

"A little bit of warning would have been nice?" Emily rebuked him.

"There may not be a second warning for him."

"I meant for me." She said trying to catch her breath.

He grinned. "You are the one who wants to be the mother bear. I won't soon forget you with your foot stuck in that tree limb."

Emily's serious expression was replaced by a smile. "Delete image."

He looked back at Galen who was picking off berries, the whole incident forgotten. "We have to start building him the outdoor cage." Daniel realized that there were a lot of things he needed to do, most importantly, get his and Anna's winter wood in. But there was no way he could swing a sledge hammer or splitting maul.

"I'm pretty good with a hammer," Emily said, sensing his feeling of inadequacy.

"You are, are you?" Daniel cocked his head, grinning.

"It takes great technique to hammer out the dents on a vintage Mustang." She said with pride.

"You're hired."

When Galen had eaten his fill, they made their way up the hill. Their progress was slow and Daniel was breathing hard. She linked her arm in his and led him to a stone to sit down. His brow was furrowed in frustration and she tried to engage him in light conversation.

"Daniel? I'm curious. Anna said her husband took her name when they were married. Pete said your mother was French. Did your father take his wife's name as well?

"I am glad you are with me and not against me, my astute detective." Daniel said trying to catch his breath. "Claret was my mother's name. My father and Anna's husband were brothers of the Abenaki tribe."

"Russell was your uncle! So Anna is really your aunt? But, Pete said that you had been taken in by a neighbor."

"Pete does not know everything. There are others in town I am related to. Had my father chosen to keep his own name, it would be Brown. If there are too many of us the words 'clan or confederacy' might be spoken aloud and may cause trouble for us."

"Still, today!" Emily shook her head in disbelief. "What are they afraid of, an Indian uprising? Now, I can see why Anna was defensive and called me a European."

Daniel started up the hill again. "It was not personal. In her mind, the Europeans in both countries have tried to rise above the land and reach for more by always standing on another's shoulders. People do this but the land always remains. No one can possess it."

She returned to her train of thought as they walked, "Brown? So you and Ila and Teresa are related."

"Not even Pete has figured that out!" He smiled. "I guess I'm going to have to kidnap and keep you here now that you know our secret."

"You can't kidnap the willing." She kissed his cheek and left him in order to catch up with Galen. "Walk slow," she called back, hooking the leash on the bear.

Daniel climbed to the level ground and put his hands on his knees, catching his breath. "My little deer, you will be caught. You just wait."

"I'll wait." Emily grinned back, the cub pulling her along.

When they were in sight of the police station Daniel mentioned with a tinge of disappointment in his voice, "It looks like Pete is back."

~~~~~

The constable tried to hang his baseball cap up on the coat rack and found it broken in the corner. There was a cage in the office, a cracked printer, and various claw marks on the office furniture whether it was metal, plastic or wood.

"Daniel? Emily?" Pete called. Silence answered him. "What happened here? Looks like a bear got into the office." He tried to put his lunch in the refrigerator and found it full of vegetables, fruits and baby formula.

"What the hell?"

The door opened and the bear cub burst in followed by Emily, who was being dragged on the end of the leash. Daniel followed a few feet behind and shut the door behind them.

Inside, the little cub sniffed and whined at Pete, then ran behind Emily's legs.

"Hey! Pete! Welcome back," Daniel called.

"Did you have a good time?" Emily asked, as she pushed the bear's bottom into the cage.

"Okay, I demand to know. Who are you, and what have you done with my wardens?"

"Sorry about the printer." Daniel indicated the wreck on the counter. "I've got another one on order. I'll pay for it."

"No, I told you I'm going to pay for it," Emily protested and gave him a playful whack on the left arm.

Cocking his jaw, Pete watched the two of them. Their eyes shone as they looked at one another. "Let's start with why do we have a bear in the office?"

"Pete, meet Galen. He won't be here long. Daniel is building him an outside run at his house, until he can live independently." Emily introduced the bear as if presenting a child prodigy.

Daniel tried to explain the rest of the story while Emily interjected from time to time with hopeful statements about turning the bear loose to be wild again.

Pete listened with his hand on his chin. Then he said, "All right, all right, I used to have two sensible officers working here. Emmy, your badge, please!" Pete held out his hand.

Emily frowned. "Because of the bear?"

"Pete, she's got 'til the end of the month," Daniel stated firmly.

"Emmy can work in an investigative role on the Faidlee case, here with me, but I'm not going to put either one of you in danger by having you both in the field together." He took Emily's badge and tossed it into the drawer.

"What are you talking about, Pete?" Daniel said with anger just on the edge of his voice.

"Pete, I promise you, I haven't let the bear interfere with my job." Emily looked at the usually easy-going constable in disbelief.

"It's written all over the two of you. I'm making a judgment call based on the fact that both of your performances may be diminished. Your actions, as officers of the law, may be exaggerated in order to defend one another while on duty together."

They both stood there speechless.

Pete continued, "Do I have to spell it out to you?" Then the constable's demeanor softened and he chuckled. "You look like two kids caught behind the barn."

"It's that obvious?" Daniel was surprised he could show his emotions so easily these days.

Emily blushed and looked at Daniel, who had just confirmed his love for her aloud and in front of Pete. "Ah, Pete, nothing unprofessional has been going on, believe me."

"Then I guess you'd better get started," Pete said and stretched. "I've had a wonderful vacation. I'm rested and raring to go. Rifle season hasn't started. After you get done briefing me as to what, officially, has happened, I'd recommend the two of you take the rest of the day off. Take a trip into the White Mountains. Ride the cog train. Look at the leaves, take a hike, get to know each other better."

Daniel looked at Emily and saw her eagerness.

"What about the bear?" Emily said, wanting very much to go.

"You don't think I can take care of a bear cub? I'll take him to the kid's school. He'll be a good PR man, if it's a he—he is? Yep, I can take him for walks, feed him."

"He's a handful, Pete, and he is getting a little rough," Emily warned. She loved the idea of going to the White Mountains with Daniel, but she was worried about pushing the bear's training back. From the sound of what Pete was saying, Galen might be dancing for peanuts by the time they got back.

"Cripes, it's only a day!" Pete said, opening the cage. The cub scooted as far back as he could. "Come here, Cubby. Come to Uncle Pete."

Galen whined, ending with his "wub wub" sound.

"That's weird, he sounds like a real baby," the constable said, looking at the animal quizzically.

"Just step back and let him come out on his own," Emily said, urging Pete to take a seat again, "Let him sniff you and get to know you. I have to warn you, he likes to suck on fingers and ears."

Pete did as he was told and then asked, "What's new with Faidlee?"

"Still across the border, we assume," Daniel said.

"Teresa still in hiding?"

Emily answered, "Ila doesn't know where Teresa is but they have been in communication."

Pete bent over as the cub wandered towards him and sniffed his shoe. "What is that thing? Huh?" The constable talked to him as if he were a toddler. "What is that?"

"Anything that has happened is in the report," Emily said, watching the bear.

"Then get out of here. Junior and I will be just fine." Pete stayed bent over and playing with the cub.

"His name is Galen. I've been keeping notes on what he likes and doesn't like. It's posted on the refrigerator," Emily informed Pete. She looked like a worried mother.

"Go! Get out of here—skedaddle," Pete commanded. "And I don't want to see you back here until tomorrow afternoon."

Emily and Daniel walked outside.

"Do you want to go?" Daniel asked, hopefully. "It's going to be cold. Might even be snow in the Mountains. The Mustang isn't going to be able to handle the snow."

"I've heard that before. Then we'll just have to go as far as we can," she declared, her green eyes dancing impishly.

"Do you want to go out to dinner or eat by a campfire?"

"Oh, a campfire, please!"

Daniel hugged her. "I'll go get the tent. I've only got a single, summer sleeping bag and winter one. The other one I left at the camp. We can put the summer bag open on the bottom and spread the winter one on top."

"Are you trying to seduce me into your bed again, Officer Claret?" she asked, feigning a look of utter shock.

"Again? I don't remember the first time."

"What a thing to say!" Emily said indignantly, and started to walk away.

He laughed and caught her around the waist. "I mean I do, honest." He drew her close to him and breathed into her hair, "I remember waking up to find the most beautiful angel in heaven lying next to me."

She bit her lip and smiled up at him. "And now that you know that I'm not an angel...?"

Daniel lifted her up and kissed her with more passion.

"Daniel, no, don't! I'm sorry. I shouldn't have teased."

"Don't kiss you?" His eyes were playful.

"Don't lift me. We have to be sensible. We're not going camping—just having dinner by the fire."

His groan was cut short by her kiss.

"No PDA's on public grounds!" Pete yelled through the door and laughed as they took off like kids.

The phone rang. He picked it up and said brightly, "Oh, hello, Mrs. Harrigan. Okay, Maureen. Yes, Susanne and I had a great time. I recommend it. Good to be back, though. Thank you. No, you just missed her. She and Daniel are gone for a drive in the White Mountains. Of course she will be safe with him! No, no I don't. Pardon me? Maureen, I hold Officer Claret in the highest esteem as I do your daughter," he said, suddenly frowning. "No, I don't think that way at all."

"Maureen, your opinion isn't justified. No, that is not true. They are both adults. What?" He looked incredulously at the ceiling. "You're going to hold me responsible, for what? You're kidding, right? You're not kidding. Is Henry there?"

He held the phone away then put it back to his ear saying firmly but ill at ease, "No, I'm not going to talk her out of coming back here, if that's what she wants. I think you'd better have this conversation with your daughter. Good-bye, Mrs. Harrigan." Pete said firmly and put down the phone. His eyes went back to the cub. "I'd rather tangle with your mother than with hers."

CHAPTER 20

Snow swirled in the winds around the white capped peak of Mt. Washington.

"I think we better stick to Route 16 and head south to the Kancamagus Highway," Daniel advised. "You have a real nice horse, lady, but it's not shod for snow."

At Conway he took Route 112 West and then at Sabbaday Falls they stopped and spent an hour admiring the roaring water and beautiful foliage. Daniel decided they would have dinner in the Rocky Gorge where the landscape was more rugged and the falls not so loud. Though foliage was about at peak, there was hardly anyone around on this weekday. The tourists would seek out the colorful leaves of deciduous trees. Here, under the evergreens, they pretty much had the park to themselves.

Daniel found a space with a fire ring. It was by the brook which skirted a wall of granite. Beneath the great hemlocks and high ridges, the air was colder and Emily was glad she had worn a wool sweater. Together they gathered fallen sticks for the fire.

The sun set swiftly behind the cliffs. Daniel had the fire going and cooked marinated chicken on a stick. Emily made a salad on one of the park's picnic tables and pulled out an unopened pint of Peppermint liquor and marshmallows for dessert.

"I've had it since Christmas and brought it in case I was desperate to sleep. The trouble isn't going to sleep, it's staying asleep." She handed him the warm drink. "This seems like a better use."

Both were sticky by the time the feast was over. They went to the brook to wash their hands and faces.

"Whoo, that's cold," Emily exclaimed, shaking her hands in the stream.

"The water runs down off the mountain," Daniel said, washing briskly.

Back at the fire, she put on her parka.

"Are you warm enough?" he said, amused at her three layers of clothes.

"I will never be as cold again as I was that night we looked for you."

"You really went into the swamp to try and rescue me?" Daniel held out his arms for her.

"Even with those awful leeches." She shivered at the thought and then looked through the limbs of the trees. "It is so light out!"

Daniel pulled her closer, smiling. "Tomorrow will be the full Autumn Moon. Nohcihtowipisim."

"No-tsh-towe-wee-o-pee-sim." Emily repeated looking up at it and nestled against him. "Tell me about you. Not the Cree stories, but the real stuff."

"There isn't much to tell." He spoke into her hair.

"What was your mother like?"

"I don't remember her. People have told me she was beautiful with black hair and blue eyes." He looked at the fire as if trying to conjure up an image of her. "I don't have a picture of her."

"Do you miss her?"

"You cannot miss what you cannot remember."

She let that train of conversation go and asked, "Tell me about Rusty."

"Emily, I don't want to…"

"What did you do as two little Indian boys?" she asked, grinning up at him.

"We got into a lot of trouble."

"You? Mr. Quiet, straight man?" Emily asked in feigned disbelief.

"Well, as a matter of fact, I probably got into more trouble than you ever did," he said, pulling a strand of her hair until she felt it.

"Oh, I never got into trouble. I was a perfect child," she claimed and took another sip of the peppermint liquor.

"I don't believe that," he said, wrapping his arms around her.

"Well, maybe just a little. I got caught playing with matches."

"All kids get caught playing with matches."

"Yeah but the matches also included a little Fort McHenry cannon my uncle gave me, BB's and gunpowder."

"I've seen one of those. It's a toy. It just snaps when you put a cap in it."

"Ah but for the child with an inquisitive mind, it can do so much more, like shoot a hole in the hot water heater."

"You could have killed yourself. How did you…" He leaned back against the tree laughing.

"You know that barrel is just big enough that a BB can go into it. Scrape enough gun powder off the caps, a little tissue wadding, drill a hole for a fire cracker fuse, add a match and voila—you have a flooding basement."

"Ow, that hurts," he said, laughing so hard there were tears in his eyes.

"I couldn't sit down for a week." She loved watching him laugh but tried to stop him because of his side. "Okay, Mr. 'By-the-Book', your turn."

"I don't think I can top that." He chuckled, wiping his eyes with his thumb.

"Sure you can." She took another drink of the warming peppermint liquor and handed it to him.

He took a small sip, and then screwed the top on. Keeping her circled in his arms he began, "Once there was this time…"

"Go on," she urged playfully.

"You won't like this," he warned.

"Try me."

"Rusty and I decided to climb up this tree to shake a porcupine out of it."

"Why would you do that?"

"I told you, you wouldn't like it. It was just a guy, kid—whatever possessed us, I don't know," he looked up at the bright moon, hoping for an answer.

"Well, go on, tell the story," she encouraged him and took the liquor back.

"Anyway, it had been snowing. We started up this tree, me in the front, Rusty behind me. He always made me go first. I guess he was afraid I'd back out of it. The more we climbed, the higher the porcupine climbed until it couldn't go any further. Ah, hah, we thought we had him. I gave that old branch a good shaking," he said, shaking her arm.

"Then what happened?"

"The porcupine started backing down the tree," he answered with a laugh, as he remembered the look on Rusty's face. "Rusty and I started to scramble down that tree as fast as we could."

Emily was enjoying the story now. "Did he get you?"

"Well, that wasn't the whole problem. Half way down the tree, we looked down and another, bigger, porcupine was coming up it."

Emily rolled over on her stomach laughing and gasped, "What did you do?"

"Well," Daniel said seriously and made a futile throwing motion, "We kept trying to hit the one below us with snow balls. But eventually we ran out of snow on the branches we could reach."

Emily was breathless, she was laughing so hard.

"And the one up top just kept coming down and the one below just kept coming up, with me and Rusty in the middle."

Emily was hysterical.

Daniel laughed at her, taking the bottle away, "No more drink for you tonight, young lady."

Emily cleared her throat and tried to give him a somewhat concerned look, but then giggled, "How did you ever escape?"

"Eventually we climbed out on a limb and jumped," Daniel said matter-of-factly, and caught her when she tried to crawl off, gasping with laughter. He sat her back down between his knees and confided, "I would like to say it was a controlled jump, but by the time we got enough courage to execute a proper evacuation of the tree, it turned out to be more of a fall through the branches."

"Did you get hurt?" she said giggling, with teary eyes glistening in the fire light.

"It doesn't sound like you would care much, if we did."

"No, seriously," she said, waving her hand making a poor attempt to actually be serious.

"Only after we got home—Anna was so mad at us. We had our school clothes on. She took that broom and kept swinging it at us and if she had ever made contact I think it would have killed the two of us, but you know how short Anna is…"

Emily nodded with a fit of giggling.

"Every time she swung that broom, we'd jump over it. That made her even madder and she tried swinging it the other way. For me and Rusty it was a matter of survival at that point. We got pretty good at hopping over that broom backwards until Anna got tired of swinging it."

"Oh, I've got to get a tissue," Emily said as she pushed away from him and got up. "I don't know when I've ever laughed this hard."

"It has been a long time for me too." He wondered if he had ever laughed like this in his whole life, even with Rusty.

Emily blew her nose and then came out of the tent with the straight stick Daniel had found for her to walk with.

"Show me how you and Rusty jumped over the broom," she said, waving the branch.

Daniel got up, saying with a warning smile. "Drop the stick and put your hands in the air."

"Oh, come on."

"My slightly inebriated love, you're not going to be swinging that at me." He caught the stick in a movement she hardly saw, and took it from her hands, before she even knew it was gone.

"How did you do that?" Emily looked at her empty hands in wonder. "Show me how you did that."

"Country boys can't give up all their secrets especially to city ladies."

"Who says I'm a lady?" she said, grinning up at him.

"Oh, boy…" He looked at her with an unsure smile. "All right, I'll show you how we jumped backwards over the stick. Rusty and I used to practice this, to get ready for Anna's assaults." He put the stick behind his back, holding it with his hands close to his sides. In a quick and graceful movement, he shoved the stick down, to the back of his sneaker heels and jumped over it so that the stick was still in his hands, but in front of him.

Emily clapped. "That's neat! Can you teach me how to do that?"

"Not tonight, little one," he said, wincing, and tossed the stick away. "Come back to the fire."

He sat down on the blanket and she curled up in his arms staring at the flames for a long time. Seriousness settled on her face. "You miss Rusty terribly, don't you?"

"Yes."

"Tell me about him."

Emily was surprised when he began to talk.

"There wasn't any malice in him. He saw humor in everything. He could even make my father laugh. Everyone loved him, old people, young people, children—everyone. My father did not want him to join the service. He said he was naive about war. He wanted me to join. Finally, Dad gave in to him, knowing he was going to do it anyway."

"How was he killed?"

"They were parked outside a mosque. Rusty took his Kevlar vest off because it was too hot in the Hummer. A sniper must have been watching. He died instantly. I should have done what my father said. I should have been the one to go. It should have been me who died, not him."

"Why would you say such a thing?" Emily asked with all giddy effects of the alcohol gone.

"Rusty was more my father's son than I was. He also had a mother he should not have left." Daniel stated without emotion.

Emily curled up against his left side. "Don't say that."

Slowly he lifted her chin to see streaks of tears glittering in the fire light. He kissed her eyes and then her mouth softly. "Can you really love me that much?"

"I love you more." She settled back into his arms and they talked about their lives and dreams for hours. The waxing moon was beginning its descent when, almost in mid sentence, her eyes blinked, and then closed. Daniel was content holding her, watching her face in sleep and smiled when she started to snore. He could have held her all night but the fire needed wood and his first duty was to keep her warm. He tried to tenderly lift her up.

Emily was the cold dead nurse, lying naked in the basement under a clear sheet of plastic. The dark figure of a man was coming down the steps to her once more. She could think and feel and her only thought was to get away, back to her children. But she couldn't move. He kept coming. Then he was standing over her. She tried so hard to move. Something was holding her down. If she didn't move now she could never go home.

"No!" Emily screamed, her hands flailing towards him, catching his cheek with her fingernail.

"Apisci-mosos. It's okay. Wake up!"
She struggled against Daniel's arms and afraid he would hurt her, he released her.
"Emily!" He shouted as she twisted away then fell forward, towards the fire, her hand in the coals. He grabbed her to him and she woke up, the side of her hand smarting.
She looked up at Daniel, saw the cut on his cheek and realized what she had done.
"Oh, God, Daniel. I'm so sorry." She touched his face, crying. "I'm so sorry."
"It's all right Apisci-mosos; let me see your hand. Emily, let me see it." He took it forcibly. The side of it had a blister forming already. He tried to pick her up to take her to the cold brook but she wouldn't let him and walked down to the water with him, apologizing the whole time.
He put her hand in the icy water and held it there.
"Oh, Daniel, how bad did I scratch you?"

"No more than a willow branch in the dark. I know how you hate the cold water, but hold your hand there a little longer." He took off his jacket and shirt. Tearing his undershirt, he wrapped it around her hand. "It's clean."

She held the make-shift bandage to her nose, "It smells like you. What would you want with a nut like me?"

"You are not a nut. It is the dead, as Anna says. They want you to be there for them, speak for them. You would be greatly honored in Anna's tribe but it is a gift that draws the life out of the giver."

"That's crazy."

"No, this is crazy." He held up her bandaged hand. "You are being tormented. We'll use the police psychiatrist. I'm going with you."

"You need to stay to help Galen."

"To hell with the bear!"

"Don't say that Daniel." She laid her head against him. "If I see the psychiatrist—if I'm considered unstable—how am I going to defend myself in court?"

"Maybe you can't. People will believe what they want to."

"I only wanted to stop that child from killing himself. He was so young. He had his whole life ahead of him." She sobbed, her face buried in his arms.

"I know, Apisci-mosos. The only thing which concerns me is the fact that you can't keep up with this lack of sleep and the stress of these nightmares. Anna is afraid the dead will take you with them. I am beginning to think she is right. I can't lose you."

Emily's tears ceased. With the sound of the brook and wind in the pines, they were quiet and content to be in each other's arms. But the night grew colder. Daniel spoke around three in the morning, "Come on, we'll head back to town. Neither one of us can sleep but I know you're not going to go along with another idea I have."

"Does it have to do with that little motel we passed?" She looked up at him. "Be patient, for both of us, my love."

"Just call me Job."

~~~~~

196

They returned to town around seven o'clock that morning. Pete's cell phone number was on the door in case of an emergency. Through the window they could see the cub was asleep in his cage. Without going inside Daniel called Pete on his cell phone, knowing he was usually up at that time but that Susanne and the kids weren't.

"What are you guys doing back already?" Pete said, sounding surprised.

"What's going on?"

"What do you mean?" Pete returned the question.

"Sounds like a chain saw," Daniel handed the phone to Emily to listen.

"I'm just cutting up a little wood here," Pete shouted into the phone.

"You go ahead," Daniel replied. "I'm going to drop some things off at the house and I'll be at the office." Daniel flipped his cell phone shut. "He's getting his wood in for the winter."

"So why do you have that look?" she asked.

"What look?" He exaggerated a frown.

"The one before the fake one?"

"It's just that, getting Anna's and my wood in for the winter is something I need to do before long."

"That's right," she remembered somberly, "you don't have any other kind of heat."

He didn't ask if he could drive but took the wheel, his mind elsewhere. Emily didn't mind if he wanted to drive the Mustang from now on.

"How can you cut wood?" she asked.

Daniel said nothing but slowed the car, trying to size up the situation. "That's Pete's car and George's truck."

Emily smiled as she opened up the window and heard the sound of chain saws going. She said happily, "Sounds like maybe your problem is being solved as we speak."

Daniel got out of the car and walked over to Pete, who had brought down his hydraulic wood splitter on the back of his tractor and was slicing cylinders of wood into fourths. Pete's father and George were running chainsaws with hard hats and ear protectors, so they were oblivious to their arrival. Joe was there too, and his friend Ike. They were taking armfuls to the shed out back and loading it.

Pete shut off the tractor, which eased the noise a little. He waved to his father to turn off the chainsaws. Suddenly all was quiet.

"Pete, I don't know what to say," Daniel looked at piles of wood, already split.

Pete's father came over and lifted off his hard hat with the attached ear protectors. His clothes were covered with chips of wood and he was grinning as he said, "Hey son, good to see you up and moving."

"Thank you. Emily, this is Pete's father, Bill Hines." Daniel hastened to introduce her.

"I know this little girl," he exclaimed, and kissed her on the cheek. He smelled like gasoline and chain saw oil, "but she's not so little anymore. Good to see you, Emmy. Tell your Dad I'm going to be heading down his way for some ice fishing this winter. Is he going to put his shanty out?"

"I don't know. You guys better stop talking about fishing and start doing it," she admonished him with a grin.

"I don't know how I can repay you for this." Daniel looked awkwardly at them all.

"Like you wouldn't do it for us? What did you do to your face? Did Emmy do that to you?" Pete looked at the others smiling, pretending to know some secret they didn't.

"Tree limbs can get in the way. I'll never forget this." Daniel said humbly.

"How do you like my wood splitter?" Pete changed the subject, uncomfortable with the gratitude.

"Nice. I'll have to think about getting one when I'm old."

"Very funny! Hey, everybody! Daniel made a joke!" Pete shouted.

There was a chorus of masculine woos and good-natured derisiveness. Emily hugged Pete. "How is Galen?"

"He's been a good guy. I gave him a long walk yesterday afternoon, and this morning. The kids and I took him all around town. I think his belly's full from all the handouts."

So much for wilderness rehab, Emily thought, but smiled gratefully at Pete and asked, "What can I do to help?"

"What did you do to your hand?"

"Just a little burn from the campfire. It's fine."

"Anything you feel like doing. Last night we filled Anna's shed. We just have to finish Daniel's. We could use some coffee and some breakfast soon?" He asked it like he wasn't sure she'd be happy about taking on this domestic role.

Emily grinned and got back in the car. "Need to get eggs. Be right back."

"And you, Daniel, can work the splitter lever. Ah, ah, ah! Take it like a man."

That night Daniel walked Emily to her car and held the door open for her.

She brushed off the wood chips and got in. "I'm going to leave at the end of the week. I need to do this alone and you need to work with Galen for me."

He squatted so he was face to face with her in the window. "That only leaves us tomorrow."

"I know, but Pete has returned and I want to get this done and get back here."

He looked at her seriously, "Before you go, I want to make a commitment to you."

"I'd like that." She smiled.

His heart leapt with happiness. By her consent, it seemed that she had already said 'yes'. "I have to work until six tomorrow night. Would you meet me at the cabin then?"

"I'll pack, take Galen for a dinner walk, and be there at six."

"I don't want you out in the woods after dark."

"I promise I'll come in before it gets dark." She kissed him.

"I love you and I am proud of you for your decision to get help. But I don't want to lose you."

"You will never lose me. Someday you may be sorry you said that."

CHAPTER 21

Freed from his leash, Galen padded along in his flat footed stride, sniffing, turning rocks and dead branches over as he went. He seemed to have grown since yesterday. When she would get him out of the cage there still would be the moment of finger or ear sucking and pawing. However, she could sense him becoming more independent.

"Galen, what do you have?" Emily asked, walking over to him. She watched as the cub ate dirt. "Is that good? It doesn't look good. Are you after a root? No, it's the dirt, your just eating dirt. Whoops, there goes a worm with it. Was that yummy?" She screwed up her nose and sat down next to the bear. "I think that worm just got in the way of the dirt, that's what I think." Emily scratched behind the cub's ear, happy and hopeful.

The sun was lower on the horizon, making the tributaries of the swamp below shimmer as if gilded. She and the bear maneuvered down the steep hillside. Emily looked at her watch. She had promised Daniel that she would be back before dark. There was still time to satiate Galen's appetite at Symond's orchard. At the bottom of the hill she turned right.

Emily was filled with joy, thinking about tonight and the commitment Daniel wanted to make to her. She wanted to run up the grassy road. But Daniel said that running with the bear wasn't a good thing to do. Even as a cub, he might get over excited with the chase and confuse her with prey. So she walked briskly, arms swinging and calling to Galen if he went off the trail too far. A thrush piped in the pines. It was a beautiful melodious call. Emily tried to imitate it. The bear cub looked up at her, his little eyes attentive, his head slightly turned, listening.

Galen wandered into the sea of berries and was happily licking off the fruit. He'd look at her from time to time as if conveying that this was the good stuff. Then he would shut his eyes and nose into the brambles for more.

"Better than ants?" Emily asked him, picking some of the fruit for herself.

The cub seemed to smile with his rubbery lips as he continued to pick off the berries. They were everywhere, but like a kid, he moved deeper into the prickly thicket for the biggest bunches.

A sound made her pause and listen. It sounded like waves of yelps. It took her a minute to identify the sound of hounds on a chase. Though she had not actually heard dogs bay in pursuit, she knew what it was. This was not barking but a high pitched, haunting rhythm of a predatory pack, growing louder as they loped towards her.

"Galen," Emily called, looking around for the cub. He was nuzzling deeper into the arched vines. "Galen, come over here," she said, fishing for the leash in her pocket.

The baying was coming this way. A flock of migrating cedar waxwings flew out of an old crab apple tree, sensing danger.

Her heart beat faster. She walked towards Galen but he was moving farther into the thicket, having found what he wanted to fill the empty space in his tummy. "Galen, come here," she tried to keep her voice calm.

How could the hounds tell the difference between a big bear and a baby cub? They couldn't. They would run whatever was in their path, run it to death.

"Galen!" her voice grew desperate as she tried to follow him through the thorny brambles. The baying grew louder. But the cub, never having seen a mother bears' reaction to this sound, didn't seem to notice or care. His eyes were on a juicy clump of raspberries a little farther away.

"Galen. Come here!" she screamed frantically. Her face and hands were being torn by the sharp needles of the vines. Emily continued to struggle towards the cub.

And then the dogs were on them. She wrenched free of the tearing thorns, time and again, as she tried to reach the bear. Twisting out of her snared coat, she frantically climbed through the vines, shouting the cub's name as the dogs ran past her.

At first Galen just arched his back like a cat and stared at them. But as one bite after another penetrated his heavy fur, he turned and started to run.

"The tree!" Emily screamed, the thorns tearing into her flesh now. "Run to the tree!"

It was as if he understood her and with the hounds nipping at him, he started up a pine. He went up it a few feet and stopped, then tried another couple of lunges upward. The teeth of one leaping dog found him and lacking the muscle development to keep his weight close to the tree, he fell back into the pack. His panicked cries were like that of a small child.

Emily picked up a stick and ran into the pack of dogs tearing at the cub. Screaming, she hit one animal after another, but the drive of the kill was boiling inside them. They were supposed to just tree a bear, make it a target to be shot, but they'd never had an animal fall into their midst and it was small and did not fight back like a full grown bear.

By the time the dog hunters arrived and shot into the air to stop the horrifying attack, the cub lay torn, bleeding and bawling. She knelt beside it and its small eyes were on hers.

"You okay, lady?" Josh Anderson said.

She didn't answer, putting her hand on the bloody fur. The cub kept crying.

"You want us to shoot it—get it out of its misery?" Josh asked.

She nodded slowly for the cub's intestines were spilled on the ground.

"You're going to have to move then." Bailey Wigman spat out tobacco juice on the ground next to the cub.

She studied the spit, squinting as if she couldn't understand what it was. When she didn't move Josh hauled her up by the arm and dragged her a few feet away.

She wrenched herself free in time to hear the gun go off.

With a furious scream, she swung back to the cub in time to see his feet stop pawing the air, stop trying to run away. Inside her, hatred erupted for all those who had ever hurt an innocent being. The dead, living within her, broke their chains, and burst forth with a cry of vengeance from her lips. She rushed at Bailey, knocking the gun from his hands and hitting him in the face.

Josh Anderson tried to grab her arm. She swung around, and stared at the man, her eyes so full of hate that he backed away.

"You crazy bitch!" Bailey rubbed his grizzled cheek, picked up his gun, and called the dogs.

The dogs trotted around them, antennae jiggling from their collars, red foamy tongues and tails wagging with expectation of a reward. One was limping, throttled hardest by her stick.

Emily dropped to her knees, once more, beside the cub.

"Bailey, it's that warden woman," Josh Anderson whispered. "She's going to know we got our bears already."

"Will you shut up? It's just a cub!" He looked at Emily. "We were just exercising the dogs."

Emily said nothing. Her mind was emptying of them. They were talking faces only.

"It was just an accident, right, lady?" Josh said.

"You know I could bring you up on assault charges," Baileys spat again, his pride hurt more than his face.

Josh squinted at Emily. "She doesn't look so good. Maybe the dogs bit her. The dogs bite you?"

Emily said nothing.

"Nawh, they didn't bite her," Bailey said, wiping the tobacco from his lip. "Lady you gotta' get to know the facts of life out here. These things happen. If that cub had been where it was suppose to be, up that tree, this wouldn't have happened. Come on, Josh."

"I don't know if we should leave her like this."

"Come on, Josh! She'll get over it," Bailey insisted, still rubbing his cheek. They called the dogs and left.

Emily knelt. Her fingers idly pawed at the earth, her eyes on the dead cub. The trees seemed to move away from her, out of her sight.

Her mind was seeing the little hand protruding above the leaves at Bow Park, the face of the nurse twisted in horror, the boy's sad blue eyes as he pulled the trigger, the cub and many others. These images whirled about her head.

Emily began clawing the ground with her hands, then used stones and sticks. Soon she was covered in dirt and her fingernails black.

The more the images flashed by her, screaming for revenge, the harder she dug, scraping at the earth with raw hands, tearless yet gasping for breath. She wanted to stop their screams in her mind, and she cursed with effort to pull stones from the grave. She would bury the bear, bury the child—bury them all! Then she wouldn't have to think about them anymore. It was just too hard to keep them with her. She could not survive it. She couldn't fix them. She couldn't fix all the wrong in this world. Emily dug harder.

They would go into this grave and she wouldn't have to think about them anymore. Thoughts of anything else, besides these macabre images, began to jumble, make no sense.

There was no present tense but the grave itself. Sanity would fly through her mind like a leaf in a wind storm, impossible to catch hold of. A tree root became a barrier to her nothingness. She clawed it, hacked it with the rock, pulled on it. It wouldn't budge. She'd simply have to dig more to the left. Emily desperately tore at the soil. Her eyes were dry and determined while she bludgeoned the breast of the earth. The flesh of her hands became torn, but she did not feel pain. All sensation was leaving her.

The more she crashed her stone against the earth, the more her mind relaxed into an unfeeling world where the only thing she saw was the widening hole beneath her. Only physical now, void of thought, she dug, relishing the blankness of mind. She clawed, exhaustion eliminating all memories. All thoughts were gone but the need to dig this grave. No more pain. If she buried the cub there would be no more pain. Her thoughts could not transcend this moment. They would all be in the grave and she would be at peace. She wouldn't have to think of them anymore.

It was dark by the time she had the hole big enough, but she had one last conscious act to do. Trying to be as gentle as possible, she felt for the lifeless bear-child, pulling him to the hole and eased him in. Breathing like something wild and beaten, something ready to collapse from exertion she scratched the excavated dirt over the dead ones, all of the innocent ones. Once done, she patted the earth and caressed the surface smooth, tossing aside any stone that might blemish her perfect monument, her memorial to all the victims who had lived in her mind. Her bloody hands massaged the dirt with love, as if it were a garden plot, which she would leave forever behind her. Emily lay against the mound, her breath slowing. There was a peaceful smile on her lips. She had succeeded.

When she lifted her head, the bear, the child, all of them were gone from her mind. Everything was gone. Slowly she started to walk down the dark, moon-lit trail, only because it was the path of least resistance. She had no idea where she was going. Not one thought could stay in her mind; they would flit by her, like moths, unrecognizable. A thought would be there but vanished before she could grasp it. As she moved through the darkness and she eventually just stopped thinking, stopped caring, and stopped walking. She stood still. There was nothing left to do.

~~~~~

"You're still here?" Daniel walked into the office and put the remaining 'No wheeled vehicle' signs back on the shelf.

"Yeah, where have you been?" Pete said, looking up from his magazine.

"I told you I had to drop those signs off with the Reynolds."

"Oh, I thought you were out with Emmy and the bear."

Daniel looked at the empty cage and his heart thudded in his chest. "They're not back yet?"

"Guess not."

"She promised me."

Pete put down the magazine slowly. He had never seen such emotion in Daniel's face.

"She promised me she would be back before dark!"

"Whoa, I'm sure they're okay, probably went to visit Anna."

Daniel was unlocking a rifle from the gun cabinet.

"It's not even six o'clock. Aren't we overreacting just a little?"

"Pete, she promised me."

"Daniel, you got to understand something about women, they change their minds."

"Not Emily. Not after last night."

"Damn it, Daniel. I'm supposed to be at the kid's school play at seven. I'm sure she is with Anna. Maybe she is at the cabin."

"You go on." Daniel released him from any obligation.

"Maybe she took a wrong turn. Here, take a flashlight."

Daniel shook his head. "The moon is full. It is a clear night."

Leaving the truck at the station, so his eyes would adjust to the dark sooner, he went to Anna's first.

Anna knew by his look what was wrong. "You must let her go, Daniel," she cried. "If she is to come back to you, you must let her go."

Daniel turned angrily away from Anna, not understanding her words or wanting to. He ran to his cabin next but it was dark. Her car was parked there, packed with her suitcase and hanging clothes, but the engine was not warm. He realized that she had intended to stay at the cabin tonight and his heart felt it would burst from his chest.

There was no sign of Emily or Galen anywhere around the cabin. He ran to the path and hurried down the steep trail. The water of the swamp glistened in the moonlight. A moose stood in the wet grasses, chewing. It sensed Daniel's descent and uttered a rapid 'hey, hey, hey', sound. A female was with him.

"Mooswa nistes, Akawac n'kaskihtan ci-pimohteyan." *Brother moose, I can hardly walk I am so winded.* Do not fear me. I am not going to chase after your beautiful woman." Daniel said in a quiet voice and the huge animal dropped his head into the grass again.

At the bottom he hesitated, making a choice. He knew she wanted to go to the 'ageless face'. Maybe she tried. Perhaps the trickster used the moon to tempt her. The boulders were large and the path to the waterfalls was difficult. It would be easy for someone inexperienced to turn an ankle. He searched the ground with his eyes, his breath leaving his chest in painful puffs of vapor in the cold air. Walking a few steps each way, he found the darker indents of a small bear's paw leading to Symonds orchard and he began to run once more. It could have been yesterday's print but he made his choice by it. He was almost at the orchard when the moonlight revealed a figure kneeling on the path.

"Apisci-mosos?" Daniel started to walk towards the figure as if it were a ghost which might suddenly vanish.

He dropped the rifle. The woman kneeling before him was Emily, but she did not speak. She did not look at him, but remained motionless, as if he wasn't there. Her hair was in tangles, her face and hands were bloody and dirty and her clothes were torn.

"Apisci-mosos?" Daniel took her face in his hands, but she did not respond to him. Her body was like a board and her eyes were fixed on nothing.

He took her raw hands. "Tell me what happened!"

There was no reply.

Daniel put his arms around her staring into the darkness from which she had come. She remained stiff against him, where only the day before, her body had curved into his. Anger welled up in him. "Was it Faidlee?"

Had any soul, guilty or not, moved toward them from the woods, Daniel would have murdered with his bare hands. But no one came. All was quiet. He could not even hear her breathing.

Daniel clenched his teeth, eyes welling with tears and shook her shoulders. "You see me! You must see me!"

His breathing became more labored with despair and he cast angry eyes towards the sky, shouting, "What is it you want from me? You take all I have! Just take me! Leave her alone! How can you do this to her? She trusts in you. If you want me to suffer, fine! Send your worst, but leave her alone, leave them all alone. I am the one you have cursed from the beginning. I deserve this, they do not!"

Daniel held her close, rocking her body but she did not react. He put his hand against her face, lifting it so that he might meet her eyes. The moonlight cast a deathly glare on what had been warm green pools of life. It was as if she wasn't there anymore. There was no one inside her.

He closed his eyes in anguish. "Why? God, why? "

When he opened his eyes, they rested on the gold circle hanging by a chain inside Emily's torn shirt. The moonlight made it glow like a tiny orb. Carefully picking it up, he squinted at the figure in the center of the medal and whispered, "Meriyana nikaawiy? *Mother Mary*? He won't hear me, Mother. Please ask Him for me. He is deaf to me. Beg your son to help me, Meriyana. I cannot do this without Him, my Mother!"

A drum beat started. Was it his heart, or the drumming of a grouse? He stopped breathing, and looked around.

"Look at me!"

He stared in Emily's face. But she did not move; her eyes were void of feeling. The beat continued softly, as he searched for the voice who had called him.

"Taaniyal, look at me!" The voice came again from a great distance. Now it sounded like Rusty.

"Rusty?" he questioned, puzzled by the realization that all of this, which looked so real, existed only in his own mind. Or did it? Where was the drumming coming from? He closed his eyes. When he opened them, a giant bear stood before him. Startled, he almost let go of Emily, but grasped her to him, bending over her, trying to protect her from the bear.

Rusty, as a child, was calling him. "Taaniyal, look at the bear."

Daniel looked up. The animal was fierce and glowing. Beside him, Rusty was motioning to Daniel to come. Maskwa raised its great forepaw sweeping at the moon, scattering the stars.

Then Rusty was right in front of him, reaching for him. "Run to Maskwa! Run! Maskwa is in the light. Kika-kiskinohtahitinaawaw! *I will guide you!*"

"Rusty?"

The pounding of the drum beat got louder.

"Come, Taaniyal, look at me! Come with me to Maskwa. Run hard, Run very hard. Don't be afraid. Stay with me!" The child seemed to pull on Daniel's hand. He felt it.

"Rusty, let go! I need to let you go."

"Taaniyal, come with me. If you run hard you can come with me." Rusty laughed and tried to take Daniels hand again, but Daniel pulled it away before Rusty could touch him.

"I can't Rusty. Go. Go now, alone. I will come later, my brother."

The bear began to shrink until there was only the boy. Rusty waved good—bye with a grin and ran to the figure of a woman in the distance.

Daniel felt he could barely breathe when the drum beat faded.

"Daniel, look at me!" The voice came again.

He looked down at Emily, lightheaded.

She remained void of all expression.

Suddenly the memory came flooding back. "Daniel, look at me!"

It was the morning at the cabin. The pain was so great he had wanted to die. Emily's voice, her eyes locked on his, holding him onto the earth, "Daniel, look at me!"

And then Daniel knew what he had to do. "I'm so sorry, Apiscimosos."

He kissed her, laid her on the ground and removed her tattered clothes, aching that this was the way he would first see her body. Then he removed his clothes and picking her up, walking slowly into the cold swamp water, the moon bathing their bodies with golden light.

Daniel waded until he was waist deep in the wilted grasses, his bare feet on the matted roots. The moose, though fifty yards away, lifted their great heads and watched. Once more he cried to the heavens for help then slowly lowered her body into icy water. He had to let her go so that she might come back to him. Her face drifted below the surface, her hair a golden halo around her. An eternity passed.

Emily came up out of the water with a cry of self preservation, coughing and breathing hard. She saw Daniel and those once blank, green eyes held accusation.

He grabbed her to him laughing and crying at the same time. "I thought you were lost to me forever."

She gasped, crying, "What are you doing? Daniel, I'm so cold—I'm so cold. What did you—why?"

He picked her up, and waded out of the water, crying aloud with joy, "Thank you, Meriyana nikaawiy."

"What's wrong?" Emily demanded of him, as he quickly tried to dress her, and himself. "Why were we in the water? Where is Galen? Why are you naked?"

He glanced back at the cold water with frustration. "Believe me, this is not the way I wanted you to see me the first time. We must get dressed before we freeze. Lift your foot, Apisci-mosos. Help me get your pants on. They are dry. They will warm you. We need to get up the hill, to the cabin."

"Daniel what is going on?" She held onto him for balance. "Why am I naked?"

"You are naked? I am trying not to notice. Here, put your shirt on, quickly."

He put his jacket around her. "I will explain when we get home. Come Apisci—mosos. I need you to help me get up the hill. " He knew that needing her help would penetrate the confusion in her mind.

"Are you all right? Daniel, are you okay. What are we doing down here?"

"I need you, Apisci-mosos. Together we must climb the hill. Okay? You'll help me?"

"Oh, Lamb. Of course I'll help you." She squinted at the moon resting in the tops of the trees. "It is so light out here."

"It's the moon."

"I've never seen it so big." She stared at it and her face became stricken for her memory began to return. "Nohcihtowipisim! The Autumn moon! The campfire! Oh, Daniel—Galen—the dogs!"

"Emily, I need your help to get to the top."

Holding back the desire to cry, she put her arm around him and together they slowly ascended the path back to the cabin. Neither of them spoke, neither of them could. At the top of the hill Emily stopped.

"What is it?"

"I'm not going in," she said with resolve.

"Why?" He looked both confused and hurt, "Emily, why?"

"Don't be angry. I won't be gone long, but I have to find out why this happened to me." She laid her head against his chest.

"I am afraid you won't come back," he spoke into her hair with misery.

"I will, I promise. But I have to go right now."

He held her to him. "I thought I had lost you. I cannot bear losing you again."

"Daniel," she whispered, "I will never be anyone's but yours. But why did I shut down like that? My mind still can't seem to focus on anything. Everything is jumbled."

"The despair took you," he explained simply. "But you are all right now."

"I can't be a part of your life. I can't be a part of an investigative team. I can't be anything to anyone until I come to grips with this, find out why it happened and if it will happen again," she said, gulping a breath as a tremor shook her whole body. "I have to go—now—or I won't go. I may not be able to talk to you for awhile."

He pushed her back and studied her face frowning. "Why can't you talk to me?"

Emily took off his jacket and handed it to him. "Because the first time I hear your voice I will weaken and run back to you," she choked on her tears but managed to explain, "It would be so easy to just stay with you, ignore what happened. I should have gone for help in the beginning."

"Then we would not know each other. I'll come with you!"

"This is something I have to do by myself. If I have to, I'll put myself in that hospital for awhile, that retreat—to help—to think."

He tried to hold her but she backed away.

"I will do anything and everything to get back to you as quick as possible. Just give me a little time to work this out. My mind is in turmoil right now. I need to figure things out on my own, but I don't know how. I don't know anything except that I want to tear things up with my bare hands. I want to break windows, and break them and break them—I have to go." She got into the Mustang. "I will write you. As soon as I know what is going on, I will write."

He caught the car door, gazing into her eyes with hope. "I will write you tomorrow and every day after. I promise not to interfere. But as soon as I hear from you, a hundred letters of my love will descend on you. But tonight, Emily, let me drive you. You don't realize what happened to you."

"Daniel, I can do this. I know I can. Believe me, I am focused on doing this. I can drive. Just don't give up on me, please."

"All right, then I'll follow you. God has given you back to me." He held onto the door though she started the engine. "I will give you until Thanksgiving. If I don't hear from you by then I am coming to get you, but tonight, let me follow you down—make sure you get there. I'm going to get the truck. Emily, please wait!"

He had run only a few feet to get his truck at the station when she drove away.

CHAPTER 22

When Emily left Daniel, she didn't stop in Mica for the last of her things. She was so focused on getting back to Manchester that she was afraid a side trip might break her resolve. Arriving in the city, she went to her apartment to clean up, but did not go in, feeling watched, even at this midnight hour. Her suspicion was not without reason for a man sat in a parked car, possibly an unfortunate rookie assigned the graveyard shift by the press.

She was without means to call the police psychiatrist. Kaskitesiw had claimed two of her cell phones, one in the swamp, the other probably buried with the little bear. She could go to her parents and call but she couldn't face her father's concern and her mother's overwrought reaction to her sudden arrival with scratched face, and torn clothes. Maureen would blame Daniel and Emily knew she would lose her self-control, completely. For some reason, she despised both her parents right now, but had no idea why she felt this way.

So Emily waited out in front of Bradford's office, dozing in the car. The secretary arrived at seven forty five and Dr. Bradford at eight. By eleven o'clock she was admitted to St. Claire's.

With its barred windows, orderlies and truly ill people who existed in a state of limbo, Emily immediately decided she didn't belong there, that she had made a mistake. When she told Dr. Bradford this, he simply said that was a good sign. After that she didn't see him to discuss anything for almost two weeks.

When the initial panic of confinement eased, Emily realized that her emotions were out of control, and St. Claire's was a safe place where she owed no one a reason to cry. Crying, sleeping, screaming, anything was okay here and Emily indulged in all of them.

She stayed secluded, out of touch with everyone, only asking the hospital to let her parents and Daniel know she was safe. When Emily wasn't grieving, she was sleeping hours on end, at all times of the day. After two weeks of this, one morning she woke but did not turn over greedy for sleep, for escape. She got up, showered, and had breakfast.

Dr. Bradford found her and said they were ready to talk now.

She was surprised to find her anger, sadness and guilt went back even further than she thought. In an effort to be her father's "partner" and "rescue" him from her mother's disdain, she had crept into his den as a young child and studied his gruesome reports. These images remained with her. Her hope of fixing what was wrong in her family, led her to try and fix what was wrong in her father's cruel and terrifying world. It wasn't enough to solve a homicide; she wanted to stop it from ever happening. Emily suffered tremendous guilt and sadness when she could not.

Concerning her mental and physical "shutting down", as she called it, Bradford had an answer. The psychiatrist, who had served in the military, explained that she experienced "disassociation" triggered by Galen's death. With soldiers who experienced this condition under the stress of battle, it was usually marked by paralyzing grief and culpability when a fellow soldier died. That which they could not control or fix shattered them. They were forced, by their own minds, to relive these traumatic situations nightly, through horrible dreams, until fatigue affected the way they performed their duties. Misunderstood, they were often branded as cowards.

Bradford said physical or mental abuse as a child was a common thread in the soldier's affliction, and Emily argued that she had never been abused. He said that she had, in a subtle way, for her parents were dependent upon her to keep them together. When they didn't get along, she felt it was her fault. Through exercises designed to confront her effigial parents with this truth, Emily found herself freed of their dependant hold and with a renewed ability to love them for who they were.

Dr. Bradford didn't laugh when Emily told him of Anna's diagnosis that the dead wanted her to come with them. In her case, he said it could certainly manifest itself in that manner. It was her need to nurture, project empathy, which caused her to feel failure when people died in spite of her efforts.

When she asked him if this "disassociation" would ever happen again, Bradford was serious when he said that after therapy, probably not, but she might want to consider another line of work; one in which she could use her nurturing and empathetic qualities on the living instead of the dead. A month ago she would have been defensive about keeping the job which was passed down to her by her father, and which she was good at. Now she told the doctor she would take his advice into consideration.

After a month at St. Claire's, she could see Dr. Bradford as an out-patient. Emily walked out of the hospital full of hope and expectation, eager to renew her relationship with Daniel and face the challenges ahead. But instead of a joyful emergence, Emily walked into a world of grief and chaos.

The second week in November, the trial began. Emily stayed at her parents because the press had staked out her apartment. She had to be content with the clothes she had packed in the Mustang.

Her parents were tremendously supportive, opening up her old room until Emily felt ready to return to Kaskitesiw. Emily wanted to be with Daniel more than ever, and wrote to him expressing how she felt like a woman freed of her own enslavement. No letter came back.

Meanwhile, the male prosecutor for Cathleen Droger found out about Emily being under psychiatric care and made a great deal of her 'irresponsibility' as a police woman. At the trial, he expounded that Emily pushed Alex Droger over the edge, so that he had committed suicide rather than surrender. This made the papers and Bailey Wigman apparently could read. With encouragement from the prosecutor, Mr. Wigman showed up to claim Emily assaulted him. Under oath, she admitted to striking Wigman once. This, along with the dog hunter's baleful account of the madwoman beating him and his dogs, took root in the mind of the jury. Emily admitted it had been the wrong thing to do, and that she had acted irrationally as a police officer. It was the truth, but now Wigman was ready to sue her as well.

The prosecutor would not allow the school principal's testimony that Cathleen Droger had been advised four times to arrange for her son to receive mental help, that Alex had strong feelings of inadequacy and his sensitivities far exceeded the normal range of a child's reaction to grades, classroom and social interaction. The lawyer claimed Alex Droger's school history was inadmissible as evidence.

Had there been any kind of eye witness or physical evidence, Cathleen Droger's passionate demand for justice would have left Emily making substantial monetary payments to this woman, probably for the rest of her life. However, there was no witness for the prosecution on the day of the shooting. In addition, there was no evidence that anything, other than what Emily said, happened in that school hallway. The jury was also aware that a catastrophe had probably been averted, sparing teachers and other children.

Still, Emily would, in all likelihood, be dismissed from the force after the psychological evaluations were completed in December. Captain Horan was kind, though Emily had refused to see his son since she had returned to Manchester. To her face, he said she was saner than he was, and told her she could remain on the Faidlee investigation through the end of the year. Her instincts were sharp, her investigation techniques flawless, but he sadly agreed that the story surrounding her mental health was too widespread for Emily to ever recover her respectability as a police officer. Her actions would be in question from now on. Horan also confided in her, saying that he saw in her what he had seen her father. Too much of themselves died with the dead they investigated.

This, and the fact she had not heard from Daniel caused her much grief. He hadn't called or written. He hadn't even responded to her mother's invitation to come for Thanksgiving.

~~~~~

It was now the 23rd of November and Emily was seeing Dr. Bradford for the last time. Through this psychiatrist, she had grieved for the loss of many. Now those losses included Daniel.

Dr. Bradford was kind and sympathetic saying that, sometimes when we grow, others find it hard to grow with us. Perhaps Daniel just stepped back and found that, with his own issues and Rusty's death, he couldn't deal with anyone else's problems right now. Possibly, that after seeing her in that frightening state, he decided he couldn't handle the relationship.

Emily couldn't believe that and tried to call him. Her parent's phone had been recently downgraded "because of cost", prohibiting them from making long distance calls. Maureen had a cell phone but didn't have many minutes left and didn't offer to add more. Emily bought a new cell phone. Somehow, it simply vanished from the pocket of her coat along with the phone card she had bought earlier.

Though she told her mother she had bought them, she couldn't bring herself to tell her she had lost them. She was embarrassed. But she told Dr. Bradford that she still wasn't thinking as clearly as she wanted to, misplacing things and forgetting parts of her daily agenda. He said that people dismissed mental recovery as something instantly achieved or impossible to achieve all together. People seldom allowed the mentally afflicted time to heal, as they would the physically injured. She must allow herself time and patience.

The day after Thanksgiving, Emily would be back in her apartment with a phone and electricity turned back on. The press would be on to fresher pieces of meat by then.

Though she could have pursued other means to call Daniel, Emily made the decision not to try to call any longer. He had her letters. He had the number at her parents. He had their invitation. He could get in touch with her. If Daniel's love for her had died, it was not something she wanted to hear over the phone, anyway. She would make a trip up there, right after the holiday, to follow up on the Faidlee investigation and confront Daniel.

"So, I guess this wraps up things," commented Dr. Bradford, "Emily, in my years of trying to help people, I have never known anyone so determined to help herself."

"I had a lot at stake," she said, smiling sadly.

"And yet all that remains is just you at the end. You lost your job and the man who you loved and you're okay with that?"

"I have my mind back and my faith," she said, gratefully. "And I'm not done fighting for the rest, though I am considering your words on alternative employment."

"Call me if you need anything at all, especially after you go up north. I'd like to know how it went. How does your mother feel about you going back up there?"

"I know she wouldn't want me to go—if she knew about it," Emily confided. "She's been great though, even said she sent an invitation to Daniel for Thanksgiving."

"Scary." He smiled, having come to know Maureen Harrigan through discussions with her daughter. "Did she ever tell you why she was so dead set against him?"

Emily shook her head saying, "Just prejudice I suppose."

"Well, I think you're doing the right thing going up there. This chapter in your life needs to re-opened or closed completely."

"May I use your phone? My mom needs some rolls and she might have thought of something else she needs for tomorrow. It's a local call."

"Be my guest."

Emily dialed home and a recording said that the number had been disconnected.

"Dr. Bradford, thank you again," she smiled and left, wondering about the phone.

Emily found herself feeling happy as she picked up the rolls her mother wanted for Thanksgiving dinner. The whole family would be here tomorrow. The air was damp and pungent with the smell of wet asphalt. Shoppers were cramming the stores. This was a world she knew, the city, teeming with life, lights on every corner, deafening sounds.

Kaskitesiw, Pete, Anna and Daniel seemed planets away, almost as if they were all a dream she had and never really existed. Yet she wondered what they were doing and how they would spend the holiday. She wondered if Daniel's father had made it home, as he told Daniel he would.

The mall traffic was heavy this time of day and she avoided it by getting on the turnpike, driving past the old river mills, to her mother and father's house. She didn't need to think about Kaskitesiw. She loved her aunts, uncles, and was especially excited about the new baby nephew, who was coming to visit for the first time. Emily was home for the holiday and in spite of her thoughts of Daniel, she would put up a good front. After the anxiety she had put her parents through this past month, Emily owed them a joyous spirit.

Tonight she would write one last letter to Daniel. She had written him four letters since departing the safe walls of the hospital, none of which had produced a reply. Emily had promised Lisa some maternity clothes and she needed to follow up on Faidlee's case with the state police and Canadian authorities. Then she would face Daniel, in person.

Emily pulled into her parent's driveway. The home was from the factory era when the machine tool and woolen industries were booming during the Second World War. Though most of the leaves were gone, the white clapboard house gleamed with the care her father put into it. Flaming red leaves of woodbine climbed the chimney. Mature and well sculpted evergreen shrubs graced each side of the porch.

The air had changed from a chill to downright cold and she hurried up the front porch steps. Gripping the sack of rolls, she pushed open the door and drew in a breath of apples and cinnamon.

"Hi, sweetheart, did you get the rolls from Bernie?" her mother asked.

"Here they are," she said, handing her mother the package, "You're making apple crisp?"

"Your favorite!" Maureen said, kissing her. "How did it go with Dr. Bradford?"

"We're done," Emily said happily.

"Come, tell me all about it." Maureen clasped her hands in excitement.

"A little later. I'm going to write one more letter, and if I don't hear back, that's it!"

"Oh, honey, don't torture yourself. He's probably wed to Princess "Winterspringsummerfall", or was it "Summerfallwinterspring"—that one on *The Howdy Doody Show*? Anyway, sweetheart, let it be."

"The what show?"

"Never mind."

"One more…," Emily said smiling, and started up the steps. Then she turned around. "Mom, is there anything wrong with our phone?

"No, Sweetheart, why?" Maureen said, "The new number is working fine."

"New number?" Emily asked, coming back down the steps quickly. "You have a new number here? Why didn't you tell me?"

"We decided to get an unlisted number because of the trial. There were so many phone calls from the press. I'm sure I told you. Did you try to call home?"

"Yes," Emily said, concerned, "When did you change the number?"

"Sometime before the trial started. I know I told you. You even put the new number in your coat pocket. Maybe you misplaced it with your new cell phone?" Maureen realized what she said and held her breath.

Emily hastily began to root through her pockets, unaware of her mother's faux pas.

"Sweetie, you have been under such strain," Maureen said, smoothing her daughter's hair back as Emily found a tiny piece of paper with a number on it deep within her left pocket.

Emily stared at it. "I don't remember you giving this to me. What if Daniel has been trying to call?"

"It's understandable that you can't remember. You have been so ill." Maureen put her hands on her hips and spoke firmly to her daughter. "That man had plenty of time to call you before we changed the number. It hasn't been new that long. He's police. He could check up on an unlisted number. Besides, you've been writing him so much your fingers are about to fall off. Have a little pride in yourself, Emily."

"I suppose you are right," Emily murmured and continued to look at the scrap of paper.

"Sweetheart, you have been through so much," Maureen softened her voice, "Why don't you just rest up a bit. Then come down and we'll have tea and Apple Crisp—hum?"

Emily nodded and put the paper back in her pocket. "Did Daniel know you changed the number?"

"Of course!" Maureen watched her frowning.

"When did you talk to him?"

"I told you he called while you were in that asylum. I told him about the number change. Just because we don't have long distance calling doesn't mean he couldn't call us."

"I'll be down in just a little bit."

Maureen let out her breath as Emily's door closed. Her daughter's future was at stake. She had persuaded Henry that they needed an unlisted number because of the press, but not before that Indian called to see how Emily was the first week. In spite of the fact she told him that Emily was confused and didn't want to speak to him, he had called again a few days later. Maureen told him that Emily didn't want to see him anymore and that they were going to change their phone number because of his persistence. When Emily came home from the hospital, Maureen stuffed the minuscule piece of paper in her left pocket and discovered the new cell phone. A further inspection found a phone card. She confiscated both.

As the days passed, Maureen had disposed of Emily's letters before they went out. Throwing away the first and second letter had been easy. The third and forth took some real art in getting Emily to release them to her care. Maureen actually felt that Emily might be getting suspicious, but her daughter's life hung in the balance.

Emily didn't know what was best for her. She was confused during this traumatic time of her life. The last thing she needed was to become an abandoned squaw, like her grandmother had, married to a heathen in that hovel they called a town up north.

~~~~~

Thanksgiving Day dawned gray and cold. Emily came down the steps in her nightgown and tossed the letter in the basket for tomorrow's post. She went into the kitchen for a cup of coffee. Her mother was already up and basting the turkey.

"What can I do to help?" Emily asked, sitting on the counter stool.

"Want to make the dressing?" Maureen posed the question, knowing the answer.

"I figured as much," Emily said, laughing. "Every year I'm the one who is up to my elbows in egg, sausage and breadcrumbs."

It was good to hear her daughter laugh again. "It's the seniority system," Maureen said, "When I'm gone you can give the job to someone else."

"Hope that day never comes." Emily kissed her mother quickly on the side of the head then went to the sink, staring out at the shadowy lawn.

"Don't think about him," her mother said, shifting her teasing eyes from the turkey to her daughter.

"I'm not." Emily pulled her hair back in a band and washed her hands. "I just find it so hard to believe that there was nothing sustainable between us."

"It was probably that miserable woman, Anna. I'm sure she wanted him to marry a girl of his own kind."

"I think the only thing she wanted was for Daniel to be happy," Emily said, smiling sadly, "and she wasn't miserable. Just because she called you strawberry hair or head or whatever it was."

"Nobody calls me a strawberry and gets away with it," Maureen snapped with disapproval, "You do like this color better, don't you?

Emily looked at the chestnut dye job, wondering if she had ever seen her mother's naturally colored hair. "Much better!"

"Here! I chopped the onions for you. You've done enough crying lately. Aunt Marge and Uncle Rick will be here soon. Dad went to the airport to meet his brother and his girlfriend. They're coming with her kids."

"Billy and Lilly, Pauline and Uncle Jerry—be nice, Mother. They do have names. I can't wait to see the baby."

Maureen huffed, "We'll be lucky if we eat before five o'clock tonight."

"Why?" Emily questioned, cutting up the celery.

"Because your father just called saying the plane was delayed."

Emily finished the dressing and pressed it into a baking pan. Then as with every year, she scrubbed and scrubbed her hands, trying to get the greasy sausage off of them. She had just succeeded when the door bell rang.

"That's probably Aunt Marge," Maureen sounded excited, "You go change and I'll see them in." She wiped her hands on a towel.

Emily double-timed it up the steps in her nightgown.

Maureen waited until she had shut her bedroom door and then went to the front door. Her eyes fell on the letter and taking it, she went back into the kitchen, sliding it under the onion peels in the garbage. If Emily asked, she would say that after letting Marge and Rick in, she walked it down to the corner post office box for a breath of air.

"Hi, baby sister, what were you doing? Chasing the turkey?" Aunt Marge wheezed through the door, smelling of cigarettes. "It's freezing out here."

"Good thing, I've got every stove burner in the house lit. Hi, Rick!" Maureen kissed them both, taking their coats.

~~~~~

Emily pulled on a festive vest which her mother had bought her. It contrasted nicely with her camel colored slacks and beige polo shirt. She drew her hair back on one side with a leaf barrette and dabbed a bit of blush on her cheeks. The smells of cooking drifted up the steps. The whole house smelled wonderful. The sound of family chatter was carried up along with the fragrances. It would be good to see Aunt Marge and Uncle Rick again, especially Aunt Marge. Her aunt had a dry sense of humor which, when coupled with her sister's spontaneous wit, made every occasion a vaudeville act.

But Aunt Marge had decided not to stop smoking, even with her diagnosis of lung cancer. There probably wouldn't be many more holidays with her. Even now, her boisterous voice filtering up to the second floor was raspy.

Emily started down the stairs when it felt like ice cold water ran down her back. She stopped with a look of concern.

Maureen, having heard the first foot falls on the steps, came around the corner and stared up at her daughter, fearful that she had noticed the letter missing.

"Baby Doll! Come here to your Aunt Marge!" Her sinewy aunt held out her arms.

Emily finished the steps, disconcerted but smiling and hugged her aunt warmly. "Mom, call Dad and see if he is all right," she whispered.

"Your father's fine. Come in here and see Uncle Rick." Maureen pulled at her hand, dragging her into the kitchen where, for the next half hour she was besieged with questions, carefully devoid of Kaskitesiw and her treatments.

"Emily, would you put butter in the crystal dishes?" Maureen called from her place in front of the oven.

Aunt Marge sat on the kitchen stool sipping eggnog, which she had spiked herself at the stroke of 10:00 AM. Uncle Rick had gone into the living room to watch the Thanksgiving Day Parade, in hopes of catching the first game before dinner.

"Sure, Mom," Emily hopped off the stool where she had been laughing with her aunt and opened the cabinet, reaching for the butter dishes.

"Apisci-mosos." A voice whispered. Emily tried to steady the fine crystal but the dishes broke against the floor.

She stood there looking at her shaking hands as if the dishes should still be in them and cried, "Oh, no. I'm so sorry."

"No harm done, Baby Doll," Marge said, sliding off her seat and bending down to help Emily clean up the mess. "Here look, all is not lost," she remarked and picked up the broken glass. She pulled the trash can towards her. "One top isn't broken and one bottom isn't broken. I'll get your Mother another set for Christmas."

Aunt Marge tried to stand, steadying herself on the edge of the garbage can. But in her frail condition, or perhaps it was the effects of the early Eggnog, she pulled the garbage can over. Glass, potato peels, apple peels, onion peels tumbled onto the floor, along with a sodden letter addressed to Daniel.

Emily helped Aunt Marge to her feet, staring at the envelope. Her eyes shot to her mother across the room.

"I must have picked that up with the newspapers. I'm sorry, dear," Maureen said and gave her a weak smile. Then she realized what Emily knew. There were no newspapers today and Maureen couldn't have know it was Emily's letter from where she stood, unless she had put it there herself.

"Oh Mom," Emily said, tears filling her eyes, "What have you done?"

"Sweetheart, you have been through so much. You didn't know what was for your own good," Maureen's eyes also flooded with tears at the possible consequence of losing her daughter's love now. "You didn't know your own mind."

Aunt Marge looked back and forth, between the two of them and excused herself, "I'm going in with Rick. Call me if you need me, dears." She tiptoed over the mess on the floor.

Emily turned and leaned against the wall, her face in her hands, then whirled. "Is the phone not working long distance, or is that a lie too?" Emily picked up the wall phone and called the Kaskitesiw Police Department but there was a fast busy signal. She tried dispatch, but the phone made the same sound.

"I told the truth. Emily, please, it was for your own good," Maureen pleaded. Her hand went to her daughter's shoulder.

"Don't touch me, Mother!" Emily snapped. "How many did you throw away?"

"All—all of them I think. Sweetheart, I did it for you," Maureen said, "I did it for all of us."

"I'll deal with us—if there *is* any us later. Something is wrong with Daniel," Emily said and grabbed her mother's sleeve. "I'm going to need you to drive while I try to get through to him. If anything has happened to him, I will never speak to you again."

Maureen gave a helpless shrug to Marge and Rick, as she was pulled passed the door of the living room and her coat thrown at her.

"You drive," Emily ordered and threw her mother the keys. "I've got to reach Pete. Give me your cell phone."

"Where are we going?" Maureen asked, stunned. "Emily, its Thanksgiving!"

"Get on 93 and head north," she commanded.

Using her mother's cell phone, which had more minutes than expected, she dialed the number for Kaskitesiw PD. It continued to ring but she hung up before the call was transferred to the State Police dispatch.

CHAPTER 23

The smoke from chimneys and stove pipes hung low in the cold air of Kaskitesiw. Thanksgiving morning was quiet. Hardly anyone was on the street. Snow was expected and the low, gray sheet of clouds confirmed the forecast. Daniel opened the door to the office and tossed yesterday's mail on the desk without turning on the light. He had gone through it already, and there was still no letter. He sat down, pushing his hair back. Once more, he had been delinquent about cutting it. He didn't care if his father noticed or not.

Right after Emily had left, he had contacted a chiropractor in Plymouth. With the doctor's help he had gone through active release to break up toxins in his injured muscles, deep massage and a series of exercises designed to strengthen his side and right arm. He could stand much straighter now, lift his arm higher and he could run, not as a marathoner for sure, but as he built up stamina, the chiropractic treatments continued to break up the toxins and stretched his striated muscles almost normal length once more. It had taken a lot of work and he couldn't wait to show her his progress.

The stronger muscles in his side even filled in some of the depression, nearly hiding the nubs of his ribs. Time and Anna's herbal oils had diminished some of the hard ropy scaring. He wanted to be as normal as he could be for her.

But why had he ever allowed himself to think Emily would be content with him in this back-water town? She was city woman and it probably only took her return to the urban world to make her realize that.

Daniel pulled a ring out of his pocket. The little emerald glinted under the desk lamp as he turned it on. The green gem was like her eyes. He had planned to give it to her the night the cub was killed. Then it was too late and she was gone. Try as he might, he couldn't wait for Emily's letter and had called. Her mother said she was in the hospital and did not want to hear from him. As yet, there had been no word from Emily to prove her mother wrong. He called once more, and Maureen threatened to change the number if he called again. So he honored Emily's wishes and waited for that first letter. It never came. He had written many letters of his love for her, his encouragement, his understanding. Anna had added notes to his letters. They sat in a pile on the kitchen counter, waiting, as he had promised.

This weekend was the last of the hectic deer season. After that he was going to Manchester. If she no longer loved him, she must tell him to his face.

His father would not be arriving until late morning. Anna declared that they would eat in the evening. Daniel would work this day and give Pete time to be with his family for their noon feast.

The less time he had to spend with his father the better. He didn't feel like answering questions, didn't like the lectures and didn't want to listen to the argument that Anna and Kirk would invariably start, over Rusty or the most insensible of things.

Daniel did his job efficiently but mechanically these days. He was back to being the person he had been after Rusty died and before Emily had come. No one on the street asked him how he was anymore. They knew the answer.

Today, the promise of snow also disturbed Daniel. The longer stride and wider print of the big bucks would be easier to follow on the white landscape. The winters here were just too harsh up here to remove the strongest males and still expect the herds to thrive.

The office phone rang. He put the ring back in his pocket and picked it up. The thin frightened voice of a woman whispered over the receiver, "Daniel? It's Ila. I'm at Teresa's. Faidlee is here!"

~~~~~

North of Concord, Emily called the office again almost afraid to hear Daniel's voice, afraid his reaction would be angry because of not hearing from her. The phone was busy. She tried Pete's phone. It too was busy. Next she called the State Police Barracks.

"This is Detective Emily Harrigan, badge number, 2724. I am unable to contact the constable or the game warden in Kaskitesiw. What is their status?"

"Constable Hines is off duty until sixteen hundred. Warden Claret is on duty. Office line is busy and his radio has been activated for the State Police frequency. Do you want to send a message?"

"Negative. I'll try again in a little while."

Was she going off on feelings alone? She had no evidence anything was wrong. Emily felt Maureen's glance and demanded, "Keep your eyes on the road, Mother."

"Honey, I am so sorry. Let's go home and talk this out."

"We have nothing to talk out."

"I just wanted you to be happy."

"The only person you wanted to be happy was you. How long did you think you could keep up this ruse? You even lied to Dad. No, don't start crying."

~~~~~~

Daniel lowered the radio receiver and picked up the phone. "Pete, I'm sorry to bother you."

"Hey man, Happy Thanksgiving! We're going to eat about noon. If all's quiet why don't you come over and join…"

"Faidlee has taken Ila as a hostage. I'm in touch with the state police. They're going to meet me at Teresa's trailer."

"Faidlee has them both?" Pete asked.

"Just Ila. She went over there to take some things to Teresa. They were going to meet someplace tomorrow." Daniel continued, "Ila can't tell Faidlee where her is, but she is afraid he is going to kill her anyway."

"He would, damnit."

"It won't get him what he wants so he wants to make a trade."

"For what?"

"Me, along with making sure no one follows us to Teresa. Couple of cruisers just pulled up. Gotta' go!"

"Daniel, don't you go—damn it—I'll be right there," Pete hollered into the phone. He hung up and turned to find his wife and two kids standing there. He grabbed his jacket and said hurriedly, "Keep it warm for me. Daniel is going to try and get himself killed again."

~~~~~

"Dispatch, this is Emily Harrigan. Have you heard anything from either the constable or warden?"

"They are involved in a hostage situation."

Emily's heart sank as she asked, "What is the status?"

"I can't page them for you. Lines are open for Littleton barracks and their Special Weapons and Tactical Team'."

"Can you tell me who is involved in the hostage taking?"

"Richard Faidlee and a woman," the dispatcher informed her.

"Teresa," Emily whispered and then said, "I'm chief investigator in that case. I'm opening my line to patrol cars in the area."

"Copy that."

~~~~~

Pete slid behind one of the cruisers and asked, "Any shots fired?"

"No," a state trooper said, "we're waiting on the SWAT team from Littleton, but it's going to take awhile. It appears holidays bring out the worst in people. They're on another domestic abuse call, children involved."

"Have you heard from Faidlee?"

"Yes, sir." The trooper indicated another officer helping Daniel to tighten his Kevlar vest since his range of motion was still compromised.

"What the hell do you think you're doing?" Pete growled as he crawled behind the car. "Get down here!" He yanked Daniel down to the ground for protection as the warden buttoned his uniform shirt over the vest. "You are not going to do this. He's going to kill you. What has he got to lose?"

"If I don't go in, he is going to kill Ila. I have a better chance of surviving than she does." Daniel knelt and tucked his shirt in, leaving his jacket off. "I know where Teresa is, and Ila knows that I know and so does Faidlee."

"Wait a damn minute," Pete hauled him back down when he started to get up. "The SWAT team will be here soon. What is the update on the SWAT team?" he called to one of the State Police.

"Be here in about an hour," the trooper said, checking his watch. "The last domestic impasse has been resolved."

"By the time the SWAT team gets here she'll be dead," Daniel said. "He's already roughed her up. You'd go in." Daniel stood up in full view of the trailer.

Pete wondered if he would, searched his soul, then nodded solemnly.

A shot went off from the trailer and everyone ducked.

Faidlee shouted, "I swear I'll kill her, Claret, if you don't get in here and tell me where my wife is."

~~~~~~

"Mom, pull over. I'll take it now."

As Maureen slowed to the shoulder, Emily got out and ran to the driver side. "Get out!"

"Oh, Emily, you're not going to leave me here."

"Don't tempt me," Emily said, holding the door open and her mother got out and ran to the passenger side of the car.

"Put your seat belt on," Emily snapped and reached under the dash to turn on the police bar lights in the back and the alternating blue lights near the front grill.

Emily picked up the radio and said, "This is Detective Emily Harrigan, anyone in range?"

"Got your lights, Detective," the voice of a state trooper came back.

"I have reason to believe manhunt suspect Richard C. Faidlee, F-A-I-D-L-E-E, is back in the country, in the vicinity of Kaskitesiw, New Hampshire. He's wanted for shooting a game warden and killing another man and now may be involved in hostage situation."

"We have that report. What can we do for you, Detective Harrigan?"

"I headed the investigation and may be able to help with the situation, if I can get there in time. I could use you to pave the way for me."

"10-4."

A minute later, from behind her came a state police cruiser. It swerved around her and took point. "Mom." Emily reached for the cell phone again and handed it to mother. "Hit re-dial."

"Busy." Maureen said with a worried expression for her own future.

~~~~~

"Anna, is Kirk there yet?" Pete whispered into the phone as Daniel stepped over the caution ribbon.

"Mestacaakanin just walked in," Anna huffed.

Pete didn't know what she said but assumed it was an insult and that Colonel Claret was there.

"Let me speak to him, Anna, now!" he said and looked around at Daniel. "Daniel, wait a minute!" Pete shouted.

Pete turned away as Daniel's father came on, and spoke in a low voice, "Colonel, I need you down here. It's Daniel. If you want to see him alive get down here fast, and talk some sense into him. I'm at Faidlee's trailer. Park at the station and come in low. We've got a hostage stand-off here and your son is going in as a trade. I can't stop him," Pete said in desperation and turned off the phone. He got up and walked over to Daniel, regardless of the danger.

Daniel put his fingers in his shirt pocket and handed Pete the ring.

Pete looked down at the small gold band with a delicately cut emerald stone. "What's this?"

"Just in case, would you give it to Emily, if you see her sometime? Maybe she will keep it as a memento."

232

"What's the estimated time of arrival on SWAT?" Pete shouted at a trooper.

"ETA, 13:17."

"Daniel, put this off twenty minutes," Pete moaned, his eyes on the trailer.

"Pete!" Daniel commanded the constable's attention again. "Will you give it to her?"

"Yeah, I'll give it to her," Pete agreed then looked up from the ring, ready to say something else but Daniel had walked in front of the cruisers shouting, "Faidlee, let Ila go. I'm coming in."

"You come in first," Faidlee shouted back.

"Daniel!" Kirk Claret called to his son. He was breathing hard from the run across backyards and was being urged, by the police, to crouch down behind the cars.

"Hi, Dad," Daniel said, only turning his head slightly to his father. He was afraid Faidlee might think he was doing something suspicious and harm Ila. "Sorry about Thanksgiving Dinner," his voice was flat and without emotion. "You'd better get down."

"Son—I," his father started to say. A police officer yanked him to the ground for safety. "Isn't there another way to handle this?" Kirk Claret questioned Pete.

"Let her go, Faidlee!" Daniel shouted again. "Half way, and then I start."

"Just wait, Daniel." Pete pleaded.

"He's got the door open. I see Ila," Daniel said, relieved.

"Wait!"

"Faidlee sees more police and it will be over for her," Daniel said urgently, looking at her raw and bruised face, pleading for his help. He started forward.

"He has nothing to lose by killing you both," Pete hissed.

Daniel took a deep breath. He spoke without looking at his father, "Sorry Dad, I never was the brave one like Rusty. But, I don't want to live with myself if something happens to Ila because I did nothing. She is frightened. She isn't the only one." He stepped forward and called towards the trailer. "Faidlee let Ila go. I'm coming in. You've got my word," Daniel spoke loud and firm in spite of his feelings.

"I've never known a hero who wasn't afraid," Kirk Claret's quavering voice came from behind him, "I love you, son."

"Love you too, Dad," Daniel said and began walking towards the trailer. He did not look back again. At the halfway point, he stopped and waited. In the silence around him he could hear a blue jay scolding a few houses away. School was out for the holiday, but children were playing on the swings of the mission playground. Looking up he felt snowflakes against his face. With another deep breath, he fixed his eyes on the trailer door. "Let her go, Faidlee," Daniel said in a demanding voice.

The door creaked open further, and Ila was pushed out.

"Come, Ila. Don't run. Just walk to me," Daniel coaxed her softly.

She glanced back, afraid that the man would kill her at any moment.

"It's going to be okay." Daniel persuaded in her native Abenaki, "Baji. *Come to me.*"

She started to walk toward him in little pigeon-hops, her hands over her ears as if to shut out the sound of her own death. "Alida hosia bashomek! *I think he is going to shoot me!* "

"Debestamaso! *No, listen to me!* Baji dodosa ! *Keep coming!* Now, just walk past me. Don't stop."

"Daniel, I'm so sorry! I told him that you know. Ozigalda, *I was afraid,*" Ila cried, her cut lip trembling. "Nahlomek! *He'll kill you!* "

"Cabosa. *Just walk by me.* That's my girl," Daniel said gently.

As soon as Ila was safely past, he started to walk toward the trailer. He could hear his own heart beating rapidly with dread.

~~~~~

The static on Pete's radio made him jump. "Conway dispatch. I have a Detective Harrigan on the line."

"Patch her through. Emmy, where have you been?"

"What's going on, Pete?"

"We've got a standoff. Faidlee took Ila hostage in Teresa's trailer. She's safe though, thanks to Daniel."

"Where's Daniel?"

"The only way Faidlee would let her go was if Daniel changed places with her. Ila told Faidlee that Daniel knows where his wife is. He's just about in there now."

There was silence on the other end.

"Emmy, he would have gone in anyway. Where have you been?"

"I'm on my way, Pete," she cried. "I'm on my way! If you get a chance, tell him I love him—I couldn't help what happened."

Emily snapped the cell phone shut and picked up the radio receiver as it sounded.

"Handing you off."

"Thanks, Officer."

"Happy Thanksgiving," her mother called to the radio.

Emily stared at her in disbelief.

The radio's voice came again. "Passing you to Conway."

The state police cruiser slowed and pulled to the right. As Emily sped past he gave a salute.

"Thanks, officer." Emily let up on the button.

At Conway limits, a cruiser appeared before them. Emily was driving faster than he was. She slowed somewhat. Still, ninety miles an hour wasn't bad for the Crown Vic and the Mustang. She stayed on his lights like a shadow, changing lanes when he changed, passing cars when he passed.

Maureen had her red fingernails pressed into the dashboard. Once she yelled, "Go! Go! Go!" as a semi-truck threatened to break the invisible thread between the two cars.

"How could you have done this to me?" Emily cried to her mother. "I loved you so much."

"I'll make it right, sweetheart, I promise, I'll make it right. Watch the road and don't think about it now."

~~~~~

"Close the door."

Not seeing Faidlee, Daniel glanced down at the knob to shut the door. The next thing he realized was that the back of his head hurt and Faidlee had cuffed his hands behind him.

"Nice to see you again, Warden," he snickered. "I really thought you was dead."

Getting to his feet, Daniel remained silent.

"Nothing to say?" Faidlee asked sarcastically and, in a move too quick for Daniel to dodge, jammed the point of the rifle into Daniel's stomach.

Daniel struggled for balance and straightened up, the Kevlar taking the brunt of the blow. By stature and by presence, Daniel looked down on the man and Faidlee didn't like it.

Faidlee turned the gun, slamming the rifle butt into Daniel's cheek bone. The bone did not absorb the shock like the vest. He went to his knees, almost falling forward on his face, but the kitchen table caught him in the shoulder.

"You ain't gonna yell out, are you, Indian boy?" Faidlee sneered. " That's what I figured. Gonna' be a hero. You ain't gonna' be such a hero when I gut you out. By the time they get antsy and come in here, I'm gonna' be gone to get my wife. Now, where is she?"

Leaning his shoulder on the table, Daniel staggered to his feet. "You can't get away. The trailer is surrounded."

"You just think you know everythin', don't you?" Faidlee barked. "Why, that grass is three feet high around these trailers. I've been known to sneak up on a buck and gut him out while he was standin' in grass half talls is this."

Faidlee did have camouflage on. It was possible he might escape; but, he would leave without knowing where Teresa was. Daniel fixed his eyes on him. They were dark and piercing. Faidlee drove the rifle butt into his right arm, causing Daniel to drop to both knees.

"That's better," Faidlee commented, feeling the dominance. "Now, where's Teresa?"

When Daniel didn't answer Faidlee kicked him in the right arm and side. The vest took some of the blow but not all.

"I said—where is my wife?'"

"Where you won't find her," Daniel managed to say, breathing hard.

"Ila says you know."

Daniel got up on one knee, but did not answer.

"Don't you be actin' like no dumb Indian!" Faidlee spat and swung the gun butt towards Daniel's forehead but the warden avoided it by leaning back.

"I've just about had enough," Daniel said with contempt. Steadying himself against the wall, he got to his feet.

"Oh, you've had enough?" Faidlee pursed his tobacco blackened lower lip and sneered, "The Indian boy had enough. Well, I've had enough of you meddling in my affairs. First you mess up my business, and then you tell my wife to leave me. Man's got a right to defend hisself from this kind of thing."

Faidlee aimed the rifle at Daniel.

~~~~~

The cruiser pulled to the right lane and flashed its high beams. "God speed, Detective," a voice came over the radio, "I'm handing you off to Gorham."

"You guys are good," Emily commented, smiling in spite of her fears.

"Happy Thanksgiving!" Maureen shouted again.

"Would you stop with the 'Happy, Happy', Mom? Have you called Dad yet?"

"No, I guess I'd better." Maureen took the cell phone. "What am I going to say to him?"

"The truth, Mother! God bless them! Here comes Gorham." Emily picked up speed as the cruiser pulled in front of her.

Maureen had dialed the number. "Henry? Yes, I'm all right, Emily's all right. Honey, we are on the way to Kassy—that place Emily was.

I've done something wrong, really wrong." She glanced at Emily. "I threw away the letters she wrote to Daniel."

Maureen started to weep, her mascara streaking down her cheeks. "I know. I know! I'm so sorry. Emily knows how sorry I am. Henry, don't be mad with me. Please. Just come get me, Henry. Emily's not coming home. I've really messed up. Please come get me. I love you."

Maureen shut the cell phone and bowed her head.

"Did you mean that?" Emily asked.

"I'm so sorry, Emily," Maureen said, trying to wipe away the mascara smudges.

"I mean the part about you loving Dad?"

"I've taken him for granted," she sobbed and stared out the front window, "I knew he'd always be there no matter what I did. I thought I could give you more than a plodding ox like your father, but I was actually—actually I was trying to give you less. I'm so sorry, Emily. I am so sorry! God, what have I done?"

"It's okay, Mom, but we are going to have a very long talk later." Emily brushed at the tears on her own cheeks and said, "Just pray Daniel is safe.

Maureen nodded and pulled a rosary from her coat pocket. She was silent for a long time, though her lips were moving.

~~~~~~

"Aren't you scared, Warden? I want to see you beg for your life. That pretty-boy hunter begged for his life. Last time, where's my wife?"

"Did you kill Eric Patterson?"

"Not the right answer."

"Did you kill him?"

" 'Course I killed him! Killed the Kirby boy too—not that it's going to matter much to you in a minute. Now, where is she?"

Daniel didn't answer.

Faidlee, pretending to sigh with regret, adjusted the bolt to be sure a bullet was in the chamber.

With all the strength left in him, Daniel launched off his one knee and dove under the gun barrel into Faidlee's lower stomach with his shoulder, driving him backwards onto the breakfast table. He got to his feet before Faidlee, and hopped backwards over the plastic restraints. With his hands in front of him now, he swung his fists across Faidlee's jaw.

Faidlee stumbled to the side, losing the gun. They both scrambled for it but it slid beneath the table and Faidlee grabbed the nearest weapon, a cast iron skillet. He kept swinging it at Daniel. The warden managed to maneuver out of its way twice before the heavy metal pan connected with his right arm and what was left of his rib cage. The blow doubled him over in pain. He felt something snap between his cuffed hands and then he was being dragged by a chain.

Daniel wrenched backwards, but it was no use. He was lifted off the floor by a pulley system at the ceiling. His arms strained in their sockets, and his extended right side blazed with pain. He looked down and found the floor with the toes of his boots, not enough to support his hanging body.

Faidlee tied off the rope and looked up satisfied. "I want to remember you this way," he said and pulled out his buck knife, "Gutted out like a deer. You sure as hell are gonna' tell me where my wife is now, while you're beggin' me to stop."

"You don't have time to show off, Faidlee," Daniel tried to talk, his breathing an effort. "They gave me ten minutes. Time's just about up." His hands were numb and turning blue.

"You've got a damn vest on!" Faidlee could see its outline in Daniel's stretched torso. He spat tobacco on the floor of the trailer and said, "You're takin' all the fun out of this. Have to be a head shot. By the time they hear the gun go off, I'm gonna' be long gone. One more chance, where's my wife?" He picked up the rifle and aimed it.

Daniel raised his head, pressed between his arms, and looked at the thick plastic ties. They were tightened up to the pulley on the ceiling, pinching off the circulation in his hands. There was no hope. He groaned and looked back at the man raising the rifle to his shoulder. Pain radiated along his side, pulsing with each heart beat. He wouldn't have to suffer this for long.

Faidlee aimed the gun at Daniel's head.

"Apici-mosis," Daniel breathed.

The gun went off.

~~~~~

"Oh, no! Not now, Lord," Emily looked up at the sky through the front windshield.

"What's the matter?" Maureen asked, pausing in her prayer.

"It's snowing. This car has no traction in snow. I'm not slowing down, Mom. Keep praying."

"All Errol units available have been called to the hostage scene in," the Trooper's voice came over the radio. "There's no one to hand you off to."

"Thank you, officer. I'll take it from here."

"Honey, I have never known the kind of love you feel for this man. Why this man?"

"Why not him?" Emily started to slide, counter-steered and pressed the accelerator.

"You do look a little like her."

"Who?"

"My mother—your Grandmother."

Emily quickly glanced her way and riveted her eyes back on the white road.

"How she loved your grandfather," Maureen mused, "She loved him so much that she died—after he killed himself with alcohol." Maureen said bitterly, "She didn't care that she left me and my sister alone. And the stinking Indians wouldn't help us, wouldn't take us in."

Emily frowned, but concentrated on the slippery road.

"She died from grief," Maureen went on, "for my father and his damned crossed blood. And now you're doing the same thing."

"Crossed blood? Mom? Grandfather was Indian?"

240

"No, the government said he wasn't. We'd have been better off if he'd been full Indian. We were Metis." Maureen smiled ruefully. "I hardly remember him except that he made my mother laugh. He made us all laugh with his dancing and his fiddle. She never laughed after he died, never smiled again. Marge and I tried to make her laugh. She wouldn't. She only lasted a year after he killed himself with liquor."

"Mom, you told me you were Scottish." Emily tried to touch her mother but had to grab the steering wheel as a pile of slush caught the tire. "I wish you had told me this."

"It didn't fit the image I wanted you to have of me. Not as a half breed. Why do you think I always dyed my hair? It's black, Emily, black as coal. Thank God, you took after your grandmother, like Marge—and your father's side. Your father doesn't even know Marge and I changed our last name."

"Daniel isn't like that. Mom! Daniel is not that way!"

"You've known the man less than a month."

"Look, wrong as it was, I understand now why you did what you did. But you have to give Daniel a chance. I can't change my feelings for him. I love him with all my heart."

"Funny. You always did remind me of your grandmother. Do you still wear that necklace she had?"

"Our Lady of Guadalupe? I've never taken it off."

"All right, Mother." Maureen tilted her head back. "You win. She's your granddaughter more than my own daughter. Just don't let her suffer like you did—like Marge and I did."

Emily fought to keep the Mustang steady going around a curve.

~~~~~

At the sound of the gunshot, Pete and the troopers rushed the door and kicked it open. One trooper stopped at Faidlee but Pete ran around him, took out his pocket knife and began cutting the rope holding Daniel.

"I've got the situation under control," Daniel said, wincing between his painfully stretched arms.

241

"Sure looks that way," Pete retorted, as he struggled to cut the rope.

In spite of the rules, Kirk Claret had pushed his way into the trailer. He caught his son as the rope severed. Daniel crumpled in his arms.

"Are you all right, son? Have you been shot?" He clamped his hands against the sides of Daniel's face and stared at him hard, trying to get an answer.

"Dad?" Daniel looked up at him, dazed. "How could he have missed from there?"

"You scared the hell out of me," Kirk Claret said, as Pete cut through the plastic. He fervently tried to rub circulation back into his son's hands.

"What did you do to him?" Pete asked, looking back at the man on the floor, "and how the hell did you do it?"

"I don't know," Daniel said as bewildered as they were. "Is he dead?"

The trooper bent over the man on the floor after kicking the rifle away. Faidlee was gurgling blood from between his tobacco-stained lips, and his eyes showed that he realized he was dying, but he couldn't move or speak. The bolt from the rifle had gone through his mouth and severed his spinal cord. Before his eyes fixed in death he stared at something in the distance with fear. His terrorized expression was enough to make the trooper turn to look. Finding nothing, the trooper looked back at the man. "He's dead."

With gloves on, another officer lifted the weapon. "This old rifle decided to malfunction right now. You are alive only by chance, Warden Claret."

"Here!" Pete held out the ring. "You give it to her. She's on her way. Said to tell you she loves you."

"Emily—coming?" Daniel struggled to a sitting position, trying to focus on the ring in order to take it with his numb, tingling fingers.

Pete put it in Daniel's shirt pocket. "We're going to go see Doc. That cheek looks nasty. What'd he hit you with?"

"Rifle butt. The vest saved my life though. Faidlee wanted to dress me out like a deer, but he didn't think a knife could cut through Kevlar."

"And you didn't tell him different?" Pete grinned and grabbed Daniel's one arm. Kirk Claret took the other, getting him to his feet.

Daniel laughed. "No, I sure did not!" Though he was wobbly from the abuse his body had taken, he was ecstatic to be alive, overjoyed that Emily was coming home.

The colonel looked at his son, surprised, having never heard him laugh before. Not even as a child did Daniel smile. He looked so much like his mother when he did. "Daniel?"

"What, Dad?" The smile still remained at the corners of his lips as he looked at his father, but it faded quickly.

Kirk began to ask for forgiveness. Daniel stopped him, encircling him in his arms.

"You are taller than me," Kirk said, laughing, as if seeing his son for the first time, "and stronger."

"And smarter?" Daniel teased.

"Don't push it," Kirk said, "But you have chosen a woman who is returning to you. Better than I did, son. What is her name?"

"Emily," Daniel said, and allowed his father to take his arm to support him. "You will love her, Dad. She is like a deer, delicate, and beautiful but very smart and a heart so good."

"Was she the one at the hospital?"

"Yes."

"I could tell she loved you."

"You could? Even then?"

"You think your old man is senile too?"

"No," Daniel laughed. "But I think it is time we learn more of each other."

As they went into the snow, Ila hurried up to them, putting her hands against her face in sorrow as she looked at Daniel.

"It's okay, Ila. You did the right thing." Daniel tried to ease her mind at seeing him beaten. "Your sister is in Littleton—the convent. Her husband can't hurt her anymore. Go to her."

As they stepped over the yellow caution ribbon, a red Mustang came around the corner, out of control and squealing, spinning in a complete circle. It circled twice before crashing into the Fish and Game truck.

"Well, that's two down," Pete mumbled and watched Emily bound out of the car. "We're getting mighty low on vehicles here. I told her that car was no good in snow."

Emily started to run to the trailer. With her dress shoes on, she was having trouble getting her footing on the slippery ground.

"Pete—Dad, let go of me."

"Oh, now that would look good. Fall flat on your face in front of her," Pete said to Daniel, then raised his voice, "Emmy! Oh, geezum, she thinks that's you!" The body of Richard Faidlee was being taken out of the trailer. "Officer, son," Pete called to one of the troopers nearby, "You're younger than I am. Would you go catch that girl?"

"Arrest her?"

"No, just catch her for me, please."

The young trooper sprinted across the lawn.

"Don't hurt her," Daniel yelled after him.

"Don't you get hurt," Pete shouted.

The young police man quickly maneuvered in front of a panicked woman. She tried to run around him but the officer caught her around the waist.

"What do you want me to do with her?" the trooper yelled back.

Emily stopped struggling and looked in the direction the trooper was shouting. Then she started to strain against the man, laughing and crying when she saw Daniel.

"Just let her go, son. Let her go," Pete grinned.

Daniel wrenched free of his father and Pete. He caught Emily and they both dropped to their knees in the snow, holding onto each other for dear life.

Pete walked over to Emily's mother as she managed to crawl out of the driver's side of the car; the passenger door wouldn't open.

"You okay, Mrs. Harrigan?"

She nodded, pushing back her disheveled hair.

"What happened? Why didn't Daniel hear from Emily?"

Maureen shifted her eyes away, and then smiled. "Hardly looks like that matters now, does it, Constable?"

CHAPTER 24

"Anna has invited me to Thanksgiving dinner," Doc said. His eyes were bright as he smiled at Emily behind his surgical mask.

"Thanksgiving! I forgot all about it."

"Yep, there is going to be quite a feast at Anna's tonight." The doctor concluded his examination of Daniel's cheekbone and pulled off his gloves.

Emily couldn't help but think of her own family's ruined Thanksgiving dinner.

"You're fine, Daniel, just bruised. Thank God you have as hard a head as you do. Okay, out of here, you two. I've got to whip up my wife's famous Waldorf salad. We had it every year. Only reason I know how to make it is because my wife hated to peel apples," Doc added wistfully and kissed Emily on the cheek. "If I need an assistant again, I'll call you."

"Please do," she said. "I'm between jobs at the moment."

"Well, consider yourself hired."

"Wow!" She grinned. "Can you give me just a little time to think about it?"

"Take all the time you need."

Emily and Daniel left Doc Pomfret's and started up the street, holding hands, not caring who saw them. "Oh Daniel," she turned into him, "I have so much to be thankful for."

He held her close and when he released her there was moisture in his eyes. "I thought I'd lost you. Why didn't you write me? Your mother said you didn't want to hear from me. I promised you that I wouldn't interfere with your healing time. But I didn't know what was going on. As soon as hunting season was over this weekend, I was coming down there, regardless of what your mother told me."

"And I was coming up here to look you in the eye when you told me you didn't love me anymore. I thought I'd lost you, too. I will never go away again."

"Promise me?" he asked, his eyes yearning.

"I promise with all my heart!" She smiled, taking his hand again, and they walked in silence.

Emily wasn't as angry with her mother as she thought she would be. She had left her mother standing, alone, in a crowd of people, to go with Daniel. Her mother had looked frightened and out of place. Pete said he would take care of her until Emily's father arrived. Emily guessed that they had left by now, gone home to the rest of the relatives.

They turned past where Martin's garage used to be and headed up the street to Anna's. They hadn't gone past the red and white bungalow when they started to count cars. It seemed like every car in Kaskitesiw, and beyond, was there. Even her father's car was parked in the single line on the only side of the street. Five children ran by with Uggh, Andre's drooling mastiff. She recognized two of them as her niece and nephew and the others as Pete's children and Tracy Wright. They vanished around the corner of the house, the dog now in the lead. "It looks like everybody really is here!"

"I just want to go home with you," Daniel protested, tired and sore. "Can we grab a bite and go?"

"We don't even have to stop to eat, but I think we'd better say hello," she advised, taking his arm and leading him to the porch. "I need to see if my mother is all right after slamming the Mustang into your truck. Pete said she was fine, but I guess I need to see for myself."

"That was quite an entrance," he remarked.

"I happened to be a little upset at the time," she upbraided him, "I thought it was you coming out of the trailer on a stretcher. I've never been so frightened in all my life."

He bent and kissed away her frown.

The door opened and one of the children ran out giggling. Emily and Daniel stood in the doorway in a mild case of shock. Joe from the gun shop and her father had just finished setting up tables in a line that what went from the doorway, through the living room, to the other side of Anna's small house. The chair and sofa had been moved to the bedroom. Father Paul, Tommy from the gas station and some other parishioners from the mission church were setting up folding chairs. Ila Brown was with the frail woman whom Emily had seen at the gas station the first day. It was Teresa Faidlee. They were spreading sheets and table cloths over the train of tables.

There was a group of men, out in the chilly November air, cooking on the grill. Anna's stumpy figure was moving about the room like a little general, issuing orders both in Cree and English. The counter in the kitchenette was stacked with food in plastic-ware and foil.

"Does this happen every Thanksgiving?" Emily whispered in awe.

"Not in my lifetime," Daniel whispered back. "I think everyone in town is here."

"Including some of my relatives, too! My father must have brought them. That's my uncle and aunt, Marge and Rick. Over there is my other aunt, well, soon to be Aunt, Pauline and Uncle Jerry with her kids and—oh, and the baby!" she said happily and started to drag Daniel in that direction but didn't get far.

"Emmy, Daniel!" Pete announced their arrival. Everywhere the bustle stopped at once. All eyes turned on them. There was the sound of a single clap started by Kirk Claret then the room became a crackling din of hand against hand.

Daniel looked shocked and embarrassed. He turned to Emily but she was clapping too, tears brimming in her eyes. The boy whose mother hadn't wanted him and whose father left him behind was being honored as the hero he was.

Anna came over and pulled on their hands. Daniel leaned down to her. "Anna, this should be for Rusty, not me. His spirit still needs to be honored."

"Rusty lives inside you, my Taaniyal. It is for both of you," she said and urged them to step between the crowd of people, who continued to clap until they were both seated near the end of the table, closest to the door. The food started to go on the table: turkeys, dressings, hamburgers, hot dogs, pizza, and something a little scary looking in a bowl which Andre brought. There was every kind of salad you could name. Susanne and Pete's family meal had arrived intact and was for the sharing.

Father Paul hurried over to Daniel and Emily. "Bless you, bless you." he said quickly then hesitated before he asked, "Emily, will you be staying in Kaskitesiw?"

She blushed and said yes, wondering the reason for the little priest's personal question.

"Forgive me for being so bold but might you be looking for a job?" He sounded desperate.

"Oh my! Ask and you shall receive. I'm not sure, Father. Doctor Pomfret just asked me about working for him."

The priest looked crestfallen, "Yes, well, he would be able to pay you more than I can. God bless you both," he said softly and started to leave.

"Father, what is it?" Emily asked, catching his hand, feeling as though God was intervening somehow.

"I need a substitute for the sixth grade. After the holidays, Mrs. St. Marie is moving to the city with her husband. I thought there was no harm in asking."

"Am I qualified for that?" Emily asked.

"To be a substitute? Yes, I am sure. You have had some college?"

"Yes, but not in education," she said, "but I don't mind studying and taking courses if they are not too far from home." Emily looked at Daniel, remembering her promise to never leave him again.

"Tomorrow, could you come to the school? We can talk about it," he said.

"Okay," she smiled, releasing his hand.

The little priest was so excited he practically danced away. Doc Pomfret came in and put the freshly made Waldorf salad on a scarce patch of linen. He looked curiously at the uncharacteristic, almost smug little smile on the face of the priest as Father said 'Hello', and went by chuckling.

Emily looked into Daniel's shining eyes. "Do you think I could be a teacher? I mean the responsibility of molding little lives—I don't know if I have what it takes."

"You won't know until you try," he said, smiling. "But I think you would make a wonderful teacher."

In a fashion more orderly than Emily could think possible, people took their seats.

"Do you mind me sitting next to you?" Emily's mother looked at her daughter, pleading, and Emily put her arms up and hugged her. No one but Daniel needed to know what she had done.

"Are you ever, ever again going to do something for my good, without asking me?"

Maureen put her hand over her heart and shook her head.

"Hi, Daddy," Emily said, cheerfully.

Her father bent down and kissed her, "I'm so glad to see you I don't even mind the dent in the Mustang." He then shook Daniel's hand, saying, "Son, you have made me very proud to know you."

"You too, sir," Daniel replied, unaccustomed to praise.

When everyone was seated, the priest from the mission church blessed the people and the food they had brought. Along with almost everyone else, Emily and Daniel made the sign of the cross.

Maureen looked at her daughter surprised. "He's Catholic?"

"Yes Mother, and you, most especially, can't fault him for that."

As Father Paul took his seat, the crowd erupted in cheers again as Ila Brown came over and kissed Daniel. Teresa was standing next to her older sister and Daniel took her hands with apology in his eyes. But with a grin she kissed him too, and it wasn't merely a peck on the cheek.

So much for mourning the loss of her husband, Emily mused.

Kirk Claret stood at the head of the table next to Daniel and shouted above the crowd, "I have an announcement." Eventually the room became quieter.

"My friends, I want to tell how proud I am of my sons," Daniel's father said. The remaining chatter settled down. Someone had to shush Aunt Marge.

"My sons grew up without me, Daniel and my adopted son, Rusty." The Colonel said with authority, as if addressing troops.

Daniel looked down at the table, quickly, his hair dropping over the side of his eye so that Emily couldn't see his expression. There was no smile on his lips.

"They became men, better than me, wiser than me, more caring than me, thanks to Anna."

Anna covered her face in her gnarled hands.

"I give thanks to Almighty God that this good woman has been here for my sons." Looking more Native American than ever before, Kirk raised his hand and his voice to the ceiling, "I give thanks to God for the sons I did not deserve."

There was no sound, except a chickadee noisily searching the window feeder outside. Emily watched Daniel. He hadn't moved. The bruise on his face reflected blue in the candle light. She could see by his jaw that he was clenching his teeth to suppress emotion. He seemed to know what was coming next and he hardly breathed.

Kirk Claret took a small piece of bread and a napkin. He moved around the table to stand at the side of Anna who knew exactly what was coming. In an ancient ritual of feeding and wiping the tears of those who mourn, Kirk knelt and gently wiped the tears from Anna's cheeks with his hands. Then he put a morsel of the bread tenderly in her mouth. Through both their tears, he smiled at her. Anna took the piece of bread handed to her and fed him, wiping his face over and over with her palms, chanting, grieving, softly in Cree. Those at the table did not have to understand the whole ceremonial offering to be deeply moved by two grieving people, caring for each other. Emily found tears for Rusty, for the bear and child, running down her own cheeks and when she looked at Daniel, he too was grieving for his little brother.

This was the ceremony of letting go. This was the ceremony which convinced the spirits of their loved ones that those left behind on earth would be cared for. Rusty could go on his journey to God now, free of earthly concerns.

A woman touched her gently on the arm and she looked up to see Ila. With compassion, the Indian woman wiped her cheeks with a dark hand and placed a piece of bread at her lips. Emily took the symbol reverently. The same was being done to Daniel by Joe. Then Daniel rose and beckoned Emily to come with him. Together they performed the ritual with Anna and then his father. When the ceremony was over, Emily felt purified of all the grief which had ever held her captive.

Daniel smiled at her, as if feeling the same peace and proud of her for participating in the ceremony. She may not have understood it but she had accepted the ways of his people with reverence. And though it was a shadow of what it once was, the ceremony achieved the sweet blessings of a physical prayer shared by a community.

Emily's mother and father looked at her with approval as she sat back down.

"Daniel?" Maureen spoke and reached over Emily. "How old does a person have to be before they stop learning?" Maureen looked down at his bruised knuckles and red wrists and kissed his hand.

"There is no past with us, only now," Daniel said, pressing her palm against his heart.

Just when everyone thought the moment could not become more serious the colonel announced:

"And now, I am honored to share this special moment in my son's life."

All grew quiet again and Emily expected a continuation of the solemn ritual. The eyes of all the people were on them.

Daniel looked down at the plate, worried that his father would embarrass him with another show of pride.

Pete hit Daniel in the head with a crumbled paper cup. Daniel looked in the direction of the projectile and saw Pete patting his shirt pocket.

Daniel frowned, mouthing the word, "What?"

Emily looked at Pete with irritation for interrupting this special moment but then she realized everyone was looking at them, grinning expectantly.

"Come on, the foods getting cold!" somebody yelled.

A few more people began to ball up their paper cups, even the parish priest.

"I think they want you to say something," Emily whispered, knowing that was the last thing Daniel wanted to do.

Feigning wide-eyed annoyance, Pete tapped his shirt pocket again.

When Daniel mimicked what Pete did, his face brightened. Good old Pete, he must have told everyone here. In panic, Daniel dug for the ring and with relief found it. He closed it in his hand. His father sat down with a smile.

Daniel took Emily's elbow and asked her to get up.

Confused, she looked around her but there was no help there. She stood up.

"I had not planned on doing it this way. We have Pete to thank for this," he whispered in her ear.

"Do what?"

"Emily Marie Harrigan," Daniel said, seriously, with all the people smiling around him. "We believe that every person, every animal in the forest, every star in the sky must find their balance in another. We cannot be whole until the one arrives who is our counterbalance, the one who straightens our path to the Great Spirit. Emily, I have loved you from the moment I saw you and every day since I have loved you more."

Emily put her hands over her mouth, tears in her eyes.

"Will you marry me, Emily? Would you be my wife?"

"Yes!"

There was such cheering and whooping in the room that Pauline's baby woke up crying.

Daniel's father took their hands and folded them over each other.

"Sir," Daniel looked at Emily's father while Kirk kept his palm suspended above the two. "May I have your daughter's hand in marriage? I will love, honor and protect her with my life."

Henry, eyes glistening, got up and placed his hand over theirs. Kirk finished the stack and everyone clapped again. This time, when Daniel was congratulated he was all grins.

"Let's eat!" someone yelled.

Towards the end of the feast, Daniel wiped his mouth looking at Emily curiously, "What is going on in that pretty head of yours?"

She leaned over whispering something in his ear.

CHAPTER 25

Daniel drew back, looking at her shocked, and then with elation. "Tonight?" he asked.

Emily nodded happily. "Everyone is here that I care about. Daniel, we have been through enough, already. I don't want to take any more chances of losing you before I can give myself to you.. Do you think Father Paul would?"

"I don't know, but I'm sure going to go ask him." Daniel got up and bent over the priest whispering something in his ear. The priest got up and followed him to Anna's bedroom were the sofa was standing on its side, removed to make room for the dinner.

"What is it, Daniel?"

"Father, you have known me all my life. I would not ask something on impulse, if I wasn't sure it was the right thing. You know this of me."

"You have always been a practical boy, a very practical boy."

"Father, I need to ask you a favor, the biggest favor of my life."

"Go on."

"Father, marry Emily and me, tonight, at the church, please!"

"Oh, my," Father Paul murmured and put his hand on his balding head. "This is highly irregular. You should have baptismal certificates, pre-cana instructions, six months notice—Emily wishes this as much as you do?"

"Yes."

"It has been done before but, well actually Mary and Joseph didn't wait six months." he chuckled. "Emily's parents could vouch for her baptism," he said thoughtfully, "and, heaven knows, I baptized you. Give me a minute to pray on this."

He knelt down by the window for what seemed like an eternity.

Daniel stayed quiet.

Finally, he made the sign of the cross and got up saying, "Well if the Pope can pray facing Mecca I suppose, just this once, I can bend the rules. Do you have anything to confess, my son?"

"Ah—no, Father if you're thinking—I mean probably, yes, but not what you are thinking—unless just thinking…"

"Ah, the thinking! That's the one that lands me into the confessional every time. I absolve you from all your sin in the name of the Father, the Son and the Holy Spirit. I'll go get the furnace stoked at the church. Tell everyone to bring their chairs."

The two went out to the main room. Daniel nodded to Emily, whose eyes became brilliant.

Father Paul went to Henry Harrigan. Emily's father got up and listened to what the priest said. His eyes went to Emily. She had that little girl look he could never refuse. She saw him nod twice to the priest, and then he came over to her.

"Are you sure, Baby? I'm aware Daniel loves you but you haven't known him that long."

"I have never been so sure of anything, Daddy," she said, "As far as the length of time I have known him—I have known him forever."

"How am I going to tell your mother?"

"Mom is in a pretty compliant position right now after what happened today. I'll tell her," Emily got up from the table and walked to her mother who was taking a bowl of mashed potatoes into the kitchen. Emily took the bowl from her and handed it to Anna, who looked at her puzzled.

"I don't want her to drop it," Emily explained, and then turned to her mother. "Mom, Daniel and I are going to be married tonight. Father Paul has agreed."

"Oh, Emily! No, this is too soon! I wanted to prepare. I wanted a…" Maureen stopped and looked at her daughter, "It doesn't matter what

I want. I could have lost you after what I did. You forgave me and you still love me. Oh, sweetheart! You don't even have a dress!"

"Be happy for me, Mom. A dress doesn't matter!" Emily kissed her.

The next thing they knew, Anna had hold of both their wrists and was dragging them into the bedroom.

Daniel was whispering into the ear of a couple who were leaving. The woman squealed with delight and the room hushed. People were looking at each other for an answer to the woman's glee.

Henry was talking to Kirk Claret. They were both smiling.

"This evening will not end!" the Colonel said, putting his arm around the smaller man's shoulder. He said in his booming, authoritative voice. "Too long I have ignored our ways. My son is to be married! Tonight! We will celebrate!," Kirk shouted. "Tonight, Kaskitesiw will be Abenaki, Cree, Metis, Micmac and," Kirk gripped Henry hard, "Irish!"

"Viva France!" Andre yelled, and a few cheers erupted from others.

"And English!" Doc Pomfret shouted.

"Tonight we will begin again."

The place erupted in cheers.

"Build a bonfire on the green," Colonel Claret directed, "drive the fallen snow away with its heat. It is a night with our ancestor's shining down upon us. This will be a night without end. Rouse everyone. After the ceremony we will celebrate all night!"

Aunt Marge whooped the loudest.

~~~~~

Maureen stood in front of her daughter in Anna's bedroom and said, "Honey, I can't believe you are doing this."

"Mom, Daniel and I want to be together. If I recall, you didn't date Daddy for all that long before you married him."

"But that was back then," Maureen tried to reason, "He was Catholic and he was so hot and you were supposed to get married first."

"Yeah, well, that's what we are doing," Emily laughed, lifted her chin, and looked her mother straight in the eye, "and I'm not spending one more night without loving him."

Maureen looked at her daughter in awe that she had waited for the one she knew she would love.

"I told you they were just sleeping together." Anna clucked her tongue and pulled a garment from a cedar chest, "Miskam! *I found it!!*"

Emily looked around the side of the sofa standing on its end.

"I was young, then—small like you. Mekiwina, *a gift*," Anna said and handed the dress to Emily, "It is perhaps, a little short."

"Oh, Anna!"

The dress was of white, bleached buck skin, worked into an incredible softness. Brown and yellow softened porcupine quills were carefully sewn into a lily design blossoming upwards at the shoulders where it was tied. A stem of green, glass beads traveled down the front of the dress.

"It is beautiful," Maureen had to admit. "Not what I would have picked out for you, but—it is beautiful, Anna."

Emily kicked off her shoes and took off her sweater and slacks.

Anna brought in a bowl of herb scented water and commented quietly to Emily that she should wear nothing underneath.

Emily went into the adjoining bathroom. She washed and then slid the soft shift of hide down over her body. Then she returned to the women. It was a perfect fit, just a little short and Anna laughed, delighted, remembering herself once this small. Anna, in spite of her aching fingers, tied the white latigo strands at the shoulders in a slip knot, trailing the long ends gracefully against Emily's arms

Anna dug into the chest again and pulled out a tall pair of white, leather moccasin boots which came to Emily's knees. The fringe at the dress's bottom hung over the tops of the beaded boots.

There was a knock at the door.

"Awas," Anna snapped, "it is not time."

"Anna, it's Susanne, I have something."

Anna let her in. In her hands, Susanne held a wreath of twisted Bitter Sweet, with bright orange berries still clinging to the vine. She had also bunched together more of the bittersweet into a bouquet, ringed with crow's foot and high bush cranberries.

"They're the only things left with any color in them." Susanne offered them to Emily.

Emily hugged her saying, "Thank you, my Susanne. You are the sister I always wanted."

Susanne, usually austere, bent and kissed her cheek, obliviously pleased.

Maureen began brushing Emily's hair until it shone like polished copper and then placed the wreath of the Bittersweet on her daughter's head. It looked as if it meant to be worn by her alone.

The three women stepped back and appraised their work.

"You are a beautiful bride, darling," Maureen said with tears in her eyes.

"If this weeping does not stop I will begin to do it!" Anna slammed a box of tissues into Emily's mother's stomach, and then crossed her arms over her great bosom with satisfaction.

"You look like Maid Marion of Sherwood Forest." Susanne giggled.

"No, she looks like an Irish Pocahontas." Maureen smiled back.

"Ah," Anna said, remembering, and went to the box where the merino shawl lay with its beads cupped by tiny white feathers. She put it around Emily's shoulders.

Emily kissed her with gratitude, saying, "Thank you, Mother."

Anna nodded happily, and then pulling Emily's head towards her, whispered in her ear, "At the cabin, there will be creams, lotions from the traditional ways. Use them and there will be no pain and much happiness."

Emily blushed.

"Mihkwaw!" Anna pointed to her cheeks, laughing.

When they stepped out of the room, no one was there. The food was covered and placed on the cold porch, for safekeeping from bacteria, but perhaps not a raccoon or bear. The tables were still there, but the chairs were gone.

"Anna, do you have a flash light?" Susanne asked.

"Ehe!" Anna went to the door where two torches were left with matches.

"Oh, Good Lord! We'll catch our hair on fire!" Maureen cringed. With the amount of hairspray she had on it, she had a right to be afraid.

Anna lit one and handed it to Susan. Then she lit the other and handed it to Maureen. She left them and called for Teresa and Ila who were standing nearby. They went to Daniel's cabin.

"So much for the limo service I was dreaming of," Maureen said.

The torches lit their way as they came into view of the church. Two men took the torches and carried them to where a huge bonfire in the center green was being built.

Henry was standing at the door waiting. He kissed his wife and handed her to Uncle Rick, who took her arm and led her to the front row of chairs. Pete's son, John, coupled his arm around his mother's elbow. In a very grown up manner, he led Susanne to the second row. The rest of the people sat in either fold up chairs or the half logs of the church.

Emily stood alone in front of her father.

"You look like an angel, a little woodland angel," he said softly.

"I love you so much, Daddy."

"I love you too. You know your mother is going to want a reception at home," he reminded her solemnly and linked arms with her.

"I know and we will do it soon. I'm so happy tonight."

"Wait until Daniel sees you. He's not going to be able to take his eyes off of you," he approved and gave her a little pull. "Ready?"

She nodded. They started down the aisle.

There was no music. There hadn't been time for music. But there was a sea of quiet voices acclaiming their entrance with bright smiles. Pete was taking pictures.

"Whoever said small towns were dull?" Emily grinned.

"Me, I think," her father said, shaking his head with amazement. She tucked both arms around his right elbow.

Half-way down the aisle, she searched through the faces for Daniel and found him in a game warden's dress uniform next to his father who stood in a military uniform. They looked so handsome together.

"Pssst, Pete! Take a picture of them please." Emily called back over her shoulder.

Composing herself like a bride should, she looked to her husband-to-be, smiling. Her father was right. Daniel's eyes never left her. His lips were parted slightly in a controlled smile but people would say later that his eyes shone with a light they had never seen in him before.

She kissed her father as Daniel took her arm and led her to the wooden altar.

Even Maureen Harrigan could not have wished for a more beautiful ceremony for her daughter. Father Paul was gentle, his eyes radiated with love. This was nothing like what Maureen had ever dreamed of for Emily. She had to admit, it was better.

Emily was surprised and delighted when Daniel, saying his vows, took a matching band to her engagement ring from his father and placed it on her finger. Afterwards, she would tease him about being pretty sure she would say yes, when she hadn't even shown up until that afternoon. But at that moment, panic seized her. She had no ring for him. Her dismay showed on her face and Daniel's father stepped forward taking off the wedding band he had worn for a quarter of a century and gave it to her.

"Thank you, Dad," she whispered and kissed his cheek. Emily sensed what it took to let go of the woman he loved deeply.

Daniel's eyes left her face for a moment to look at his father. He swallowed back the emotion he felt. All this time Kirk Claret had worn that ring in hope and loyalty to his marriage. He had truly loved Daniel's mother. Though he had always respected his father, for the first time, Daniel understood him and loved him more than ever before.

Emily said her vows and placed the ring on Daniel's finger. The rite of the Holy Eucharist began in which practically all took part. Then Father Paul blessed them and the congregation, concluded the Mass and told Daniel he could kiss the bride.

Daniel didn't need another prompt as he proclaimed loudly with joy and wonder, "My wife!" He gathered her to him in the sweep of his arms and kissed her as her husband. He was still in control, but his eyes said that wasn't going to last much longer.

The church congregation cheered and tossed paper balls, pamphlets and ribbons as Emily and Daniel walked back down the aisle.

Outside relatives and friends shared kisses and best wishes. Emily found herself smooching grizzly faces of men she didn't know. A procession was starting with a native chant. She and Daniel were being pushed along.

"The key to my apartment is in the office desk drawer. You could stay there," Emily said to her father, remembering that she hadn't given a thought to lodgings for her parents and relatives.

"I'm going to take the family back to Manchester," Henry shouted over the chant. "We'll be fine. The talk of this night will get us home wide-awake."

"Mom, you okay?" Emily searched for her mother in the crowd.

Maureen was doing a little shuffling dance step with her arm in Anna's. "I'm fine, dear, but I think we are dancing you both to bed. You're holding up the works."

Emily laughed trying to get a cascade of shredded paper off her lip. Someone had found a plastic coffee can and was beating it to the rhythm of the dance. Two men ran off and returned with real drums and a fiddle. The song of the ancestors began.

Someone had put a candle in the open window of Daniel's cabin and Emily couldn't help but think Nutmeg must be very upset with all this.

"Hey, Detective Harrigan, I mean, Mrs. Claret! A wedding present!" Joe shouted and held up a big, chubby, brown, puppy with a red bow around its neck. It was Uggh and Gwendolyn's prodigy. He looked much like a little bear.

"Joe had me talked into this if you came back," Daniel said, dubiously. "Is it too soon after Galen?"

With a cry of joy, Emily reached for the puppy.

But Daniel directed Joe, sternly. "I will have no competition tonight. Bring him by in the morning—very late morning. Actually, make that late afternoon."

Suddenly, Emily was picked up by Daniel who kissed her fully and passionately in front of the whole crowd, without any discipline, what so ever. Her crown of bittersweet came loose and fell to the ground.

There were shouts and claps of approval.

Someone in the crowd pushed the door to the cabin open and Daniel carried his bride over the threshold, pushing the door shut with his foot. There was bed on the floor made from many blankets and soft pillows. It was covered in white sheets and candles burned on both sides of it. The wood stove was lit and the room warm. The room smelled fragrant, owing to the dried flower petals and leaves of sage strewn over the bed and floor. Bowls sat on the floor by the bed, with different aromatic lotions in them. There was a talisman of sweet grass, representing Mother Earth and fertility, along with a statue of Our Lady of Guadalupe, pregnant with child.

Daniel set her gently on her feet and stared at her as if he didn't really believe she was here. Candlelight flickered against their bodies. Emily tossed off the moccasin boots and danced away from his arms as he reached for her.

She said, with mock concern, from the other side of the bed. "Are you sure you are up to this? I don't want you hurting yourself."

For a moment he thought she was serious, but with simultaneous tugs on the latigo strings, the wedding dress dropped to the floor.

The light of the bonfire filtered through the hastily pinned drapes and wavered like luminous dancers on the walls. Tonight, Kaskitesiw would belong to the First People once more, but for these two, it only mattered that they belonged to each other.

Would you like to see your manuscript become a book?

If you are interested in becoming a PublishAmerica author, please submit your manuscript for possible publication to us at:

acquisitions@publishamerica.com

You may also mail in your manuscript to:

**PublishAmerica
PO Box 151
Frederick, MD 21705**

www.publishamerica.com

Breinigsville, PA USA
01 March 2011
256641BV00002B/2/P